His sinews strained, and the elf grunted, pushing and pushing, gradually wheeling the catapult around towards the fleeing ogres. He saw something gold and round in the load basket but had barely registered the sight when Strongwind Whalebone chopped downward, slashing the trigger. With a loud *snap*, the catapult's arm whipped upward, hurling the sphere into the air, far, far toward the seashore below the fortress.

DRAGONLANCE NOVELS BY DOUGLAS NILES

Chaos War Series
The Last Thane
The Puppet King

Preludes
Flint the King (with Mary Kirchoff)

The Lost Histories
The Kagonesti
The Dragons

The Lost Gods
Fistandantilus Reborn

The Icewall Trilogy
The Messenger
The Golden Orb

ICEWALL TRILOGY
VOLUME TWO

The Golden Orb

DOUGLAS NILES

THE GOLDEN ORB

Cover art by Brom
Map by Dennis Kauth
First Printing: February 2002
Library of Congress Catalog Card Number: 2001089461

9 8 7 6 5 4 3 2 1

US ISBN: 0-7869-2692-9
UK ISBN: 0-7869-2722-4
620-88542-001

U.S., CANADA,
ASIA, PACIFIC, & LATIN AMERICA
Wizards of the Coast, Inc.
P.O. Box 707
Renton, WA 98057-0707
+ 1-800-324-6496

EUROPEAN HEADQUARTERS
Wizards of the Coast, Belgium
P.B. 2031
2600 Berchem
Belgium
+ 32-70-23-32-77

Visit our website at **www.wizards.com/dragonlance**

Dedication

To Mike Wesling and Pat Seghers
Friends in deed.
October 2001

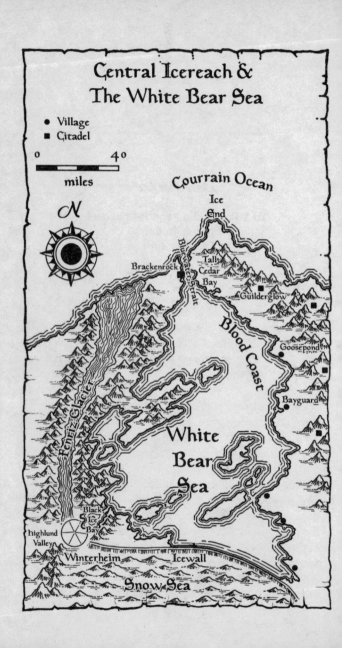

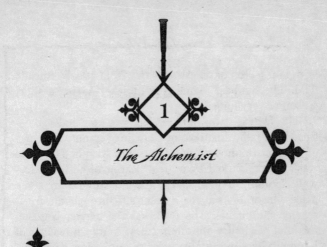

1

The Alchemist

There was a place on the world of Krynn, a remote land lying far to the south of the great centers of civilizations, isolated by ice and ocean from realms of elves and dwarves, beyond the ken of Istaran priests and Solamnic Knights. That place was called the Icereach, and it was home to bears and seals, glaciers and walrus-men, landscapes of flat tundra and craggy summits.

The cold and rugged land was also host to populations of ogres and men, the former in their ancient kingdom of Suderhold, the latter in scattered strongholds of the Arktos and Highlander tribes.

By many standards the Icereach was a poor land, producing but a small amount of food and supporting a limited population—limited, at least, when contrasted to the teeming multitudes inhabiting the fertile pastures of the Abanasinian plains or thriving on the rich fisheries of the Newsea. While fields greened for the harvest and grapevines grew heavy with fruit on the continent of Ansalon, the denizens of the Icereach counted themselves lucky to find scattered berries in the river valleys, or to take a crop of wheat or barley from a rocky hillside field. The hardiest plants grew quickly during a short season of very long days.

The Icereach was surrounded by water and ice, defined by a radical pattern of changing seasons, extremes of weather unknown upon the rest of Krynn. The place was further marked by a great barrier of cliff, the Icewall, looming a mile above the flat tundra in some places, in others scoring a great rift through the frost-scarred mountains. The wall was the barrier between the land of vitality and the farthest southern reaches of Krynn, where mountains were the only denizens, rock and ice the rugged heights' sole occupants. In the coldest season, while the blanket of snow spread across all parts of the land and water alike, the ceaseless blackness of the night sky offered contrast to the blanket whiteness of the landscape.

When spring came to the Icereach, the sun poked into view gradually, at first for only an hour or two at a time but each day rising higher, casting more light across the snow-draped landscape. Gradually the snowfields melted, streams cascading into life until, finally, the wintry cloak became a patchwork cover revealing the barren stone and frost-browned grasses covering the ground. Snowmelt came to the north-facing slopes initially—they were the first to feel the kiss of the returning sun—but soon it spread across the flat tundra, liquefying the ice-capped seas.

Summer was the time when the land truly came to life, blessed by a sun that remained constant, never dropping below the horizon for a span of three full months. Flowers burst into blossom under this day without end, while animals ranging from bears and deer to plump grouse and sleek seals fed and mated and thrived under the blessing of perpetual warmth and daylight. Fish spawned in sparkling streams, and great whales basked in the sun-drenched seas. Humans and ogres, too, busied themselves in their multitude of tasks. Men spent their time hunting and foraging, mining for gold and iron and coal, or planting crops and catching fish. The ogres did some of these things as well, but mostly they made war on humans so that they could steal the products of man's diligent labors.

As it did for the rest of the world, autumn brought a time of darkening to the Icereach, a sobering transition that sent animals seeking shelter and men making preparations for the upcoming winter. Crops were harvested, meat salted and smoked, lodges and boats secured against the inevitable and imminent storm. The span of daylight grew short until the sun barely poked above the northern horizon for a few hours, before and after the noon of each day. With every progressive sunset the interval of darkness became longer and the coming winter loomed closer.

When winter burst upon the Icereach, the fury of the Sturmfrost was unleashed. In so many ways this mighty storm, unknown to the rest of Krynn, defined the harsh extremes of this polar land. Throughout the year the tempest gathered pressure but contained its fury behind the barrier of the Icewall. During the waning days of fall, seething and churning with cyclonic force, the storm's strength swelled, icy winds chipping away at the stone and frost that formed the bedrock of its wintry world. Finally, when the Sturmfrost could no longer be contained, the blizzard erupted on the land, snarling over the Icewall like ten thousand hungry bears, roaring across the domains of ogres and men alike. Seas froze under the impact of the frigid blast, and any greenery left upon the land immediately succumbed to the killing chill.

Fish dove deep in their seas to languish in the lightless depths. Animals cowered in dens, slumbering through the months of darkness, surviving on the fat their bodies had stored during the season of plenty. If they had not accumulated a sufficient reserve of this fat, they died.

Even ogres and especially humans quailed against the onslaught of the Sturmfrost. Everywhere mankind retired to shelters, be they the great citadels of the Highlanders or the snug lodges of the Arktos. The lucky ones dwelt within the high walls of Brackenrock, the great fortress held by the Bayguard tribe. Vast wells of subterranean steam vented through the halls of Brackenrock, allowing those fortunate denizens to exist in comfort and warmth unknown to the rest of the Icereach's humans.

The ogres had their own capital, the great mountain city of Winterheim. Like Brackenrock it was heated by the world's natural steam, making a cavernous subterranean shelter of benign, even luxurious, comfort for thousands of ogres and their even more numerous human slaves. Winterheim was a great mountain, mightiest summit of Icereach, and much of the massif was hollowed into living space for the ogres who had dwelt there for more than four thousand years.

Beyond Winterheim and Brackenrock, the sentient denizens of the Icereach lived a hardier life, battling the elements even within their shelters: fires that needed constant replenishment of fuel, windows and doors that required never-ending attention, lest encroaching wind and snow claw their way inward. The Sturmfrost attacked not like a blizzard or any other violence born of nature. Instead, it was like a savage and malevolent being. Chunks of ice, some of them bigger than large houses, flew through the blinding gale, blasting with meteoric force any obstacles in their path. Stinging needles of ice flayed the flesh from anyone foolish enough to be caught in the open. The surface of the sea froze with the first minutes of the onslaught, trapping unwary boats in the water. Later, more gradually, the winter would crush the hulls under the inexorable pressure of the expanding, remorseless ice pack.

The Sturmfrost was accustomed to rage in full fury for a month or six weeks every winter, a period of utter, sunless night. Very gradually, the force of the epic blizzard would fade. Winds still came howling up from the south, and snow swept the landscape in storms that remained frequent, but these were broken by increasing periods of preternatural calm. During frigid intervals the skies cleared. Though the temperature remained well below freezing, one who bundled against the cold could safely view a dazzling array of stars. A number of weeks, perhaps even a couple of months of winter, passed before the sun again appeared, but the waning of the storm was inevitable and each year gave hope to the people. Those who had survived the Sturmfrost truly believed they could survive anything.

Even when the violence of the storm had passed, of course, there were many who never dared to emerge into the long, cold night. They remained within lodges and dens, citadels or city, until the winter was truly past and spring began to brighten the Icereach. In the vast landscape of the Icereach there were many remote outposts of men and ogres alike, places buried in deep snow and ice.

One of these remote locales was an island, an ogre territory rising in the midst of a sea, more than two hundred miles to the west of Winterheim. In temperate weather this place was surrounded by waters of deep blue, home to whales and walruses, albeit prone to sudden squalls and driving rainstorms. Now, at the tail end of the cold season, this outpost was merely a place of high, mountainous terrain in the midst of a frosty, drift-covered landscape. Named for the serpents who had dwelt here in centuries long past, during the days of the dragons, this island was called Dracoheim. It was claimed by the monarchs of the ogres as part of the Kingdom of Suderhold.

Atop one of Dracoheim's summits was a fortress, a place of high walls, deep courtyards, lofty towers. In the depths of the snow, much of the place was buried, locked in hibernation. Nevertheless, some of the wall peaks were visible, and a few towers jutted above the surrounding drifts. In one of these towers a pale light glowed through an ice-sheeted window. It was a high garret, a solitary room well-removed from the rest of Castle Dracoheim. This solitude served both the castle's mistress and the denizen of that room himself.

There was indeed but a single occupant of that lofty nest, and he was no ogre. He was a person of manlike stature, though smaller and slighter than a strapping male. Now he seemed almost childlike, for he huddled upon a bed, buried under several furs of white bearskin. With a soft moan he clutched his arms around his thin chest, and he shivered.

His tremors were not the result of cold, for it was fairly warm in this garret. A mountain of coal was piled in the corner, and an iron brazier still radiated some of the heat from the blaze the man had kindled forty hours before. Then he had been alert and active, but later he had left the stove to burn down low while he went to his bed and buried himself under his quilts.

He had slept the deep and dreamless slumber that inevitably followed the drinking of his elixir, when the magic suffused his flesh and hummed warmly through his body. It brought serene pleasure, indeed the only contentment that he knew. Yet, as it always did, that pleasure waned acutely with the fading of the magic, and so he awakened as he did now, with the hunger burning within him. It was a craving that drove all other matters from his mind.

The hunger was nothing strange; he felt it and fought it through every waking minute of his life. But now that hunger was tinged with despair, for the means of slaking his need was growing short and would soon be exhausted.

The manlike being peered from beneath a corner of his blankets at the workbench along the far wall of his room. The cluttered table extended nearly halfway around the periphery of the circular chamber. There were many objects on that bench, lining the shelves on the wall above as well: bottles and vials of multitudinous dusts, ashes, powders, and liquids; boxes of arcane ingredients; tomes of ancient wisdom—some bound and locked on the shelves, others propped on the table, open to marked pages—as well as various odds and ends, halfway sorted into piles. There was a mound of feathers, a stack of ivory walrus tusks, skulls of men, ogres, and walrus, and a scattering of marble-sized objects that were the dried eyeballs of various creatures.

The watery eyes of the figure under the blankets sought one and only one object: They came to bear with fevered intensity upon the stoppered bottle that stood on the far left end of the curved table. The glass of the container was semitransparent, smeared with scratches and blotches and ancient, grimy residue, but there was enough clarity for him to see the line marking the amount of liquid—the oh-so-precious life-giving elixir!—remaining.

That amount was heartbreakingly small, barely two fingersbreadths above the bottom. He wanted to leap up, race to the table, and lift the neck to his eager lips, sucking down every drop of that precious draught in one exhilarating frenzy. His belly growled at the thought, and saliva trickled from the corner of his mouth. For a moment he tugged at the heavy blankets and half rose before slumping back down and letting out his breath with an audible groan.

If he did that, if he sucked the bottle dry, then his elixir was gone . . . gone until the snow melted and the courtyard became passable again . . . until he could make his way to the Dowager Queen and promise that grotesque ogress anything, whatever she demanded in exchange for more of the potion, the liquid that was life itself to him.

He would do that willingly, he knew. Indeed he would go to her, as soon as he possibly could, and he would beg and grovel, plead with her. His craving would be written on his face, and her sneer, her scorn, would ridicule him. She would play with him, taunt him, tantalize and tease him, and he would sob and plead some more.

In the end, of course, she would grant him his wish. He was, after all, the royal Alchemist, and he would be no good to her, nor to the king himself in distant Winterheim, if he was reduced to a sodden mass of need, a pathetic creature of desperate craving. He could not work in that state, could barely even survive. Naturally, the Dowager Queen would make him suffer, would demand a multitude of unguents and admixtures in exchange. He would do the work she asked, and she would reward him with his potion.

He lived for that great day, that moment when she would produce a cask of the stuff, when he would have all the elixir he needed for weeks, even months, at a time. But for now he knew that time lay in the insufferably distant future. Bitter experience had taught him that even if he descended from his tower, clawed his way through the snow with frostbitten fingers and frozen feet, and forced his way into the main keep, he would find the Dowager Queen sleeping, a brace of guards at her door—brutish, hulking ogres in their own right—blocking his access until the sun had emerged into view and the great ogress decided to arise from a long winter's torpor.

So he was left, for now, with this pathetic draught, the few swallows in the jar, and he would have to make that reserve last for the rest of the winter. Despite his current need, he understood that a greedy gulping, consuming all of the potion right now, would lead only to greater desperation and pure, unadulterated misery in the days and weeks to come.

He must be conservative and careful. Very slowly, he pushed the heavy weight of bearskins off of his shoulders and his chest. The air in the room had grown somewhat clammy. Still moving slowly, he twisted, put his feet on the floor—which was lined with bearskins—and tried to force himself to a standing position.

He rose unsteadily, and the shaking of his knees was so intense that he immediately sat down again. That was fine . . . every minute of delay now was another minute he was able to survive, without replenishing his supply. So he tarried with some semblance of patience, allowing blood to circulate into his legs. There was a flagon of water near the stove, and a box with some dried fish-cake, but he ignored those. Later, after he had sipped his potion, there would be time for mundane drink, for such scant food as he cared to force down his throat. But first . . .

The bottle stood there on the bench, taunting him. His gaze remained riveted to the glass vessel as he felt the longing churn in his guts, well up his gorge and swirl, maddeningly, through his brain. At last he could wait no longer. He forced himself to his feet and in a matter of five steps brought himself to the workbench, bracing his hands upon the solid stone surface, leaning forward to catch his breath as might a man who had just completed a ten-mile run.

His hands trembled so much that he feared he would drop the bottle if he tried to pick it up right now. That thought was too terrible, so he stood very still and drew deep, slow breaths, forcing his attention away from the potion, trying to divert his mind from the hunger for even a few seconds, enough time to settle his churning nerves.

Nearby was a ceramic dish, a large bowl containing his attempts at an experiment made the previous autumn—an experiment that had yielded disappointing results. The residue in the bowl had collected little dust over the winter, for he kept his room very clean. Specks of gold gleamed in the powder, and, spotting them, he was able to force a wry chuckle. In his homeland, the amount of gold he had used for this single experiment would have bought a family food for many years, allowed a man to build a decent house, or to be outfitted with weapons and armor enough to embark on a lifelong career of adventure.

Here, on Dracoheim, there was gold aplenty, drawn from the island's own rich mines. This fistful came from a crate of gold dust the Dowager Queen had provided him for use as the basis of his experiment. He recalled the queen's purpose and command. The ogress desired that he create a unique explosive material, something that her son, the king of Suderhold, could use to aid his constant wars against the humans.

He had combined the gold particles with simple salt and black cinder drawn from the slopes of one of Dracoheim's several, mostly dormant, volcanoes. The gold, salt, and black cinder were augmented by rare ash provided to him by the Dowager Queen, something the powerful priestess claimed to have extracted from secret rituals, ordered by her violent god, Gonnas the Strong.

The Alchemist had respect for Gonnas the Strong. It was during one such ritual that the queen had also created the potion that above all else, gave him reason for living. He had set himself to his latest experiments in the fall, before the Sturmfrost, and had started out with a sense of optimism. If the ash had some concealed potency that, mingled with the other materials, could bring destructive force to life, he would discover that power, and he had every reason to expect that the queen would reward him.

He had tried for weeks, using the ingredients in a variety of concentrations and proportions, always working carefully lest he create an explosive that would destroy him in the process of discovery. His concoctions had fizzled and sputtered, smoked, and sometimes burned fitfully. At last, as the icy and snow and wind had isolated him in his tower, he had been forced to admit defeat. There was no hidden destructive power in the mix of salt, gold, cinder, and enchanted ash.

His disappointment was eased by the two full bottles of potion his mistress had brought to him, and during the long wintertime he had luxuriated in the pleasant, soothing haze induced by his elixir. He had forgotten all about the failed testing, the experiments.

Now, feeling sturdier, he collected his wits. His hand

was, if not steady, at least shaking less violently. Taking no chances, he clutched the bottle in both hands, lifting it from the table, feeling the tragically light weight of the liquid contents sloshing around. The stopper was tight—the Alchemist above all others knew the cost of evaporation—but he clamped it in his teeth and pulled sharply.

The cork came out, clenched in his jaws as he pulled the bottle away, then—horror! The glass slipped through his fingers! He grabbed desperately with his bony hands, only serving to propel the narrowing neck of the container through his slippery grasp. He watched the bottle fall as though it tumbled in slow motion.

His mouth gaped, as he croaked out a desperate word: "No!"

The bottle paid him no heed as it struck the stone bench and shattered. Shards of glass flew outward, but he ignored those jagged missiles, lunging, reaching, desperate to salvage even a few drops of his precious liquid. He saw those drops bounce from the table, jiggle tantalizingly in the air, dance between his frantic fingers. One of those spatters passed right over the back of his hand. He felt numb with a sense of irredeemable loss, as it fell with a plop right in the midst of the powdery residue of his failed experiment.

His world turned an ungodly white. A noise burst his eardrums. He felt as though the fist of a mighty god had picked him up and hurled him, bodily, across the chamber. He became vaguely aware of flames licking across the room. In another instant his vision, his awareness, his white reality merged into impenetrable black.

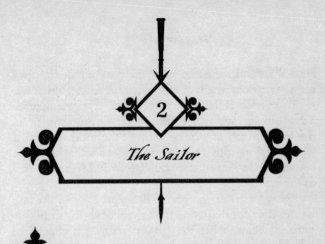

2

The Sailor

The blue of the sky was so pure, so perfect and unblemished, that Kerrick imagined spending the rest of his life in total contentment, surrounded by that color. The hue of the sky, magnificent beyond words, was actually surpassed by the intense azure of the ocean, the sparkling water brilliant under the spring sunlight, a surface of dazzling reflection extending to the limits of his vision.

Kerrick stood atop the cabin of his boat, his right hand braced on the mainsail's rigging. The sail was full in a mild breeze, the white wake trailing and sparkling behind the transom. He squinted into the distance . . . imagining, remembering, and, for the first time in many years, longing.

Of course, in some ways he raced down this same emotional gauntlet every spring, had done so after each of the eight long, sunless winters he had spent here in the Icereach. Over that time he had learned to dread the shortening days, the long darkness as autumn waned toward winter. Eight times he had joined the Arktos in cowering against the force of the Sturmfrost, the mighty blast of ice and wind and snow that marked the first and most savage onslaught of the cold, dark season of winter.

To Kerrick Fallabrine, an elf from sunny, temperate Silvanesti, an even worse ordeal than the Sturmfrost was the long stretch of sunless winter, the bleak period of weeks and months that followed the blast, when time seemed to slow, even stop, bitter cold and frozen as still as the sea.

Every year Kerrick watched the progress of the late winter thaw, anticipating the arrival of spring until this moment came, when he finally grabbed a chance to take his cherished sailboat onto the waters of the White Bear Sea.

Even in spring, of course, there could be brutal storms, a squall or perhaps even a late blizzard that might rage with but a few minutes' notice. However, the elf had sailed this sea long enough, endured the vicissitudes of Icereach springs so that he knew he could master anything the weather chose to throw at him. Once the sun returned from its winter's absence, once the warming began, there was no force on land or sea that caused him to turn back from the water.

Now he turned his face toward the sun, and though it was but a feeble flicker compared to the heat it would yield in a few months, Kerrick relished the rays caressing his skin. The wind was whipping past, still cool, but there was a hint of moisture and distant warmth in the air.

He was sailing southeast now, had been since he had departed Brackenrock Harbor a few hours earlier. His voyage was made in the service of the chiefwoman, mistress of the fortress, Moreen Bayguard. He was sailing to the Highlander citadel of Bearhearth, there to collect several chests of gold that had been promised to the

Arktos as payment by the Bearhearth thane, exchange for allowing more than a hundred women and children of that clan to shelter in Brackenrock over the winter. The Highlanders had more people than could be crowded into their frosty, stone-walled castle, while the Arktos had plenty of room and ample reserves of food. Additionally, the guests had made themselves useful in Brackenrock over the winter, working on improving the fortifications, tanning skins, brewing warqat, and making clothes, while in the steam-warmed vaults of Brackenrock they had dwelt in much greater comfort than they knew in their homeland

Kerrick was delighted to have the errand, a good excuse to take his boat out and fly across these waters, to relish the newly returned sun and race across the freshly melted sea. As the thrill tugged at him he grinned with a sudden thought, an irresponsible impulse. Once he collected this gold, he could bypass Brackenrock and sail through the Bluewater Strait, dodging icebergs on the vast Courrain Ocean, setting a northbound course. There was nothing to stop him from leaving the Icereach behind . . . in a month or two he would find himself again on the shores of Ansalon, probably making landfall somewhere on the coastline of his beloved homeland, Silvanesti. This was the month of Spring Dawning and there would be festivals, music, maidens . . .

With a bemused chuckle, he realized that he really *could* head for home, if he wanted to. For many years he had stayed here, accepting his exile as a fact of life, coming to live among the Arktos almost as one of them. All the while he had worked, been paid in gold, amassing a treasure that would guarantee his welcome back at the elven court. But did he really want that . . . and was he ready to leave, now?

Despite the Sturmfrost and the bleak winter, life in the Icereach had many benefits. Kerrick was a hero here, highly regarded by a people who, in general, were far more generous, friendly, and accepting than the hidebound elves of his homeland. He had made good friends among the humans—Mouse, Bruni, Dinekki of the Arktos, even Highlanders like Mad Randall and Lars Redbeard—better friends than any he had known in his native land. They would joke with him or listen seriously to his ideas, caring in ways beyond the interest or patience of any elf.

Of course there was Moreen, herself. She was his friend, but she was more than that. She counted on him for many things, for the knowledge he brought of the world beyond, and the skills he had imparted to her and her people. She could be cold and aloof, even haughty sometimes. He wasted no time wondering why he felt such a bond with her—but if she asked something of him, he would hasten to please her. That is why he would take the Bearhearth gold back to her, as commanded, without seriously considering the notion of running to the north.

Probably he would return to Silvanesti someday, but not now, not yet. He would return as an acclaimed explorer, demanding a pardon from the king who had sent him into exile. Someday, when he was ready . . .

He glanced back along the white trail of his wake to the headland of the Icereach, the mountainous bulwark where Brackenrock stood. It was barely a blur, low against the horizon. His gold was there, a small fortune, secured in the vaults of the Arktos stronghold. When he finally sailed north, for home, he would take that gold with him. That wealth was the key to his redemption, the proof that he—unlike his father—had *not* sailed on a fool's quest.

With a grimace and a bitter memory, Kerrick touched the scarred remnant of his left ear, where one of the elf king's courtiers had cut and scarred him on the evening of his exile. It was a wound that would mark him for the rest of his life . . . at that bitter time, he recalled, he fully expected to sail away and die. He never expected to end up here.

Here in the fabled land of gold—the land that King Nethas mockingly had charged him to find, when he had imposed his sentence of banishment. The ogres and humans who lived here possessed plenty of the precious metal but had little use for the stuff and no understanding or caring of its value to the outside world, to the distant, civilized peoples of Ansalon and the rest of Krynn.

A swell lifted *Cutter's* hull and, for an instant, the rugged skyline to the north hove clearly into view. He was too far away to see the high walls, the sturdy towers of Brackenrock. The Arktos held that stronghold in no small part because of the contributions made by Kerrick Fallabrine. He had helped the Arktos, whose previous nautical experience was limited to one- and two-person kayaks, to become a seafaring people, building large, impressive boats of their own and becoming adept at fishing and sailing. He felt a pride in the place.

The wind turned chilly, though the sky remained clear. The sun was setting already, skimming along the northwestern horizon; in minutes it would vanish for another long night. Such was the fleeting nature of spring in the Icereach, yet Kerrick was content to know that fourteen or sixteen or even eighteen hours later, he would again welcome a fresh and dazzling day.

For now, he decided to take in some sail, slowing down the speed of his graceful boat for the run through the darkness. Quickly he stowed the jib and shortened the mainsail, until *Cutter* glided through the water with gentle, lapping progress. Next he lashed the tiller in place to hold him on course during the night. He took a drink of fresh water and ate a piece of salmon that he grilled on his charcoal cooker.

At last, content and tired, he entered the cabin and lay down to get some sleep.

"Going home? Pah, you were thinking about going home without me! How far is it in miles, anyway? I bet it would take a long time, as long as it took to sail here the first time. Of course, back then we sailed without a sail, really, cuz the turtle-dragon knocked it down. Wow, I sure thought that turtle-dragon was going to kill you!"

Kerrick groaned and shifted on his bunk. He was dreaming, he knew—one of those peculiarly vivid dreams that came upon him when he was very deeply asleep.

In his dream, Coraltop Netfisher was talking to him, and the kender's presence made him irrationally happy. It had been eight years since he had seen his sailing companion, and during that time the memory of his shipmate's irrepressible cheerfulness as well as his mysteriously unexplained appearances and disappearances had faded into a sort of fairy tale recollection.

Coraltop? Is that really you? Where have you been? He wanted to talk, to welcome his old friend back, but this seemed to be one of those dreams where his muscles, his speech, would not respond to his will. So he made no sound, no acknowledgement. Instead he lay still in his bunk and listened to Coraltop Netfisher prattle on. Of course, the dream-kender was the same as any flesh and blood representative of the race, so the lack of a response to his remarks was absolutely no impediment to conversation.

"I hear you've got lots of gold now. Three chests of it in Brackenrock, right? And you'll get more from this trip to Bearhearth. Hey, did they really make the hearth out of a bear? Or is it just that a bear came in and went to sleep on the hearth? You really should ask, at least on my account. I'm just a little curious as to where they got that name."

Kerrick agreed that, yes, he could ask on Coraltop's account. He hoped he would remember that part of the dream when he woke up. It was not an important question, but Bearhearth *did* seem to be a curious name, and it would be interesting to learn how it had come to exist.

"I bet your elf king would be pretty glad to see you come home, especially with all you could tell him about the Icereach. He'd be interested in your gold too—I think it kind of bothers him that the Kingpriest of Istar is richer than the king of Silvanesti. Don't you? Think that it bothers him, I mean."

Again, the slumbering elf found himself in full agreement, even if the kender's insights into the elf king's envy rather surprised him. Kerrick once more tried to speak but still found his body unwilling to answer the commands of his mind.

"So, you've got plenty of gold, and the king who exiled you, well, he'd be happy to see you back home. That leaves just the matter of your father, don't you think?"

"My father?" Now the words came, croaked sluggishly through the thickness of his tongue. Why was Coraltop talking about his father?

"Yes, your father. Did you ever stop to think that he might have showed up back home? He might be interested in your gold, too. You know, you've been gone for eight years, and a lot can happen in eight years. Maybe he just sailed up the river, right to Silvanost, and went looking for you to say 'Hi son!' But alas, you weren't there."

"My father's dead. You know that, Coraltop." Of this Kerrick was certain, but on the other hand wasn't Coraltop dead too? Well, this was a dream, and the dead often appeared in dreams.

"If your father came home, and he didn't find you— *couldn't* find you—I would think he'd be awfully sad!"

"My father was killed by ogres," Kerrick replied, growing more confident of his speech. "You remember the ogre king's ship, *Goldwing*, don't you? Well I recognized it, knew it the first time I saw it. It was once called *Silvanos Oak*, and it was the ship my father sailed away from Silvanesti. He never would have surrendered that ship. No, he's gone, dead in the ogre dungeons . . . he didn't go home . . . and he's not looking for me."

"Maybe not," Coraltop agreed, surprisingly. "Still, don't you wonder sometimes?"

"Yes . . . I do wonder."

Coraltop surprisingly said nothing.

"He left me his ring, you know," Kerrick added, suppressing a shudder. He thought of that powerful, deadly circlet of gold—right now it was in his trunk, next to the bed where he lay sleeping. He hadn't worn it in years. He kept it as a remembrance of his father.

"You don't wear it much, it seems," the kender noted. "Don't you like it any more?"

"I *don't* like it!" That was the truth. On the few times he had slipped his finger through it, the ring's magic had infused his body with supernatural strength, allowing him to accomplish great feats, but that strength had come at a cost. When he removed it, his body was consumed with lethargy, and he was so weary that he had been known to sleep for days. Furthermore, after wearing the ring, he found himself obsessed with that magic, thinking about it and desiring it as if it were the breath of life. That feeling, as much as anything else about the magical band of metal, he found deeply unsettling, even frightening.

"No, I don't like it . . . don't want to wear it," he said, his voice growing thick again as his dream-body once more became dull and unresponsive.

"Well, still, I wonder about your father. . . ." Coraltop Netfisher was saying.

Kerrick was too tired and didn't even try to reply. He nodded back into his deep sleep. Through the rest of the long night, he had flickering dreams, glimpses of his father, his mother, his king. Always, it seemed, he was gazing at them from a distance through a small frame made by a ring of glowing gold.

3

The King

Grimwar Bane drew a deep breath to try and calm the pounding of his mighty heart. The ogre king stood still, his massive bulk planted on the two stout pillars of his legs, legs set in a wide stance with knees slightly bent. His head was cocked, ears pitched to any faint suggestion of noise that would emanate from beyond the panels of the banded oaken door. Finally he found his confirmation: a sonorous exhalation, long and measured and genuinely relaxed.

He knew that his wife, at last, was sleeping.

And this would not be just any sleep. She was exhausted, drained, and, if he knew his wife, she would be unconscious for a long time.

Stariz ber Glacierheim ber Bane was not merely the wife of the ogre king. She was also high priestess of the Willful One, Gonnas the Strong, baneful deity of the ogres of the Icereach. It was in the latter capacity that she had recently performed a grueling prestidigitation, a spellcasting that had lasted, uninterrupted, for the better part of a week. Smoke had swirled through the lofty temple chamber, a foggy murk swaddling the obsidian image of Gonnas, god of all ogrekind. Slaves brought warqat and meats to the high priestess, and dozens of lesser clerics bent their deep voices into chants that vibrated through the very bedrock of the mountain.

At last the high priestess had exclaimed her joy of revelation, and at the same time the king had felt a sick wateriness in his bowels. Bitter experience had told him that while his wife was the recipient of commands from the Willful One, it was her husband, Grimwar Bane, who was the oft-burdened executor of those decrees. Undoubtedly there was some onerous task lurking in the monarch's near future.

There would be time enough later to find out what was his next job. For the time being, for at least this full day and part of the next, he could slip away. Perhaps it would be his very last chance for a long time. He had already sent a message to his lover and knew that she would be waiting for him in the private suite of apartments he kept for their all-too-infrequent meetings. It was time to make haste. The king leaned closer, listening to one more resonant breath. He could picture the queen's broad nostrils flexing with the snore and was finally convinced that she had lapsed into her deepest stupor.

Grimwar did not depart from the front of the royal apartment, for he knew that his wife had spies throughout the mountain city of Winterheim. Any number of them could be lurking out there, watching and waiting to record the surreptitious activities of their ruler.

Instead, he crossed the great room, with its arched ceiling and massive fireplace. His feet, clad in soft leather boots for indoor comfort, made no sound on the plush rugs of white bearskin. Entering the hallway leading to his own sleeping quarters, he continued past his anteroom to the place where the corridor ended in a stone wall decorated only with a single torch sconce. The stout stick remained cold, for there was rarely need for light in this remote alcove.

The king grasped the torch sconce with his burly fist and pulled. It took all of his massive strength to wrench the metal bracket downward. Gears, well greased and huge, rumbled slightly, and a crack appeared in the corner as the end of the corridor slid back to reveal a shadowy passage. Swiftly, the king stepped through the secret entrance, turning to put his shoulder against the heavy granite slab.

He heard the knock at the door, the sound coming from the outer entrance to the royal chambers. Several sharp raps echoed explosively through the stillness, and after a moment the rude summons was repeated.

He froze, startled, trying to think. Who would dare disturb him now in his quarters, when he had left specific orders that the queen was acquiring her well-deserved rest and that the king desired to be left alone to meditate? The question was overridden by a more urgent concern—the disturbance, if it continued, would inevitably arouse his wife from her well of exhaustion.

Grimacing, unable to suppress the growl of irritation rumbling within his cavernous chest, he slipped back around the secret door to reenter the royal apartments. Hastily he pulled on the sconce until the massive portal rolled shut, then hurried into the great room. The knock on the door was repeated again, a little louder this time, annoyingly persistent.

"What do you want?" snarled Grimwar Bane in what he hoped was a loud whisper, leaning close to the double doors that gave egress from the king and queen's abode.

"Begging the king's pardon," came the tremulous reply, the deep voice denoting a large and powerful ogre.

"But there is a . . . situation . . . in the temple of Gonnas."

"Can't it wait until tomorrow?"

"I fear not, Sire. The situation is in the Ice Chamber, and Her Majesty, Queen Stariz, has left longstanding orders that she is to be alerted at once, should there be a disturbance in that most holy of rooms."

"The queen has retired and is exhausted by her previous labors. I am certain that she will want to wait until—"

"What is it?" Grimwar's statement was cut off by his wife's sharp voice and sudden appearance. The door to her chambers flew open to reveal the immense, square-faced ogress. Stariz wore her sleeping robe, a cloak of gray linen, but there was no sign of fatigue or dullness in the bright spots of her eyes.

"A disturbance in the Ice Chamber," Grimwar grunted, trying to cover up his frustration as he opened the outer door. "Enter," he declared, moving into the great room as the messenger followed behind. The king stood with his back to the fireplace and glared at the other ogre. He recognized the fellow as a captain in the Royal Guard, one Broadnose ber Glacierheim. "What is going on?"

His wife, her great tent of a gown flapping around her, shambled into the entry hall. Stariz glared at Grimwar, those small eyes glittering, and the king wondered how she could have woken so quickly and completely.

"What is the nature of the disturbance?" she demanded from the messenger.

"I . . . I am not sure I fully understand, Your Highness. The guards on duty summoned me, but of course I dared not enter the sacred sanctum. Nevertheless, as I stood without, I heard sounds like thunder and saw flashes of brightness coming from beneath the door. I know it is impossible, but I felt as though I observed a thunderstorm, bellowing and crashing within the precincts of Winterheim itself." Broadnose dropped to one knee. "I beg Your Majesties' forgiveness if I have overreacted, but I felt it best that I come at once and report."

"You did well," Stariz declared, as Grimwar suppressed the urge to kick the lackey right in the face. The queen, turning to her husband, again glared suspiciously at him. "This matter demands my immediate attention. I suspect that there is word from your mother in Dracoheim."

Dracoheim. Grimwar Bane shuddered in spite of himself. The very name evoked chilly mists, lonely images of a nearly forgotten isle, remote and barren, with ancient dragons swirling through the sky, bringing fire and death, scouring life from the land. Of course, those dragons were gone, vanished with all the dragons from Krynn some four or five centuries ago, during the time of the Knight Huma's war, but that did not much lessen the menace of Dracoheim.

Dracoheim was not uninhabited. Grimwar's mother, the Dowager Queen Hannareit ber Bane, lived there, maintaining the exile she had begun during the reign of her husband, Grimtruth Bane. She had been banished there by Grimtruth when that king, growing tired of his older, brute-faced wife, had taken a younger mistress. The elder queen had chosen to remain there in stolid isolation, even though her husband was now long dead and her son had assumed the throne—for Grimwar Bane steadfastly refused to take vengeance on Thraid Dimmarkull, the mistress his mother blamed for her exile. For her part, Queen Hanna (for she retained that honorific) had vowed never to return to the capital so long as that brazen strumpet of an ogress still lived.

Grimwar had discovered, when he visited Dracoheim five years ago, that Hanna had made herself quite comfortable in the ancient castle. The island was rich in gold. In some places it was sulfurous and scorched by the heat of infernal flames, in others honeycombed by rich mines, steam-blasted caverns, and bubbling volcanoes. More than a thousand human slaves worked the mines, and much of the fabulous wealth was sent to the capital, but Queen Hanna, who managed the mines, kept a grand share.

Also on Dracoheim, Grimwar reflected, was the laboratory of the royal Alchemist. From the chamber of that sagelike servant, with his vats and forges and diagrams and bizarre elements, came dire weapons and inventions that added to the Bane kings' power. Perhaps the current summons meant news of some discovery made by the Alchemist, something that would accrue further power and riches to the reign of the ogre monarch.

Grimwar Bane really didn't care about that, not right now. He thought with a sigh of his mistress, waiting. He watched his wife dismiss Broadnose and enter her dressing room to prepare for a return to the temple. She would undoubtedly be occupied for hours, and during those hours the king would have his opportunity. He smiled, keeping his reaction private by turning to study the great fireplace, apparently meditating upon the great black bearskin hanging on the wall over the mantle.

For Thraid Dimmarkull was not just the former mistress of his father, the ogress behind the cause of his mother's exile. Thraid, she of the full bosom and rosy lips, of soft curves and willing caresses, had been the son's lover for many years now. Currently she awaited him in their private trysting chamber. With his wife heading off to the temple for a major spellcasting session, Grimwar Bane knew that he would be able to visit his beloved after all.

Queen Stariz strode through the lofty, arched entryway leading to the Temple of Gonnas in the Royal Quarter of Winterheim. The sanctuary occupied a huge building in the mountain city and was devoted to the worship of the Willful One, the tusked and brutal god of ogrekind. The floor was black marble, the entry chamber dominated by the lofty statue depicting the god himself, a solid pillar of obsidian more than three times the height of the largest bull ogre. Twin tusks, inky black and as long as swords, jutted from the stern jaw of the implacable image, and the priestess-queen paused for a moment of reverence, bowing her head and clasping her hands before the forbidding visage.

She moved on, past kneeling slaves, into a dark hallway leading toward the deeper reaches of the temple. She moved with purpose, and the lesser priestesses who had gathered before the Ice Chamber scurried out of her way, genuflecting and chanting their mantras.

Stariz ignored them all as she halted before a broad, tall door of granite.

"Leave me!" she commanded, and waited for a short time as the priestesses all scattered to the other parts of the temple.

She could understand Broadnose's description of the "disturbance." Now she too heard the rumbling as of a great storm, saw the bright flashes—very much like lightning—pulsing across the floor through the narrow gap at the bottom of the door.

Only when she was certain that she was alone did Stariz reach forward and push on the stone portal, murmuring the word of command that released the door from its enchanted protection. Soundlessly, smoothly, it swung open, and she followed inside with a purposeful stride, marching into this hallowed room that was her province alone.

Her breath immediately frosted, for it was cold inside. The irregular walls were lined with frost, and in many places icicles draped downward from bulges, outcrops, and ledges. The far side of the chamber was different, however: There, instead of bare rock, the surface was smooth and shiny, slick like a sheet of ice made wet by a gloss of meltwater. It was as though a mirror was mounted in the rough stone, shadowy and yet illuminated at the same time.

Indeed, that smooth surface was the source of the crackling lightning, periodic flashes sparking within a roiling murk. To Stariz it looked as though she was witnessing a powerful storm from above, watching lightning burst between dark thunderheads. From the violence of the images, she knew immediately that the Dowager Queen's message was urgent.

"Cartas Danir! Boraga, Orktan Gonnas!" Stariz chanted, the words exploding from her mouth like small thunderclaps.

Immediately the roiling image faded, the churning murk pulled back from the center of the ice sheet to bluster and swirl around the edges, like a frame of black smoke around a slowly clearing picture.

As the picture gradually became distinct, Stariz beheld her counterpart, former queen of Suderhold, now mistress of Dracoheim. The Dowager Queen Hannareit ber Bane met her gaze with an expression of triumph. The elder ogress bared her tusks slightly as she allowed her pleasure to twist her face into a smile. She might have been an older version of Stariz, they looked enough alike, though the two queens were not in fact related.

Still, they both had that square-jawed face, small eyes glowering below a large, round forehead. Each wore the mantle of a priestess around her shoulders, a rippling robe of black, smooth wool.

"My Queen Mother," Stariz began, with a cool nod of her head. "I sense that you have important, and encouraging tidings."

"You sense correctly, my Queen Daughter," replied Hannareit. "Glory to Gonnas, the Willful One," she added, her words a frosty whisper in the shadowy alcove.

"May his strength be ours," Stariz responded. "What is your news?"

"The Alchemist has made an important discovery," the elder queen reported, "though at some cost to himself." Her lips curled into a smile that was as cruel as it was cold. "Indeed, it nearly cost him his life."

Stariz waited patiently, knowing that Queen Hanna would soon get to the point. She felt a measure of pity for the elder queen, living her life out in the exile of a barren island . . . a moment such as this, no doubt, would be a rare thrill of pleasure for her. Stariz valued Hanna as an ally. It made good sense to be patient, and to allow her this moment of pride.

"He spent the last two seasons seeking some unusual power of explosive, as was suggested by the communications you and I both shared, premonitions from our mighty lord."

"Gonnas be praised," Stariz chanted, remembering the dreams that she and Hanna had experienced at the same time on the previous summer. They had both reported their vision: that wooden statues, sanctified by the god, should be burned in a holy fire. The ashes, the Willful One had indicated, could be the catalyst for a mighty weapon, if the proper means of ignition could be devised. The two ogresses had agreed that the Alchemist should set aside everything and devote all of his energies to the new task. Nevertheless, when Stariz had last communicated with Hanna—well before the Sturmfrost had struck—the Dowager Queen had only disappointment to report.

"It was the potion that provided the key," Queen Hanna said. She chuckled, a dry and evil sound. "The nectar of life to that pathetic wretch—he never would have willingly included it in his recipe. There was a happy accident, he spilled some onto the mix of ingredients, and the resulting explosion destroyed half of his chamber and nearly killed him!"

"But he survives, and can continue to work and refine his discovery?" Stariz pressed.

"Indeed, though I had to use a great amount of healing magic. However, he has been able to recreate the mixture under more controlled circumstances. I had the concoction placed in a suitable vessel, and the subsequent test annihilated a camp of human slaves with a most satisfactory blast."

"You could spare a few slaves, I trust?"

"Indeed, that particular nest was a troublesome lot, always fomenting revolt, avoiding work, hoarding supplies. They will be no more trouble to me, it is safe to say. Even their buildings, stone houses and a smithy, were swept away by the impressive might of the explosion."

"And this alchemy can be turned into a calculated weapon, for use against the humans of Brackenrock?" Stariz pressed, arriving at the matter that had governed her will for the past eight years. "So that we can finally, after all this time, avenge our honor and retrieve the Axe of Gonnas."

"Undoubtedly. I am sending the secret formula to you, in the care of a loyal thanoi; even now, he has

started the long swim toward Winterheim. I think . . ."
Again Queen Hanna allowed herself that hint of a
wicked smile. "I think you will be greatly pleased."

"I will do my best to encourage your son to take advantage of this great gift," Stariz assured the Dowager
Queen, who scowled slightly in response.

"I presume my son has refused to address the matter
of that harlot, Thraid Dimmarkull?" Hanna said pointedly. "Gonnas curse his stubbornness!"

Stariz suspected that there was more than stubbornness to her husband's defense of the voluptuous Thraid.
She did not know for certain, but she had cautioned her
spies to be alert, and she was waiting to learn the truth.
There had been too many long glances shared by those
two and a number of unexplained absences.

One thing was certain, a belief she held deep within
the cold shell of her heart: Stariz ber Glacierheim would
never let herself suffer the same fate as the Dowager
Queen.

***

Thraid welcomed King Grimwar with a soft, warm
embrace and a kiss that seemed to envelop his mouth,
his breath, his very being. He pulled her tight, felt the
lush cushion of her body against him, and realized that
he was shaking with raw desire.

"How I missed you, my king," she whispered, nibbling with maddening delight at his ear, "and how delighted I am to see, to hold, to have you, again."

"And you, my mistress," the monarch replied. "It has
been far too long."

He held her at arm's length and absorbed the sight of
her, the clear skin, pale as ivory, the full lips, rouged and

swollen and curled into their alluring pout. He ran his
hands down her flanks, from the fullness of her bosom
to the waist that was so remarkably narrow for an
ogress, over the hips that rounded so invitingly, as if
sculpted for his pleasure.

They stopped speaking then, for it had indeed been a
long time since their last tryst. Desperation drove them
into a clinch. Their frenzy was shared and delightful,
and by the end the king was roaring like a triumphant
lion while his mistress, his prey, mewled with delight beneath him.

"It is a good thing you maintain such a remote chamber for us," Thraid said afterward, stroking the king's
strong jaw with her finger. "Else I fear your noise would
have aroused the whole palace."

"Indeed, the doors are well proofed against sound,"
Grimwar Bane said with a deep chuckle, relaxing on the
soft mattress, willing sleep to slowly rise up and claim
him. He looked at his cherished one, watched her
drowse, relishing the rise and fall of her breasts as she
breathed deeply.

For some reason, he was not tired, not even relaxed.
Though it hadn't taken Thraid long to fall asleep, the
king could not do the same. Restless, he worked his arm
up from beneath her and sat up, frowning. He found it
hard to relax, for he was distracted. He knew that his
wife was talking to his mother, that there would be some
disturbing bulletin from Dracoheim.

Now that Grimwar was temporarily sated, he was
preoccupied by his strong suspicion that the news, however welcome it might be to Stariz, would involve some
onerous task for himself.

The Chiefwoman

How about the third terrace? Is there enough topsoil there for plowing and planting? I don't want to lose half the crop again in the late summer rains!"

Moreen Bayguard, the Lady of Brackenrock, frowned as she looked down the mountainside, her gaze following the long slope descending from the fortress to the ocean shore, two miles away. She stood atop one of the two gatehouse towers flanking the entry to the citadel. This was the best vantage for examining the progress made by her people in their annual effort to capitalize upon the few months of precious sunlight.

"Not yet, my lady," said Lukor. The gray-haired farmer frowned sympathetically and rubbed his dirty, gnarled hands together. "We have hauled a hundred cartloads of black dirt from the fen, but there are still many rocks. With luck and hard work, we will be ready for planting within another few days."

"That will have to do, then," Moreen said, dissatisfied with the assessment but knowing there was nothing she could do to improve upon things. "You have every one of the Highlanders working on it?"

"Of course, Lady. They know that their best hopes for a good year of warqat come from the barley we grow right here. You could say that they are rather enthusiastic assistants."

The chiefwoman chuckled briefly. "Just keep them out of last year's brew until the task is done."

"Certainly," Luk replied. "I must say, they are strong men and seem cheerful enough as long as they know they have something to work for. They like life in Brackenrock as well as do we Arktos."

"Aye, the Highlanders are ripe for hard work," she agreed, then turned as she heard a loud laugh from the trapdoor leading to the gatehouse observation platform. "Ah, Bruni, welcome," she said. "What do you find so funny?"

The big woman pulled herself through the hatch and stood up, looking over the tall farmer and all but dwarfing the relatively petite chiefwoman. She chuckled again. "These Highlanders do all kinds of work," she said genially. "Marta just told me that she, too, is expecting a baby this autumn."

Moreen nodded, not surprised, but not necessarily pleased by the announcement. Of course, in a way it *was* good news. The male warriors of her tribe had been slain in battle nine years earlier—had it really been that long?—and the influx of strong, handsome, and cheerful Highlander men had undeniably given the Arktos a new lease on their future. Since she and her people had restored Brackenrock, they held the most desirable land in all the Icereach. Because of this, men were willing to come here, work, and many of them married into Moreen's tribe.

The chiefwoman understood, hypothetically, that if

her tribe had been still eking out survival in the small, vulnerable fishing village on the Blood Coast of the White Bear Sea, the migration would have worked the other way around. Inevitably the women of her tribe would have slipped away to join the Highlanders in their own citadels, sacrificing the legacy of their people for the security of a life behind stone walls. None of those Highlander forts was as tall as impregnable Brackenrock, but every one of them had been safer than a waterfront village—until Moreen's tribe had taken over and fortified Brackenrock.

After the ogres' massacre of her people, including her father, the chief of the Bayguard clan, Moreen had led the survivors—women, children, and elders—to safety, assuming leadership of the desperate tribe. In that role she had brought them to the ruins of ancient Brackenrock and made this place not just a home but an unassailable fortress. The ogre army, led by the ogre king, had assaulted Brackenrock and failed, and over the past eight years the ogres had not dared to launch another full-scale attack.

But the ogres persistently harried Moreen with raids against remote Arktos villages, and forays against some of the smaller castles of the Highlanders. Refugees from those other battles had come here to be welcomed and provided with food and shelter. Moreen knew deep in her heart that Brackenrock was only temporarily a refuge, that the ogres would not leave them alone forever.

"You were down at the waterfront, right?" Moreen asked Bruni. "What about the harbor boom?" Even though she couldn't see the protected circle of Brackenrock's little port from here, Moreen stared downward, as if her penetrating gaze might bore through the solid rock of the mountainside and bring the object of her concern into view.

"The logs and chains are in place. They need to float it across, then test it. As soon as that's done, we should be able to bar the entrance against any hostile ship."

"Such as the ogre king's galley," the chiefwoman finished grimly. Bruni let that statement pass without comment.

"Where's Kerrick? I thought he was going to be back from Bearhearth in time to help finish the boom!" Moreen wondered, her worry changing into a crossness in her voice.

Bruni shrugged and looked northward, across the newly sparkling waters of the Courrain Ocean. "I expect he's taking his sweet time on the trip. You know how he gets during the winter, all cooped up . . . and this is his first sail since the ice broke up. Still, he's been gone for three days. I would expect him back before nightfall."

"I wish he would pay a little more attention to the work that needs to be done," groused the chiefwoman.

Bruni chuckled, the sound irritating in Moreen's ears. "What's so funny this time?" she demanded.

Her friend looked down at her with an amused but exasperated shrug.

"Sometimes I get the feeling that if Kerrick marched in here with Grimwar Bane's head on a pike, you'd complain that he didn't make a neat enough slice through his neck!"

Moreen glowered up at the big woman. "If Kerrick ever brings me the ogre king's head—or any part of any ogre!—I expect I could make a proper show of gratitude! But there's so much to do here, and it seems sometimes as if he just doesn't care about anything! Anything—except that damn boat of his or all the gold he's accumulating."

Bruni nodded sagely, and the chiefwoman found that reaction similarly aggravating, especially when her friend spoke. "Remember the first gold he earned? We gave it to him willingly, so he would ferry the tribe across the strait. If he hadn't been there . . ."

"I know, I know. We'd all be living under Strongwind Whalebone's protection. I'd probably be his wife by now."

As she thought of the trials of the past years, the strength she had gained and the prosperity her people now enjoyed, Moreen acknowledged privately that she owed a great deal to the elf they had come to regard as the Messenger. Not only had he and his boat carried her people across a previously impassable water barrier, but he had risked his life in their subsequent battle for survival. Once Brackenrock had been secured, he had shown her people how to build boats, mint coins, to do so many things that were commonplace in his world. As she looked across the sculpted fields she recalled that it had been Kerrick Fallabrine who had explained the technique of terracing farmland, of bringing water through sluice gates and channels to irrigate fields, giving Brackenrock—and Moreen—claim to the most fertile granges in all the Icereach.

When she pictured the elf's handsome face, his golden hair and large, penetrating eyes—even the ragged scar of his left ear, which she secretly admired as a sign of his character—she felt different emotions. As always, she recognized a danger in those feelings and forced her emotions aside. As she turned to go, she looked at Bruni and shook her head.

"For someone who's almost ninety years old, Kerrick Fallabrine still has a lot of growing up to do, is what I think," she declared.

Bruni snorted. "You could do with a little grow—oh, never mind," she declared curtly.

Moreen immediately felt guilty. "I'm sorry—I don't

mean to snap at you," she said, then laughed. "I guess he's not really as bad as I make him out to be."

"What about you having some fun for a change, doing something just for the sheer pleasure of it?" the large woman asked eagerly. "You mentioned Strongwind Whalebone—he'd be delighted to hear from you, see you. Going hunting, fishing—something like you used to do in the old days! Who knows, the king of the Highlanders might start to look pretty good to you."

Shaking her head, Moreen laughed again, wryly now. "No . . . I think you'll have a mate long before I will," she said.

Bruni's shoulders slumped. She turned away, pretending interest in the work on the fields. The chiefwoman regretted her remark. She knew that her friend had never attracted the interest of any man. Unlike Moreen, Bruni found the lack of male interest depressing, and lately she had gone through several bouts of melancholy brought on by her loneliness.

"Will you do me a favor if you see Kerrick?" Moreen asked quickly

"Sure," said Bruni, with another shrug.

"Tell him I need to talk to him," Moreen said, before slipping through the trapdoor into the coolness of the tower. Already her mind was ticking through the rest of the list—a dozen, a score, a *hundred* things needed to be done.

As usual, it seemed as though she had to supervise them all.

———◆◆◆———

Cutter glided past the Signpost, the rocky pillar that stood at the mouth of Brackenrock's harbor. The elf had already stowed his jib, and the mainsail was tightened to a small portion of its vast surface as Kerrick steered the boat slowly toward one of the sturdy wooden docks that now extended into the placid water.

He could hardly believe how this place had changed in the years since he had first glimpsed it. Six boats, seaworthy if rather round and ungainly, bobbed at anchor. A solid quay with two long piers lined the shoreline that had been jumbled with rocky debris eight years before. To his left was the boatyard, where two new curraghs were nearly ready for launching, skeletal frames complete and awaiting only the cured leather hides that would render them seaworthy Beyond those round, tublike craft, a gleaming hull of wooden planks rested between framing beams. That boat had the sharp prow and deep keel of a true sailboat, somewhat shorter and wider than *Cutter* but nevertheless a sleek and modern craft.

A lanky young man, his long black hair bound into a long ponytail, stopped planing the hull long enough to wave at the elf.

"How did the wind hold?" asked Mouse, shouting across the rippled water.

"About like you'd expect for the first of spring," Kerrick replied, cupping his hands around his mouth to help his voice carry across the harbor. "Like I could have made it to Ansalon by tomorrow! Then I had to tack all the way back."

He turned the tiller and *Cutter* glided easily up to the longest dock. Several youths hurried to take the line he tossed ashore, and in moments the slender boat was lashed securely to the stout pilings. Knowing he had taken on a good amount of spray, Kerrick promised the boys a gold coin if they'd pump out the bilge, and they gleefully accepted.

"Do you want the sail in the locker?" asked the oldest, swaggering forward with the long experience of one whole summer as a boathand.

"Not yet," the elf replied, suddenly reluctant to abandon the freedom of the sea. "Who knows? If the weather holds, I might take another run before sunset." He knew that today's sunlight would only total seven or eight hours, but he was not willing to relinquish the good spring weather, not just yet.

Mouse had wandered over to say hello, and now he raised his eyebrows. "Another run before dark? Well, you're the captain."

"At least, on this boat," Kerrick said with a laugh, clapping the strapping young man on the shoulder, then gesturing to the nearly completed hull, the sleek boards his friend had been smoothing. Unlike the leather-shelled curraghs, the new boat was similar in shape to *Cutter*, with a keel, long deck, and single, low cabin.

"It won't be long until you've got *Marlin* afloat."

"I know." Mouse's face lit up at the mention of his boat. "Once we've got a stretch of solid good weather I'll take one of the tubs across to trade for pitch in Tall Cedar Bay. I'll get the boys to help—they're always ready for a ride in a curragh. When I bring that back and caulk *Marlin*'s hull, I'll be ready to put her in the water. I think I'll be sailing before the sun sets in fall."

"I'll enjoy the sight of another beautiful boat on these seas," Kerrick suggested. He gestured ruefully to the round shapes moored around them. "You're right. These curraghs look more like laundry tubs than proper sailing craft."

Mouse laughed. "They've changed the way we live, and that's the truth. It's hard to believe that ten years ago no one from my tribe had seen the western shore of the

White Bear Sea. Now we have small towns on both sides, and people go back and forth dozens of times in a year!"

"You Arktos are natural sailors," the elf agreed. "Taking these open boats onto the White Bear Sea is bold work."

"They're the best we can do around here, I suppose, with the materials and tools of the Icereach. You know, some day I'd love to see the shipyards of Silvanesti, or Tarsis . . . all the places you've told us about," the young man said dreamily. "To see the work of those who made *Cutter*."

"I don't doubt that if you had proper oak and mahogany in the Icereach, you'd make a vessel that's equal to *Cutter*. You've done wonders with the materials you have. Think of *Marlin*, a pine-board longboat with leather stoppers and but two sails . . . and she'll be able to ride the deep ocean as well as any king's galley. She'll take you to Tarsis, my friend, or to anywhere else you want to go."

Mouse nodded, then looked almost guilty as his eyes flicked upward toward the fortress that loomed unseen beyond the mountainside overhead. "Of course, I wouldn't want to leave Feathertail that long," he assured the elf.

Kerrick smiled ruefully. "She's as much a sailor as you are, and don't think she'd let you leave her behind. As a matter of fact, it's not exactly common for someone to sail by himself. Don't get the wrong idea just because I showed up here that way. I was unusual even among Silvanesti sailors."

"But you had Coraltop Netfisher along, didn't you?" asked the young man. "You've always said so!"

The elf winced, remembering his dream. He had felt a stab of melancholy when he had awakened to find that his old companion was not in fact present on the boat. It was rare for him to think of Coraltop or dream of him these days.

"Maybe. I'm not even sure myself, any more. It's been so long that I have to wonder if he really existed, or if Moreen is right, that he was a just figment of my imagination, created out of the long months of boredom at sea. Though I did have a dream about him," he admitted, "just a couple of nights ago." Kerrick thought of Coraltop's suggestion that his father might have returned to Silvanesti in his absence. That was impossible, of course, but it was strange how the notion, once planted in his subconscious, kept rising to the surface.

Mouse frowned. "I've never heard you say that Coraltop didn't exist! Didn't you see him right here in your boat the day we won Brackenrock?"

Kerrick squirmed inwardly. He didn't like to consider the suggestion that the kender wasn't real—it sounded far too much like madness—but somehow here, today, he keenly felt the glaring lack of evidence to the contrary.

"That was eight years ago, and I never saw him again. That day no one else saw him, either. No, that kender may as well have been pure fancy. I'm glad to say that I've put the past behind me."

"If you think so, that's the important thing," Mouse agreed, though he avoided looking Kerrick in the eye. "Um . . . how was the run to Bearhearth?"

"Smooth, no problems," the elf replied, grateful for the change of subject. "Say, do you know why they call it that?"

"No. I never thought about it."

"The thane told me that, five or six generations ago, there wasn't a castle there, and the clan was a wandering tribe. Their leader speared a bear high in the mountains and tracked the animal down to the shore and along the beach for ten miles, or maybe more. When he finally caught up to the creature, he found the bear dead, right in the middle of a flat clearing above a sheltered cove. The Highlanders decided that the place was perfect for a stronghold. It turned out that the bear perished right on the spot where they put the fireplace in the great hall."

"Bears," Mouse noted. "They play a big role in our folklore, Highlanders and Arktos alike. You've heard our own clan's legend about the black bear?"

"The one slain by Moreen's grandfather, yes," Kerrick replied. "It was a harbinger of greatness, I recall, the sign that the Bayguard clan would lead all the Arktos. I never got to see the skin—the ogres captured it that summer, before I got here—but I believe that is one prophecy that has come true."

"Maybe someday Moreen will get that fur back," said the young man ruefully.

The elf didn't see how that was possible, since the trophy, so far as anyone knew, was kept in the ogre fortress of Winterheim, but he didn't dash his friend's hopes. "Well, we have the ogre's sacred axe," he suggested with good humor, "so maybe we got the best of the trade."

"Perhaps," Mouse mused, but he was looking southward. The elf knew he was remembering the talisman of his people.

Kerrick broke into the man's reverie. "Say, when the boatmen come down for work, could you ask some of the lads to get the chest out of *Cutter*'s hold? There's a lot of gold in there, payment from the Thane of Bearhearth, and most of it goes into Moreen's treasure room."

"Sure will," Mouse agreed.

The elf felt strangely restless as he left the harbor, walking steadily but slowly up the long road that cut its way back and forth across the steep slope above the little anchorage. Yes, it had been a long time since he had thought of Coraltop Netfisher. Mouse's remark had startled him into old memories, which he had decided were best left in the past where they belonged.

Such memories made him feel all the more out of place, sometimes jarringly so. An elf among humans! They were appealing companions, of course, but could they ever truly be his people? Once again he found himself thinking of what Coraltop had said in the dream. His father, Dimorian Fallabrine, had sailed off from Silvanesti, never to return. Now *he* seemed destined never to return. It didn't seem right that the son should share the father's fate.

Finally he crested the ridge, and Brackenrock loomed before him. The twin towers of the gatehouse stood tall and proud, smooth-seamed with fresh mortar. The gate itself was open, deployed downward as a ramp across the shallow ditch before the curtain wall. As Kerrick made his way up the road toward the gates, the terraces came into view on the oceanside of Brackenrock, opposite the shore of the White Bear Sea. The soon-to-be-verdant fields descended the long slope below the great citadel. They curved along an incline. The broad hillside faced north and so caught every precious ray of the sun that would soon shine for a nightless season lasting for three uninterrupted months.

He encountered Bruni near the gate as she ambled outward carrying a large, iron pry bar. The big woman's moonlike face beamed in greeting.

"You have that look in your eye—you must have taken your boat out for a whirl," she said with a hearty chuckle.

"It shows in my eyes?" Kerrick asked, surprised and amused.

"Well, actually you got a little windburned, and that looks like salt on your tunic, so no, I guess it's not really your eyes. Still, it's nice to see you happy."

The elf grinned sheepishly. "I guess I was kind of a gruff bear toward the last month of winter there. I hope I didn't bite you too hard."

"I'm a big girl, in case you haven't noticed. No, nothing where I couldn't just bite right back if I'd wanted to." Bruni's gaze shifted back toward the castle. "At least *you* cheer up when the sun comes out again. I wish *she* would get out of the citadel for a little while, let herself go for a ride on your boat, a bear hunt . . . anything! Which reminds me: She's looking for you." There was no need to specify who "she" was.

Kerrick nodded. "About the harbor boom, right?"

Bruni nodded.

"We'll need about fifty strong men—excuse me, strong *people*," Kerrick explained, with a nod toward this woman who could lift him clear of the ground with one hand. "As soon as we have a work party, we can finish the job in one day, but I assumed she'd want to wait until the fields were planted."

"You don't have to explain it all to me," the big woman said. "I'm off to see about the lumberyard. The feeder track into the sawmill is out of alignment again."

"Good luck," the elf offered, knowing that, if anyone could align the heavy rails leading up to the iron blade, Bruni would be able to do the job. Everything he taught her she had learned to do, often improving on his own methods.

Passing through the gates, Kerrick started toward the great hall, where Moreen had her planning table and where the chiefwoman would most likely be found. An impulse moved him, and instead of going directly to the keep he turned to a side door. Following a long passage illuminated only sporadically by the light spilling from slits in the wall, he came to a stairwell. Here he took the time to strike a spark and ignite the torch that was kept here for just this purpose.

Descending the steep steps into chill darkness, he ducked low and made his way along a narrow corridor until he came to a locked door in the wall. The corridor continued on into the dark distance, but past this place the floor was lined with a thick layer of undisturbed dust.

Kerrick was one of four people who had a key to this door. He turned it, released the latch, and went inside.

The treasure room of Brackenrock was a very large chamber, especially considering that now it contained only a dozen barrels of whale oil, a few pallets of golden ingots, and a stack of small casks filled with potent, intoxicating warqat. In one corner, set apart from those possessions, were three small chests.

The elf held the torch up high as he lifted the lid, in turn, of each unlocked strongbox. He beheld the piles of gold coins, each a mass of many hundreds of coins, and he reflected on what that treasure could buy for him in the city of the elven king. Most importantly, far more significant than the wealth, the gold represented the restoration of his family's reputation, the successful conclusion to an exile issued by his king.

Kerrick knew that King Nethas had issued the challenge to find gold more as mockery than as an attainable, true goal. He chuckled dryly. Here in the Icereach he had found more gold than the king could dream of.

A few minutes later he entered the great hall. This was the largest chamber in the entire citadel, a vaulting cavern of space that dwarfed the small knot of people huddled around a table at the far end. The great shutters aligning the north and east walls had been opened, and rays of bright sunlight angled, still more horizontal than vertical, through clouds of dust mites dancing in the room.

Several large fireplaces gaped in the walls around the room, none of them as large as the mighty hearth spreading beyond the work table. Atop that hearth, bright in the illumination of reflected sunlight, the Axe of Gonnas hung in its place of honor. The golden blade was cold now, but the immaculate metal seemed deep and sinister, suggestive of the magical fire lurking there. Kerrick felt the familiar flush of pride as he saw the axe. The artifact had been an ogre treasure, and now it was the trophy of Brackenrock. It had been the elven Messenger who had wrested that prize from the hands of the ogre queen herself.

Inevitably, as he crossed the room, the sense of space diminished, and he found his attention focusing on the slight, black-haired woman looking down at plans and drawings on the table. Moreen was poring over the sketches for the third terrace, detailing which fields would be planted with barley, which with wheat. As Kerrick drew near she looked at him and blinked for a moment, as if she couldn't remember why she had asked to see him. He stared into her face, that image of pure beauty coupled with a remote, imperious sense of command.

"You're back from Bearhearth," she observed dryly.

"Yes, I have the gold." He thought of telling Moreen the tale of that place's naming but quickly decided she wouldn't be interested. More accurately, she wouldn't want to take the time to listen to him talk about something so irrelevant to all the hard work that needed to be done.

"The harbor boom," he offered. "We can finish it tomorrow, but I need fifty workers to haul the chain across the water. Do you want to spare the Highlanders from work on the terrace or wait till after you've planted?"

She grimaced at the quandary and shook her head in exasperation. "They both need to be done as soon as possible!" she snapped. "Pull the men from the field. Nothing is more important than our defense."

"All right," the elf agreed, content with her decision. Like the king in his homeland, she had the power and decisiveness to make such commands. Men like him existed merely to enact her decrees. He half turned away before he paused and looked at her. He could sense her impatience and knew that she wanted to get back to work. It was only then that he knew what he was going to say, what he *had* to say.

"After the boom is done I'll have some of the boys help me load my gold from the treasure room," he said off-handedly.

"Onto *Cutter*?" she asked, frowning. "Why?"

"Because," Kerrick said, drawing out the words, surprised at what he was saying, as his notion suddenly crystallized, "I've decided to sail north this summer, to Silvanesti. I'm going home."

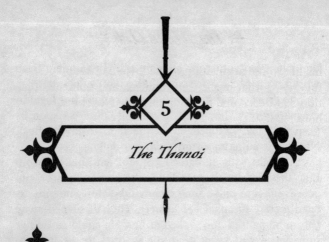

5

The Thanoi

The Alchemist sat in the chair beside his fire, the embers piled high, radiating heat through the chamber. It was after sunset, late spring, and he cherished the encompassing darkness. He was weary but not—yet—mired in that sinking despair that would clutch at him when the magic at last wore off.

In this hazy daydream his mind began to wander, into the past now, for he had no desire to anticipate his future. How long had it been since he had first succumbed to that sweet thrill of magical bliss, the enchantment that brought pleasure beyond compare? A century perhaps? Even longer? He could not recall.

The first taste of that sweet, magical nectar had changed his life forever. His days of peace, of contentment, had vanished, replaced by a constant longing that was never totally fulfilled. Indeed, for those periods when his desire was slaked, life was a dizzying thrill, darkened only by the fear that someday the magic would be gone.

Early on he had sensed the connection. Gold purchased magic, and magic gave him life. So he had devoted his life to the acquisition of gold. He had been successful enough that magic was plentiful, and that combination had fueled and driven him, and at last brought him here.

To Dracoheim.

His room had been repaired since the accidental explosion. Now he had new furnishings, surroundings appointed as well as any lord's manor in his homeland. It was a chamber of opulence, filled with treasures of gold and jade that meant nothing to him, not now, not when his need was once again beginning to grow.

The Dowager Queen had rewarded him well after his discovery. First, she had used her power to heal his burned and blistered flesh. Then she had brewed him an entire small barrel full of magical potion and had given it to him to consume as he desired.

That cask was half empty now, but still more than a hundred swallows of clear liquid remained. This particular batch was a liquid that rendered his flesh into amorphous, gaseous form. Previous batches had rendered him invisible each time he drank it, but he didn't care whether or not the magic dissolved his flesh into sentient gas or caused him to disappear from sight These were purely secondary effects. To the Alchemist, the magic was the whole thing,

Now his need was too great to ignore. He reached into the alcove and filled the dipper to overflowing, swilling down the wonderful draught, choking reflexively even as he began to take gaseous form. He floated back in the direction of his bed, but in the end he remained as an amorphous cloud in the middle of the room. The magic suffused his veins, relieved his pain, soothed his need . . .

Again he felt alive, alive!

He drifted to the window, looked into the late spring night, and saw the brightness above the horizon. It gave him some pleasure to watch the white moon rise, the full and silvery circle. This was one month before the solstice, he knew, and for his own amusement he made a few calculations, considering the converging paths of the sun and moons. The results were clear, and the news might be of use.

When, a short time later, he materialized, he wrote his findings down for the Dowager Queen. Then he went to work, laboring as if in a trance but a trance that increased his speed, sharpened his acuity, and reinforced his memory and judgment. His hands flew through the motions, mixing powders and liquids, maintaining a low simmer for a bluish solution, fanning the coals on a small forge so that a little kettle of gold nuggets gradually melted into a pool of molten treasure.

Acid simmered in the large vat, spuming acrid vapors into the air. The Alchemist coughed, ignored the discomfort as he turned the valve to draw off the noxious liquid. For long minutes it trickled away until all that was left was the powder, the stuff that was so valuable to his ogre masters. Innocuous, simple in the end, but so very, very dangerous to create. The amalgam of finely powdered gold, pure salt, black cinder, and ash, when exposed to the touch of a magic potion, would yield violence and destruction on a scale the world of Krynn had never known.

Carefully he scraped the amalgam from the sides and from the bottom of the glass container, wiping the residue into an ivory tube. Somehow he controlled the trembling that normally tormented him.

When it had all been gathered, he sealed the tube—which was nothing more than a walrus tusk that had been hollowed out and fitted with a watertight cap.

His work was done, and he was weary. With shaking fingers he reached for the dipper, removed the top of the keg to release a cloud of sweet vapor. With a quiver of anticipation, he put the ladle to his lips, tilted back his head . . . and drank his reward.

———◆———

"Begging Your Majesty's pardon, but it's a thanoi. He stinks too bad to come into the upper portions of the city, so I've got him cooling his flippers down at the harbor. He says he's got a message from the Dowager Queen."

Grimwar Bane blinked and rubbed his eyes, trying to clear away the fog of an interrupted sleep. He had just been awakened and was irritated with the messenger— once again it was Broadnose ber Glacierheim who had chosen an inconvenient time to come to the royal apartments. He stifled his displeasure as he digested the import of the ogre's tidings.

"A walrus-man? He claims that he comes from Dracoheim?"

"Indeed, Majesty, and he wears the royal collar around his neck. He bears a tusk-tube with the symbol of the Dowager Queen, your mother. I did not open it, of course, but I inspected the sigil. It seems to be genuine."

Grimwar was surprised and puzzled. The tusked, blubbery thanoi were crude and treacherous wretches, and he did not consider them friends. However, they had their uses, not the least of which was the ability to swim long distances. Although he had two stout galleys in his fleet, Dracoheim was so far away, and so remote from the rest of his kingdom, that it was only visited by ship once every few years. If one of the walrus-men brought a message from that remote island, it would likely be a missive of no little significance.

"What is it?" Stariz emerged from her own chamber, a cloud of ritual incense wafting into the hall behind her. "Who has come?"

Grimwar was annoyed when the guard, instead of deferring to the king, stepped forward to bow to his wife. "I bring news of a message from the Dowager Queen, Your Majesty. She sends a tube from Dracoheim, arriving just tonight in the hands of a thanoi messenger."

"I have been expecting this," Stariz said, which surprised the king even more than Broadnose's temerity. "Where is the message?"

"The thanoi is harbor-side, Your Majesty. I will bring him up, if that is the royal wish—though you should know that he gives off by a most pungent and unpleasant odor."

"I know what a thanoi smells like," snapped Stariz. "Bring him to us at once—"

"No," countermanded the king, drawing a sharp look from his wife. He, too, knew what a thanoi smelled like. "We will descend and interview him on the harbor level. Have the royal accounting house made ready."

He glared at his wife, who—for once—bit her tongue. Broadnose bowed deeply. "It shall be done at once, Sire!" he declared, before hastening back to the lift.

The king expected Stariz to complain as soon as they were alone, but she surprised him by bustling back to her chambers, calling for her slaves to bring a deerskin robe. Irrationally pleased at this minor victory, the king made his own preparations, draping his prized robe—the unique black bearskin claimed in a raid on the Arktos eight years earlier—around his shoulders. His slave helped him slip his feet into heavy whaleskin boots, and he waited impatiently for no more than a minute before Stariz, too, was ready.

"How did you know this messenger was coming?" he asked his wife, as they rode down through the city together.

"Several times I have spoken to the Dowager Queen in the Ice Chamber . . . about many things," she said, with a pointed look.

The king was silent, anticipating his wife's next remarks. "She repeats her request," Stariz said, "asking you to punish the harlot, Thraid Dimmarkull, for the shame she brought to your mother. I tell you, the Dowager Queen is right, my lord. Have the wench put to death, and bring your mother home!"

"I have spoken on this matter," growled the king. "I will not put an innocent ogress to death for a dalliance that was my father's fault, more than any other's." He squirmed, wanting to talk about something, *anything*, else. "Now, tell me, what is so important about this thanoi's message?"

"Be patient, my king, and you will find out," Stariz replied curtly.

He pressed further, but for her part the queen would provide no details, even though it was an hour or more before they finally reached the harbor level. Here Grimwar paused to regard his two sleek warships, *Goldwing* and *Hornet*, moored side by side in the great vault of the enclosed harbor. Both were polished and sleek after a long winter inside the mountain, and he allowed himself a moment of expectation. Soon he would take them out, crossing the White Bear Sea, perhaps even venturing onto the blessed ocean itself. He could almost smell the sea air, feel the salt spray against his skin . . .

"Husband," Stariz muttered, firmly grabbing his arm, "must I remind you that this is a matter of no little urgency?"

"Of course not," he growled, following her to the accounting office.

This sumptuous chamber was a large room located a short distance from the harbor. It was accessed by a pair of wide doors, now closed, through which cargo passed after it was off-loaded. There was a smaller door leading into the elegantly appointed anteroom, which was open, and as they approached the king detected a strong stench of oily fish.

They entered to find the walrus-man standing between a pair of ogre guards. Stariz peremptorily dismissed the men at arms, while Grimwar studied the emissary with distaste. The thanoi was bigger than a human, though not so tall as an ogre. His most distinctive characteristics were the twin tusks jutting from beneath his blubbery upper lip. Unlike true walrus tusks, which curved downward against the animal's breast, the thanoi's tusks had an outward, more elephantine bend. The king knew they made formidable weapons.

The fellow was naked, outfitted only with an ivory tube suspended from a leather loop around his neck, and a golden collar bearing the royal sigil of the Bane kings. His skin was brown and wrinkled, except on his limbs, which were relatively sleek. The fingers and toes of his extremities were webbed, allowing for that impressive swimming speed, and the barrel-shaped torso was thick with a layer of fat that caused the flesh to collect in a series of rolls around the walrus-man's middle. The thanoi's eyes were small and dark—piglike, Grimwar had often thought—and now they regarded the royal couple with a glare of pride mingled with fear.

"Who are you?" demanded the king bluntly.

"My name is Long-Swim Greatfin," replied the walrus-man, lifting himself to a semblance of attention. "I am chief of the Dracoheim Thanoi, a loyal subject of her majesty, Dowager Queen Hannareit."

"You swam all the way to Winterheim?"

"To the eastern shore of the Dracoheim Sea," corrected the thanoi. "I crossed the mountain barrier on foot, for that is the most direct route."

Grimwar nodded. He knew that the near shore of the Dracoheim Sea lay not very far west of Winterheim, just beyond the long but slender Fenriz Glacier. If the thanoi had instead tried to come all the way to Winterheim by water, he would have had to swim far to the north, entering the White Bear Sea through the Bluewater Strait and nearly doubling the total distance traveled.

"You have done well to make haste," the king declared with approval, wishing he knew what was so urgent about this foul-smelling creature's message.

"You bring us something from the Dowager Queen?" Stariz asked without preamble, as the departing guards closed the door, leaving the two royal ogres alone with the messenger.

"I have it here, my queen," said the walrus-man, lifting the narrow ivory tube, curved slightly, from a thong around his neck. Grimwar guessed the container had been made from a walrus tusk.

"I'll take that," said the king, determined to demonstrate some semblance of his authority. He clasped the smooth tube, then looked in vain for some means of opening it. He saw the Dowager Queen's sigil, the engraved "H," in the surface of ivory that formed a blunt end of the object. The other end came to a dull point, reinforcing his impression that this was the massive outer tooth of a bull walrus, but though he looked at it from every angle, he could discern no crack or seam, nothing that looked likely to allow access.

"Let me have a look," said Stariz, snatching the tube away. The king glowered, watching, as she spun it in her hands to reveal that the wider end was a cap, cut with grooves so that it screwed tightly onto the body of the tube. She unscrewed the container holding it upright as she peered into it. Her attention focused on whatever was inside the container, something she took great care not to spill.

"He has succeeded," she declared simply, as Grimwar tried to look over her shoulder.

"Who has succeeded? With what?" he demanded crossly.

"The Alchemist, of course," Stariz replied. "He has given us the means to destroy our human foes, utterly, completely, and without mercy."

"What are you talking about?"

She looked at him with her jaw set sternly, her little eyes burning with intensity. "It means that now, this summer, you must at last mount an expedition to destroy Brackenrock, to make yourself master of this land for once and for all!"

"Explain yourself!" Grimwar demanded, not liking the way this conversation was going. Brackenrock! Why, the very name gave him chills. He remembered the last time he had attacked the place, eight years before— that had been the single most catastrophic raid of his lifetime!

"I will explain, privately," the queen replied, with a meaningful glance at the thanoi, who was doing a less-than-convincing job of pretending not to listen. "You have done well, Long-Swim Greatfin. Go and find such food and drink as you desire in the harborside kitchens. Await our word before you depart. It is likely that we will give you a missive to carry back to your mistress."

"Very well, Your Highness," replied the tusked messenger. He bowed deeply until his tusks almost touched the floor, then backed to the door and departed.

"What is this madness about Brackenrock?" demanded the king, as soon as the thanoi was gone. "That place has walls as high as a mountain! Gonnas only knows how many archers the Arktos and their Highlander allies will have on the ramparts! It is a death trap, and I will not sacrifice my best warriors in a fruitless attack! I know they hold the sacred axe, but face the fact, my wife: That artifact is gone forever!"

The queen spoke fiercely. "You call it a death trap—but perhaps it may become a trap for the humans themselves." Stariz brandished the tusk-tube. "There is a powder in here, my husband—a concoction of the Alchemist with hitherto unknown explosive properties. When prepared according to the instruction the Dowager Queen has conveyed, it will make a weapon capable of destroying the entire citadel! Imagine, my lord—all of those humans dead! Their wretched fortress blown off the face of the Icereach! Surely you know that only when Brackenrock is gone will you be the true master of our lands!"

In truth, Grimwar felt enough like a master of the Icereach and didn't care to quibble about Brackenrock, but his curiosity was piqued. "How is it even possible to make a weapon such as you describe?"

"Do not underestimate the power of Gonnas or the lore of our Alchemist," the queen explained eagerly. "You can use it in two ways: a small explosion to destroy the gatehouse and breach the walls. Your warriors will be able to rush inside, to retrieve the Axe of Gonnas—I beg you, husband: We must recover that artifact!—and then a larger device will be placed. When that explodes, it will destroy the fortress and all of its contents, for once and for all!"

"You make it sound like child's play," snorted Grimwar. "Of course it will never work as smoothly as that!"

"I tell you, my king, the world of Krynn has never seen a weapon like this! Your mother was able to destroy an entire village of slaves with a minor test!"

"My mother!" he snorted again. "I should have known you two were cooking up some infernal plan. Why are you so insistent that I strike now, this summer? If what you say is true, there will be plenty of time to mount a campaign, next year or the year after! I will take the winter to plan and prepare, make sure that nothing goes wrong—"

"What do you have to do that is more important?" Stariz asked, her voice dropping to a husky whisper. "Are you planning to dally here all summer with some ogress slut?"

Grimwar's vision grew hazy, and such a rage took him that his fist clenched and clenched again of its own accord. He raised his trembling arm, knuckles white, and was pleased to see the fear flash in Stariz's eyes as she cringed away from him.

"Have a care, wife," he growled. "Even a queen has bounds she does not dare overstep."

He turned on his heel and left impressively, he hoped, but he was bothered by her words. Indeed, he had a meeting arranged with Thraid for that very night—could his wife be privy to that knowledge? Surely not . . . but it galled him to think that he might be dragged to battle, once more, by his wife.

Grimwar opened the secret door into the private chamber, palms sweating, heart pounding. It had been a long time—far, far too long—since he and Thraid had stolen a moment together, and the prospect of a quick tryst with his mistress made him feverish as he pushed through the door. "My lady?" he croaked, as a torch flared, briefly blinding him.

When he discovered that it was a human slave instead of the comely Thraid Dimmarkull who had lit the torch in the secret room, his fury rose immediately, almost causing him to do the man fatal harm.

"How do you come to be here?" growled the king of Suderhold, holding the slave—a man of graying hair and no remarkable physique—around the neck. Grimwar lifted the hapless fellow with one hand until the slave's feet kicked and flailed above the floor.

Only then in the light did the king recognize the man as Wandcort, a loyal retainer of Thraid's and one of the few slaves trusted with knowledge of the royal affair. Even so, it was with reluctance that the king lowered the man to the floor, and he waited impatiently for Wandcort's inevitable fit of coughing and gagging to subside.

"Do you have a message for me?" he demanded, urgency raising his intended whisper to a growl.

"Yes, Sire . . . forgive me," Wandcort sputtered, drawing another ragged breath. "My Lady Thraid has been taken sorely ill, a stomach befoulment that has compelled her to the sickbed. She only sends me because she is too weakened to move."

Grimwar forcibly suppressed the roar of irritation swelling within him. He wanted to demand, Why now? At last he had an opportunity to visit Thraid! His wife was engaged in the royal smithy, discussing with the metalsmith questions of the designs for her revolutionary weapon. Now, to have this rare opportunity thwarted by common illness!

Or, indeed, was it illness?

Another, darker possibility loomed in the shadows of the king's mind. He scratched his chin while Wandcort watched nervously.

"Stomach befoulment? Tell me, what has the Lady Thraid had to eat and drink, within the last day?" Grimwar demanded.

"Er, let me think, Sire. There was bread and lutefish in the morning, and for the day meal, of course. I believe for dinner she had a beeve from the royal kitchen, with shellfish."

The slave's eyes narrowed shrewdly as he followed the king's train of thought. Grimwar noticed real anger in the man's expression and was pleased—this one was indeed loyal to his mistress.

"Yes, and warqat and wine, both from her own casks. Water I drew myself from the royal well."

Now the ogre king was remembering his wife's words, all but accusing him of a dalliance. Too, just an hour ago there had been a look, cool and appraising and slightly vengeful, that Stariz had given him before she departed for the smithy. At the time he had wondered what she was thinking. Now he guessed. She was coldly content that he would find no comfort with his mistress this day!

He thought about the risks of going to Thraid's quarters, but he needed to see her, speak to her personally. If she had been harmed by that jealous cow, his wife and queen . . .

"Take me to the lady Thraid," Grimwar declared.

Wandcort, who knew the value of discretion, looked briefly surprised, then bowed his head. "Of course, Sire. We can take the Servant's Way—it should be empty at this hour."

The king nodded and followed the slave out the secret door through which they'd both entered the room. In the passageway beyond, Wandcort turned left, away from the king's own quarters and into the vast network of streets and alleys comprising Winterheim's Noble Quarter. They passed under a stone arch and turned down a narrow passageway, a route marked with infrequent doors on either side. Some of these portals were wood, others iron, all of them closed. The oil lamps posted at each intersection cast long shadows down the corridors that, as Wandcort had suggested, seemed to be empty of other pedestrians.

Soon they emerged into a roofed alley, a tunnel that led outward to the Promenade, the great ringed street and atrium at the center of every one of Winterheim's numerous levels. There, Grimwar saw ogres ambling past, while slaves bustled up and down the street on urgent missions for their masters. Turning away from the Promenade, Wandcort led the king deeper into the alley, and soon they turned onto a quiet street. Lights here were few—whale oil was a precious commodity—and the street was narrow, with numerous doors and vents branching to either side. These were the corridors used by the slaves who came and went from the noble manors, Grimwar knew. It was a part of his city that he rarely saw.

They met no one as they hurried along, crossed another alley, then stopped at an arched wooden door. The slave produced a key, and in another instant the king was inside Thraid's apartment. Quickly he made his way through the kitchen and into the great room.

He had been here once before and cherished the memory. The great white bear's head mounted above the fireplace was a gift from Grimwar, killed by the king's own spear. The bestial face was locked into a snarl, and the ogre monarch fancied it as Thraid's protector, a guardian assigned by royal decree. The rest of the room was tastefully luxurious: great couches of walrus hide, several graceful statuettes of carved ivory, lamps with cut crystal globes that scattered the light in myriad facets. One of these was lit now, the wick set low, but Thraid was not here.

A brighter light came from the arched entry to the sleeping chamber, and here the king made his way, up several steps that had been cut into the bedrock of the mountain, pushing through a curtain of soft sealskin strips. His eyes went immediately to Thraid lying upon her huge bed, with her maidservant—Wandcort's wife, though Grimwar couldn't remember her name—seated beside her. A lamp burned on the bedstand, and Thraid pushed herself up to a sitting position as the king entered the chamber.

"Oh, my lord, you have come to me!" she said, then pressed her hand to her mouth to stifle a sob.

Thraid Dimmarkull looked a mess. Her hair, normally a lush train of silken chocolate, the same color as her large eyes, now lay in a tangle of sweaty strands. Her face, the plump cheeks and lush lips once rosy with health and vitality, was pale and drawn, clammy with perspiration.

Grimwar felt a rush of fury—in his mind there was no doubt that Stariz had done this, had worked some sorcerous scheme or toxic herbal to thus afflict the king's mistress. He controlled his emotions with great effort and sat gently on the very edge of the bed. Reaching out, he took Thraid's hand, her skin cool and damp to the touch. The slave woman rose, bowed, and quietly withdrew to pass through the sealskin curtain.

"Are you in pain, my lady?" Grimwar asked gruffly.

"Not for the moment, my king," she said, making a weak effort to squeeze her fingers. "It seems as though pain, as well as all else, has been wrung from me."

"When did this strike?"

"Not long after the supper. I fear there may be some bad shellfish in the royal larder. I had Brinda send word to the cooks as soon as I was taken ill."

Such an innocent! It warmed the king's heart to see that she did not even suspect the wrong that had been done to her. Naivete was one of qualities he found so appealing about Thraid, and so different from his wife. His throat tightened as he raised her hand and kissed her fingers.

"You rest well, my dear. Has the royal surgeon been to see you?"

"Indeed, sire. He purged me, and bade me drink much water. Brinda has been faithful with the pitcher."

"Very well. You must rest. If there is anything you want or need, you will have it. Slave!" Grimwar turned to the curtain, which was parted by Wandcort. "I shall desire word, steady reports, of the state of Lady Thraid's health."

The slave bowed. "It shall be done, Sire."

Grimwar rose to his feet and gazed one more time at Thraid. His anger still burned, but the fire had been banked by his willpower. He started toward the door, and Wandcort hurried ahead to lead him through the kitchen. The slave turned, startled, as the king stalked past.

"I am leaving by the front door," declared Grimwar Bane, his voice a deep and very royal growl.

———◆·◆———

"I would speak to you, my queen," declared the king of Suderhold, stalking unannounced into his wife's parlor.

She was making a diagram of something that looked like a hollowed sphere, an array of colorful inks spread upon her table and a quill in her hand. She looked up at him crossly, her eyes, so tiny in that block of a face, glittering with guarded thoughts.

"You take a cold tone with me, my lord," she said, her own voice layered in ice. "I sense your displeasure, yet I do not know its cause."

"You have said that you wish me to attack Brackenrock this summer," he declared bluntly.

"To *destroy* Brackenrock, yes," she corrected, "and to retrieve the Axe of Gonnas.

"Bah—we can retrieve that ancient trinket next year," the king snorted. "If it bears such significance, you should never have let the elf wrest it out of your hands in the first place!"

Stariz, still seated, straightened and glared ice. "Do not forget that the elf still lives with the humans. Have you not seen his boat, fruitlessly chased by your galley on several occasions? I should think his survival would be an affront not just to you but to our entire kingdom. It is a pity that you have so little regard for the Axe of Gonnas. Remember, it was the weapon that King Barkon used to hew the ice from Mount Winterheim, thus giving his clan—"

"Yes, yes, I know all this," Grimwar said impatiently,

although he did have a little trouble remembering the details. "Do you think I forget our heritage?"

Stariz pressed ahead. "Now that we have the powder from the Alchemist, the royal smithy will be able to prepare a weapon in a matter of a few days. This is the design—it will be a sphere of pure gold, filled with the powder prepared by the Alchemist." Her pig eyes narrowed. "Have you started to organize the troops for the raiding party? And prepared the galleys for the voyage?"

Grimwar shrugged. "The troops, the ships, will be ready when I tell them to be. *If* I tell them to prepare. And I tell you now, Queen . . . I have decided. I do not choose to make this campaign this summer."

Stariz snorted in exasperation. "You know that you have been granted an opportunity that has come to no other king in the many centuries of your line? You understand that, do you not?"

"Opportunity is in your eye, or mine," the king said with a shrug. "I have no doubt but that the humans will be available to fight, whenever I deem myself ready. They are a fact of life but not a threat to our existence. And *I* did not lose the Axe of Gonnas."

"The axe is a treasure of our people, an artifact dating back to the Barkon migration!" she retorted, shocked and outraged at his statement.

"I am the king of Suderhold," he reminded her. "You have achieved exalted status of your own—*because you are my wife*! If you choose to retain that status, you will do as I tell you. This is a fact you should, you *will*, remember."

"It is a fact that is never far from my mind, Sire," she replied, her tone neutral.

He drew a breath. "Now I wish to talk about Thraid Dimmarkull."

Stariz waited, eyes narrowed now, upper lip curled in disapproval, showing her short, blunt tusks.

"I give you a warning," Grimwar declared bluntly. Stariz's eyes widened. "Should any harm come to the Lady Thraid, I will be displeased. *Exceptionally* displeased. My displeasure shall be such that your station, your rank—indeed, Queen, your very life—will be in some jeopardy. Do I make myself clear?"

The ogress managed to inject a great deal of scorn into one small shrug of her broad shoulders. "You have too many your father's weaknesses. I had hoped that the passing years would move you beyond such trite concerns."

"I am serious," the king replied.

"Very well," declared the queen, with an air of great boredom. "I give you my word. No harm shall come to the, er, *lady* at my hand."

"Neither at your hand, nor at your bidding," Grimwar pressed. "You must swear upon the Willful One."

"You test my patience, husband," snapped the queen. She shrugged again, apparently unconcerned. "But suspicion is not a bad thing in a king. Perhaps it is even a sign of the strength, the maturity, I seek to cultivate in you. So I agree. I swear upon the sacred name of Gonnas the Mighty that I shall neither command nor commit any assault against the person of Thraid Dimmarkull."

"Very well," he said, although he felt the vow had come too easy. However, he believed Stariz was not likely to abrogate a vow sworn on the god she served.

"My lord," the queen said, in a more deferential tone, "I acknowledge your mastery of your realm, and indeed, of myself. I ask for one small consideration. You have made your decision about Brackenrock—you will not go there this year—and I, as your wife, must be content with that. However, are you certain, absolutely certain, that the Lord of Us All, Gonnas the Mighty, the Willful One, is pleased with your decision? Should you not seek some guidance from our god?"

"I obey the will of Gonnas," Grimwar said guardedly, "but you are the voice of that will, and there are times when you discuss prophecies and visions, when I suspect that I am hearing *your* desires, and not those of our god." He glared at her challengingly, expecting her to react with fury. He was surprised when she nodded in apparent understanding.

"That is a fair assessment, Sire," she said, as meekly as he had ever heard her say anything. "But what if you speak directly to the god, without using me as an intermediary?"

"How could I do this?" Grimwar wondered, still suspicious.

"The Ceremony of the Midnight Sun is but a few weeks away," the priestess-queen reminded him. "You will be on the King's Roost, atop our mountain, as is your right and duty as king of Suderhold. There you will address Gonnas directly. I merely suggest that you ask him for a sign of pleasure or displeasure with your choice."

The monarch scowled. It was some kind of trap. Everything had been going so well, up to this point. "If there is no sign?" he asked warily.

"Why, that would certainly be proof that he is pleased with your rule and that your mandates are right and correct for Suderhold."

Grimwar nodded, pondering her words. "If Gonnas shows his displeasure," he continued hesitantly, "that will be an indication that you are right, that I should pursue the campaign against Brackenrock at once?"

"I could not have stated it better myself," she declared, surprising him again by dropping her face and clasping her hands before herself, a gesture he could only interpret as a sign of her respect, and obedience. He left her chamber rubbing his palms together and whistling, thinking the Ceremony of the Midnight Sun held no fear for him.

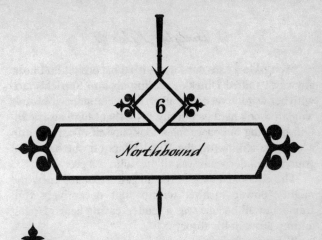

6

Northbound

The sun climbed higher into the sky with each day, and the nights became shorter, marked by extended twilight. The harbor boom was completed with the cheerful assistance of more than fifty Highlanders, with Bruni and many Arktos also contributing. When it was installed, it became a barrier that could be floated across the narrow mouth of Brackenrock Harbor, secured with iron chains, and studded with steel spikes. Any ship that tried to pass would at the very least become stuck and would very likely have great holes ripped in the hull.

Kerrick concentrated on his boat, preparing for the transoceanic crossing. He caulked the hull carefully, repaired his lines where they showed signs of fraying or wear, and mended the few tears in his three sails. A week after the harbor boom was done, the day of his departure dawned clear, with fair winds. These were good omens to start a voyage, but as he went around the fortress and down to the waterfront, making his farewells, Kerrick found himself feeling strangely hesitant and melancholy.

"You have a care out there—it's a big ocean! So I hear, anyway," sniffed Dinekki, peering up into Kerrick's face with her watery, yet penetrating, eyes. The stooped, elderly woman shook her head firmly. "Not that I have any intention of going out there for a look, myself. That one trip across the strait with the Highlanders on our heels and your boat underneath was all the sailin' I'll ever want."

The elf looked back at the ancient shaman, knew the mighty power lurking within that deceptively frail frame, but all he saw was a tender, caring heart. He felt a lump grow in his throat.

"I have a feeling you could tame those waves if you wanted," Kerrick said, "and I *will* have a care."

She pressed something into his hand, a small circle made of interlocking bones. Fish bones, he saw, the frail slivers barely thicker than coarse hair. "This may help you in a time of danger . . . throw it on the water, if you want to hide your boat and yourself. Everything else, for that matter," she said. "Chislev Wilder will watch over you, but you'll still have to take care of yourself."

"Thank you, Grandmother," he replied, using the honorific the Arktos used for their most esteemed elders. He was truly moved. He gave her a hug, conscious of her skinny frame and careful not to hurt her, then was surprised when she pulled him close with a crush that almost expelled the air from his lungs.

"We'll miss you," she said, sniffing. "Damned pollen! Never could keep my sinuses clean this time of year." She turned away, dabbing her eyes with a cloth, and Kerrick took a moment to catch his breath. The emotions of these humans, so obviously displayed, were affecting his normally reserved elven nature. There were so many here to see him off, and this evidence of their fondness touched him deeply.

He looked at *Cutter* and was instantly reassured. The teak deck shone, the sails were neatly furled but ready to snap upward and snare the ocean wind. The locker was full of smoked and salted fish fillets and his two barrels topped with pure spring water. He had fashioned a new pair of oars, sturdy paddles that might be useful in an emergency, and these were strapped, one on each side, to the gunwales. Two of his three chests of gold were already stowed below deck, secured in the hold. He knew the third strongbox would be coming along shortly.

He turned to look along the dock, noticing that more Arktos were coming down the road from the citadel or following the mountainside trails leading down to the harbor. A few Highlanders—tall, bearded, distinguished by their buckskin kilts—were also coming from the boatyard. A pretty young woman, her long hair bound into a black plume and her eyes, like Dinekki's, swimming with tears, came forward and grasped Kerrick's hands.

"Do you have to go?" Feathertail asked. "Will you come back?"

"Someday," he promised, believing it to be the truth. "Meantime, keep an eye on Mouse for me, will you?"

She smiled through her tears. "Oh, you can count on that. If he gets too careless, I just remind him that it wasn't so many years ago that we used to call him 'Little Mouse.' He blushes then and usually forgets what he was talking about!"

"I'm sure he does," the elf said. "He's lucky to have you—take good care of him." He embraced this girl who had become a young woman seemingly overnight. He had to remind himself that it had been a process lasting the whole eight years of his time here. To an elf, that time might be a mere eyeblink, but not to humans.

"Here's the last chest," Bruni said, genial as ever as she rolled up the wheelbarrow with the third of his treasure boxes. The other two had required Kerrick and two strong men to cart down from the fortress. Bruni had brought this one by herself. "Do you want me to throw it onto the deck?" she asked, joking.

"I appreciate the help," he replied hastily, "but I think it would crash through the floorboards, and I'd like to have it stowed it a little more carefully than that!"

"Well, you're the sailor," she said with a grin. She looked around at the boatyard, the nascent fleet of boats bobbing in the harbor. "At least, the *first* sailor. It's nice to see this legacy of yours, floating all over the place. We're a seafaring people now, and that will forever change our lives." She turned her moonlike gaze upon him, very serious for a moment. "It's going to be different, though, with you not here."

He drew a breath and it came out a sigh. Second thoughts assailed him. He hadn't realized how much he was going to miss these people. The big woman drew him into a smothering hug, and though he couldn't lock his arms around her massive waist he clutched her as tightly as he could.

"You're someone very special," Kerrick told her. "If you lived in Ansalon, I think the bards would be singing about you from Tarsis to Istar. As it is, you'll have to be sure to keep an eye on your chiefwoman and all these people, won't you? They rely on you more than you know."

"Oh, I help out when I can," she said, shrugging dismissively. "You come back sometime, and see for yourself how we're getting along? Okay?"

He nodded wordlessly. More of the Arktos came to bid him farewell, friends he had made over the years, and the sense of uncertainty only grew stronger. The Highlander berserker called Mad Randall—always a genial and gentle fellow, except in the midst of battle— shared several sips of warqat with the elf, then cried lustily as he clutched the departing sailor to his breast. Mouse came hurrying along, and he gave Kerrick a gift: a splendid long harpoon, with a polished shaft, a coil of supple line, and a head of shining steel.

"That's the metal Hawkworth is smelting now, thanks to you," the young man declared proudly. "He says that you could shave with that edge—if you had a beard, that is."

Kerrick rubbed his smooth elven face and shook his head. He was moved by the gift but even more moved by the all the people crowding around. Many times he had embarked from the Silvanesti docks, sometimes for voyages that would last more than a year, and never had he entertained this kind of farewell. His friends had been too casual to depart from their comfortable routines. On those occasions when he left a lover behind, she was inevitably petulant about his trip and likely as not would fail to see him off or send him away with angry words ringing in his ears.

He thought of Moreen for some reason and was startled to look up and see her standing all alone on the dockside. The rest of the Arktos had melted away all of a sudden, and were now busily watching the boat builders or fishers, leaving the chiefwoman and the elf with a circle of privacy. He heard the waves lapping against the stone wharf, punctuated by the keening cry of a gull. The bird, he thought, articulated his feelings far better than Kerrick himself could.

She came toward him dry-eyed, serious. He found himself drawing up straight, standing as tall as he could, feeling strangely vulnerable. Wondering what he would say, he was taken by surprise by the first words out of her mouth.

"That boom," she said, gesturing to the long construct of chain-wrapped timbers. "Are you sure it is going to work right?"

He felt a familiar flash of irritation. "Yes, of course it will work," he snapped. "That is, if the watchmen get it pulled across the harbor mouth in time. It won't work if the ogre galley is already in the harbor!"

"No, I suppose not," she commented, taking no visible offence at his harsh tone. Instead, she made a show of studying the length of the boom and the large winch attached to the Signpost rock. The boom itself lay in the water, opposite the spire, attached by a submerged cable. The winch, they had learned through testing, was strong enough to pull it across the harbor mouth, if ten or a dozen strong people could gather to crank the device. There was a rickety framework of scaffolding leading up the Signpost and a sturdier, more permanent-looking platform on top. A lanky Highlander leaned on the railing of that platform, momentarily noticing their eyes on him, so he quickly turned his gaze back to the sea.

"I will have to make sure that we put only the most alert people, whether Arktos or Highlander, on that duty."

"Yes," he agreed, his ill temper quickly fading. "You will." You will have to do lots of things, he thought, feeling for an instant the leadership pressures weighing upon Moreen every day. She would have to look out for all of these people, leading them against a harsh environment, protecting them from the onslaughts of an even harsher enemy. She was strong—unbelievably strong—but he was terribly glad that he did not have her responsibilities.

"That boom . . . it's a nice piece of work. One of many nice things that you leave us," Moreen said, her voice surprisingly soft and nervous. "I cannot dispel the feeling that we have not changed you in such a . . . so many fundamental ways, as you have done for us."

Kerrick blinked, surprised at the moisture that burned in his eyes. "I think, perhaps, that I have been very much changed by my time among the Arktos. Changed for the better."

She smiled wanly, then nodded to the chest in Bruni's wheelbarrow. "I see you've had the gold brought down. Do you think that will make a difference to your king?" She didn't know the full story of his exile—none of these humans did—but she had gleaned enough of his past to know that he had departed his homeland under something of an shadow.

"I know it will, at least in these modern times. Centuries ago, in the time of Silvanos and the great houses, who knows—I'd like to think the elves had loftier pursuits. Now we might as well be Istarans, dwarves even—we are as enthralled with gold as any people on Krynn."

"You know . . ." Moreen hesitated, choosing her words. "I . . . that is, *we*, will miss you very much."

He almost winced. That was how it was with her—everything was about the tribe, nothing about herself. "You should know that I will miss all of you. I'm only starting to realize how much," he responded levelly. He would miss her the most of all, Kerrick knew, but he lacked the words, the human brashness, to articulate that sentiment.

"You are welcome to return, any time you want to come back," Moreen continued. "In fact, I do hope we—I—will see you again." She gazed across the harbor, out the narrow gap onto the sea beyond. "Perhaps it won't be during my lifetime," she mused ruefully. "You could still be a young man, and come back to find our grandchildren as the new masters of Brackenrock."

"I . . . I want to be back before then," he said awkwardly. The difference in their life spans—he had centuries of adulthood waiting before him, a trackless road ahead of him, while she would become an old woman in forty, fifty, or some other finite number of years—had always yawned like a gulf between them. Now he felt an irrational tickle of guilt.

"Know that if you don't come back for a hundred years, the Arktos will remember you and make you welcome," she said quietly. For the first time ever he saw a tear shimmer in her eye.

"For all those years, and longer, I will carry the memory of this place, of your people—and of you—close to my heart," he said somberly.

Kerrick held Moreen for several heartbeats, feeling the fierce strength of her embrace, the wiry muscle of her body, and he found himself wishing it could be forever. But it was she who broke the embrace, blinked, and said, "May Zivilyn Greentree ride with you across the waters! And Chislev Wilder wait for you in the forests on the other side!"

The blessing of their two gods was like a benediction around his shoulders. Kerrick could think of nothing else to say, so he climbed aboard his boat, raised the mainsail, and started toward the beckoning sea.

Cutter burst from the Bluewater Strait like a cork exploding from a bottle. A cold south wind gusted from the direction of Winterheim and the Icewall, a reminder of winter so lately departed. Still, Kerrick welcomed the breeze, for it had strength and would bear him in the direction he wanted to go.

The sky was cloudy now, a slate color perfectly matched by the sea. The hue matched the elven sailor's mood. Playing out the jib, riding straight before the wind, he flew northward until the bulwark of land that was Brackenrock vanished from his view. Even then he continued, reckoning by compass, imagining the miles . . . twenty, fifty . . . eighty and more . . . passing under his keel.

Only when the sun angled into the western sea did he haul in the jib and turn the mainsail to lessen his headlong speed. He watched the long, slow sunset, realized that it was prolonged by his northern position. Within a week the sun itself would remain visible, low on the southern horizon, throughout every night, and many weeks would pass before it again set below Brackenrock's horizon. He chuckled as he thought of the phenomenon that the Arktos called the midnight sun. Certainly he would describe it to the elves of Silvanesti, but he didn't expect that they would believe him.

Setting the tiller and boom with ropes tied to hold a steady course, Kerrick went into his cabin and opened his sea chest. From there he took out a delicate tube, a container shaped by Dinekki from a whale's tusk. Carefully he extracted the scroll of sheepskin and spread the supple cloth across his table, where he could see clearly in the daylight spilling through the porthole.

It was a crude map by the standards of cartographic mastery, but it was a work that had occupied him for much of the past eight years. Every voyage he had taken in *Cutter*, every trip back and forth on the White Bear

Sea, had been logged here, with coastlines drawn and re-drawn, islands discovered and circumnavigated, great glaciers rendered into ink strokes, a mockery of their dazzling majesty.

The shore of the mostly landlocked White Bear Sea Kerrick had completely mapped several years ago. Despite the bothersome presence of the ogre galley *Goldwing,* the elf sailed those waters with impunity. Virtually constant winds swept the sea, ensuring that the sailboat could easily escape the much heavier, oar-powered ogre ship. On several occasions the elf had dared to taunt the minions of Grimwar Bane from within hailing distance, only to cast up his jib, cut a new angle across the wind, and whisk away like a swallow in flight.

So he had allowed himself to be diligent and meticulous in his explorations, poking into every cove and bay, doing numerous soundings across the tidal flats, rendering the coastline in as accurate detail as he could manage. It was on these voyages that he had taught Little Mouse to sail, watching the lad grow into a sturdy young man. Later, Feathertail had accompanied them, or the Highlanders Randall and Lars Redbeard. Even Moreen had sometimes sailed along, and he cherished those moments especially, laughing with her as spray washed across the deck or both of them staring in wonder as a huge iceberg calved from the face of a lofty glacier. Even in rough waters, with foaming crests breaking across the prow, she had never displayed any fear. Instead, she had been curious about the sea and as a result had learned a great deal about sailing.

His bold sailing had continued last year, even when the ogre king had launched a second galley. Even Kerrick had to admit that Grimwar Bane had built quite an impressive, seaworthy craft. No doubt he had employed human slaves for a great deal of the work. The design had borrowed heavily from the model of the *Goldwing*, which had been launched as *Silvanos Oak,* once his father's ship and pride of the elven fleet.

Despite the presence of those two great ogre ships, however, the elf sailor had continued to regard the White Bear Sea as his personal body of water. He sighted the galleys only rarely, and always made a nimble escape. In his mind his boat was the undisputed master of the sea, and his thorough surveying had given him a sense of certainty and confidence whenever he sailed in the area.

The same could not be said for the Icereach shore of the Southern Courrain Ocean. Here his map indicated broad strokes, a rough sketch of coasts extending eastward and westward from the mouth of the Bluewater Strait. From the point of Ice End, the northernmost outpost of this land, the eastern shore was backed by rugged mountains. The landscape was stony and inhospitable, without the gentle tundra that marked the Blood Coast or the stands of tall cedar and pine that characterized both sides of the strait. In his voyages that had extended for two or three hundred miles in that direction, Kerrick had failed to find a single attractive anchorage. Nor were there any settlements of Arktos, Highlander, or ogre along that desolate coast.

To the west, the headland of Brackenrock rose up against a lofty ridge of mountain. Beyond those summits, in a frontage of something like twenty-five miles, spread the massive face of the Fenriz Glacier, which was followed by another impressive spine of lofty summits. Beyond there, the shore devolved into a series of deep water fjords, extending an unknown distance into the interior.

Kerrick had been reluctant to explore these regions, for they were too much like traps—it was easy to imagine his little boat snagged like a helpless fish by the appearance of a great ogre warship, barring egress from the narrow channel. Still, he had sailed farther in that direction than to the east, for he had at least found several sheltered valleys of lush forest. Furthermore, there were remote villages of Arktos to the west, and he had stopped at these to trade and to learn. Eventually that shore turned south, creating the expanse of another sea, a body of cold water separated from the Courrain by a string of rocky, barren islands. The Arktos had called the place "Dragons Home Sea," though none could recall seeing a dragon anytime within their, or their ancestors', lifetimes. Now the elf felt a thrill of excitement as he gazed at his map and made up his mind. He would, at last, explore the far side of that sea, as it was convenient for his longer voyage to the north.

There was reputed to be a place called Summerbane Island, that lay far to the south of the continent. Traders reported carrying a variety of goods from the mainland, receiving payment in gold ingots, heavy enough to weight the hull for the return voyage. In ancient days it had been a place of dragons, and even now icebergs and frigid storms made it a dangerous place to which to sail. The tales were consistent, though, and came from many different sources. That was enough to give Kerrick a measure of confidence, a belief that Summerbane Island was a real place.

Kerrick had originally heard these stories in his younger days, when he had sailed the coast of Ansalon. During his years in the Icereach he had put the tale together with his gleaned knowledge of this new land. He had concluded that Summerbane Island was probably an outpost of the Icereach, laying far to the west of Brackenrock. It was his hope to find that place in his westward sail. Then he would turn north, follow the current to Tarsis and the coastline to Silvanesti, and come home with the first complete map of the great southern ocean.

With this plan in mind, he returned the map to his sea chest. His eye noticed the small strongbox inside, poking out from beneath a spare cloak. The ring was in the strongbox, the gift of his father that had the power to bestow great strength . . . but at such a cost. He suppressed a shiver—whenever he thought of it, it was with a sudden hunger to take out the golden circlet, slide it over his finger, feel the sudden rush of pleasant strength. Grimacing, he shut the lid and turned away to the cockpit.

He continued on the northward run for some time but turned westward while he was still within a hundred miles of the Icereach. After another day he swerved back to the south until, two days later, he came into view of the gray-white face of the Fenriz Glacier. A cold front swept off of the mainland, and he endured two more days of icy winds and steady, penetrating drizzle. Remembering the many outlying rocks along this shore, he stayed well north of the glacier, cruising slowly through the hours of poor visibility. Despite spring, the spray froze overnight, and when the storm passed the pale sun revealed a boat encased in glassy frost, with icicles draped from every line, and the boom as well.

The wind was faint, but the sun brightened his spirits, and as the ice melted and the dampness evaporated he raised every shred of sail in his locker. He contented himself with gliding along a few miles north of the glacial coast. Finally Kerrick began to settle into the lonely rhythm of life at sea. He rose with the dawn, slept at least half of each night on the deck—unless there was rain—and ate only sparingly. The locker was filled with salted fish, and he had a cupboard of hardbread. With his water barrels topped off, he could survive for many months without fresh provisions. With even moderate rainfall and some luck with his fishing net, he could extend that span indefinitely.

He chuckled as he thought of fishing, for the thought inevitably made him remember Coraltop Netfisher. When the elf had first encountered the kender, the little fellow had been adrift in the ocean, cast away upon the back of a monstrous dragon turtle. *Cutter* had bumped into the monster, and Kerrick had found himself a passenger. Unfortunately, the dragon turtle, awakened from its slumber, had smashed across the boat, snapping the boom and all but crushing the elf with a blow to his head. He would have died on that crossing, except for his kender companion, who had kept him alive.

"You *had* to be real, I know it!" Kerrick said, musing aloud. "There's no way I could have survived, if you hadn't been there to take care of me!"

Yet no eyewitness in the Icereach had ever seen Coraltop Netfisher. He was aboard the boat only when Kerrick was alone, then seemed to vanish into thin air whenever Kerrick brought aboard Arktos passengers. The elf had last seen his passenger on the day Moreen's tribe had won Brackenrock, and in the years since he had come to regard his memories with at least some measure of suspicion.

Now, alone on the ocean, he wondered anew. He spoke again, calling out, making conversation. Nothing, no one, replied, and the rocky coastline continued to slide past.

The sound came through the mists, like a guttural moan, a noise full of mourning or pain. Kerrick had been dozing at the tiller. Now he jerked upright and blinked into the gray dawn.

The wind remained low, almost still, he noticed, as it had been through the night. *Cutter* glided through placid water, moving very slightly, the gentlest of waves lapping against the hull. He guessed the hour to be just past dawn, though the fog was thick enough to obscure any direct glimpse of the sun.

For several heartbeats the elf strained to hear, replaying the noise in his brain. It had originated to the south, of that much he was certain. Had he heard the cry of some wounded whale? Such a thing was possible, according to old sailors, though never before had such a sound reached Kerrick's ears

"Hello!" he called out, speaking in the language of the Arktos. "Is anyone there?"

His words were swallowed by the mist, for he was too far from shore to bring an echo. After a long pause, however, he heard the groaning noise again. It was a plaintive cry, clearly indicative of pain and distress. If not quite human, it was not the noise of a beast either.

Kerrick hauled on the tiller, and *Cutter*, very slowly, came around toward a southward bearing. The slight breeze luffed the sail until he angled farther to the west, tacking through the placid sea, barely moving.

"Hello!" he called again, scrambling atop the cabin, straining to peer through the mist. The rising sun had some effect, brightening the fog, but he could see no feature marring the smooth surface of the sea.

A trace of rippling disturbed the placid surface, at the limit of his vision off the starboard bow. Hopping down into the cockpit, he adjusted the tiller, angling toward the place he tried to picture as the source.

The wind was so faint that the boat hardly moved. Impatient, the elf took up a paddle and propelled *Cutter* slowly forward. He strained to hear something, but the fog seemed full of silence. Kerrick didn't call out again— he was making enough noise with his paddling. Raising the paddle from the water, he listened, hearing only the musical notes of the water droplets falling from the blade back to the sea.

Then there was a louder splash, like a fish jumping, and he saw a fresh series of ripples expanding from the mist. Fully alarmed now, he considered ducking into the cabin to retrieve his sword, but he didn't want to take the time. Instead, he picked up the harpoon Mouse had given him and carried the well-balanced weapon above his shoulder as he crept forward.

Something splashed, to the right, and he turned in time to see the flash of a limb—or a flipper of some kind—just break the surface. He raised the harpoon and stared. Was it a dolphin? A seal? Or something more dangerous?

The sun was brighter now, and when Kerrick glanced upward he saw the gray sky shading toward blue. Again he saw something splash at the surface, unmistakably an arm. The stroke was followed, however, by the kick of a broad, webbed foot. A moment later he saw a rounded, whiskered face, turned upward toward the sky. The eyes were closed.

At last he understood. This was a thanoi. He saw the blunt tusks breaking the surface of the water above the creature's chest. Again it kicked one foot listlessly.

Kerrick braced his foot on the railing and stared. The thanoi's eyes—a deep brown, rimmed with blood-red—

flashed momentarily, and the walrus-man was gone, vanished into the depths. The elf's fingers tightened around the shaft of the harpoon, and his body tensed, ready to cast the weapon at the next sight of the brute. A moment later he saw another splash, this time to the left, but by the time he shifted the creature had disappeared again. Obviously it could move under the water with surprising speed.

He wasted no time wondering what it was doing here, so far from shore. The walrus-men were aquatic creatures, secretive and deadly. He couldn't allow it to hover nearby, a threat to the boat in this placid, windless water.

The next splash of sound surprised him. It came from the other side of the boat, very near the hull. He crossed the deck, his harpoon still raised, when once more he heard the plaintive groan. Another step took him to the gunwale, and he glimpsed that broad, tusked face looking up at him from the water. The creature raised one arm from the water, palm upraised as if to ward off a blow, and grunted again.

"Wait!" the thanoi cried, the word guttural and thick, but recognizable. "No kill!"

The thanoi floated sideways, waving that one arm, and Kerrick saw a ghastly wound scarring the creature's flank. One of its legs drifted loosely in the water, and the elf could see that the other arm had been chopped off, a ragged wound that left raw strips of flesh draped from the walrus-man's elbow. The elf was startled to see a thick ring of braided gold encircling the creature's neck, a collar of intricate workmanship and great worth.

"Help," groaned the thanoi, finally dropping the arm and floating on its back. The belly, leathery-skinned but unprotected, offered an easy target for the harpoon.

But Kerrick had lost the impulse to harm. Instead, he stepped to the stern and rolled the rope ladder off of the rain to trail into the water.

"Why you here on Dracoheim Sea?" asked the thanoi, seated in the cockpit, leaning against the transom. Despite the grievous wounds, the creature showed no sign of suffering pain. Perhaps the salt water had cauterized the flesh, Kerrick guessed. The raw cuts were not, at this point, bleeding.

"I'm sailing home, to Silvanesti," Kerrick replied. "I heard you make a noise. What happened to you, anyway?"

"Shark," spat the beast, the voice a guttural growl full of scorn. "I killed fish—it swallowed my knife hand, and I kill it."

The elf grimaced. "Why were you here, so far from land? Are these waters claimed by your tribe?"

"Who can claim water?" asked the walrus-man. "No, I was on my way across the sea, to the dark island."

"Dark island? What's that?" Kerrick asked.

"Dracoheim. I work for the Alchemist." These words meant little to Kerrick. The grotesque creature looked at the terrible wounds on its flank, the missing arm. "I will not return, this time, but I thank you for sparing my life, even for just a few hours longer."

The elf nodded, solemnly. "Can I give you something to comfort you, food . . . water?"

The walrus-man blinked eyes that looked very old, very tired. "Yes, water."

Kerrick fetched a ladleful as the thanoi pushed himself upright on the bench.

"I am called Long-Swim Greatfin. I thank you for mercy, strange as it be. No ogre nor human would show such care."

For the first time Kerrick noticed the manlike features of the thanoi. True, the nostrils were broad, the upper lip split into two overhanging lobes. A pair of tusks, sharp and upturned, grew from the upper jaw. But there was also real intelligence in the brown eyes, and the chin was square and possessed a certain dignity. The musculature of the walrus-man's chest rippled in an approximation of a man's, and the thanoi had arms and legs—sort of—with webbed feet and fingers broad and flat. Kerrick noticed a tusk suspended by a leather strap from around the creature's neck.

"How far away is this Dracoheim?" Kerrick asked.

Long-Swim shrugged. "A swim for many risings of the sun. In the direction of the sunset."

"Why made you come so far?"

The thanoi closed his eyes and leaned his head back against the gunwale. Kerrick wasn't sure the creature had understood the question and was about to repeat himself when the walrus-man opened his eyes and shrugged. "Took a message to the ogre king," he said tonelessly. "Got a taste of warqat, and now I swim back."

With that, he slumped backward again, and his chest rose and fell in a rhythmic pattern of slumber.

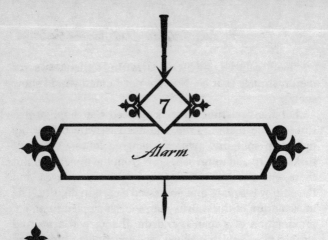

The thanoi called Long-Swim Greatfin died during the short, ghostly night, not with a sudden collapse but with a gradual slumping along the cockpit bench. He uttered no distinguishable sound, made no dramatic final gestures. Indeed Kerrick didn't at first notice that the soft, sonorous breathing had ceased.

The elf had fully raised his three sails and marked a course along the Icereach coast, still heading west. The winds were strong from the north—the night had brought the first real rush of summer air—and *Cutter* heeled hard against the pressure, fairly flying over the waves, bumping rhythmically into the crests before lunging into every trough. With water slapping against the hull, and clouds often obscuring the waxing moon, the elf failed to notice his passenger's lifeless state until the first predawn light suffused the sky.

The walrus-man's eyes stared dully in death. Gently Kerrick closed them. He removed the golden collar and set it in the cabin. After a pause, he lifted the tusk on the leather strap from around the creature's neck, setting the surprisingly lightweight object on the cockpit bench. Then he covered the body with a tarp, wrapped it tightly, and slowly eased it over the side. He shivered, even though the sun had appeared above the horizon, spilling rays that warmed the elf, his boat, and the sea. From the depths of his memory came a short prayer for the sea-dead, a chant from the early days of the Fallabrine clan:

> *From the waters to the waters,*
> *Ending and beginning,*
> *There is always the ocean.*
> *There is only the ocean.*

The watery burial site quickly fell behind as the boat surged eagerly forward. Kerrick stayed at the tiller, clenching the wooden shaft far more tightly than he needed to.

"What's in there?"

The elf looked up in shock as Coraltop Netfisher ambled around the cabin to join him in the cockpit. The kender's hair was tied in a long topknot, and he was clad in the green tunic and leggings that had—eight years earlier—been his standard outfit. It had been that long since Kerrick had seen his old shipmate, and the elf found the sudden appearance stunning and disconcerting.

"Coraltop?" blurted the elf. "Is it you!" He paused, shaking his head against a sudden, disorienting sense of dizziness. "Or did I fall and knock my head?"

With a sudden lunge Kerrick reached out and seized the kender by his wrist. The elf squeezed hard, feeling the most astonishing thing he could imagine—flesh and bone beneath his grip. He stared into Coraltop's face, saw his old companion scowl angrily, squirming and pulling away with startling strength and energy.

"Hey—that hurts! Let go of me!"

Only then did Kerrick realize that he was still clutching the thin but wiry arm. "Sorry," he said, released his grip. "I just . . . had to see if you were real."

How could he be real? But if he wasn't real, what was he? Looking at him, Kerrick found himself chuckling in amazement, for whatever was the explanation he felt himself pleased at the sight of his old shipmate.

"It's good to see you, old friend," he said.

Coraltop breezed past, sat down, and kicked his feet against the locker under the bench. "So, what is in that tusk?" he asked. "Did you look yet? Are you *going* to look? Cuz I'll look if you don't want to, but I think *one* of us should take a look—"

"Yes, I was going to take a look . . . eventually."

"It's hollow, isn't it?" Coraltop asked enthusiastically. Yes, Kerrick realized, it was hollow, some kind of storage tube that seemed tightly sealed. A glance revealed the cap at one end, which he promptly unscrewed, while Coraltop hopped to his feet, stood at his side, and danced from foot to foot trying to see.

"Look! A piece of paper! Is it a map—maybe a treasure map? I wonder if there's diamonds! You know, I've always wanted to have a nice diamond or two. I hope it's a map to diamonds! If it's a map, can we go there—will you take me?"

"It looks more like a letter," Kerrick interrupted, having removed and unrolled the piece of parchment while the kender prattled on.

"A letter, not a map?" Coraltop said with an exaggerated pout. He plopped down on the bench, crossed his arms, then brightened. "Well, what does it say?"

"I'm trying to figure it out," replied the elf, squinting at a script that was exceptionally ornate, apparently inscribed by a rather clumsy hand using a very blunt pen. The words were vaguely legible. It was a struggle to recognize the symbols and the words.

"Read it out loud!" insisted his companion, and Kerrick obliged. Even though the missive was short, deciphering the fancy script made his progress somewhat halting.

" 'My Dear Queen Mother,' it begins. Let's see, mmm . . . 'Thank you for the treasure you sent, in the hands of this loyal thanoi—' "

"I *told* you it was about treasure!" the kender proclaimed with glee. "Does it mention diamonds? Does it say how many there are?"

The elf ignored the questions, speaking slowly, concentrating. " 'We now have the means to our end, as you are no doubt aware. I cannot tell you exactly when we will act. My wife and I are in some disagreement on this point. However, I assure you that we *will* take action. When we do so, our objective will be accomplished. Brackenrock will be utterly and completely destroyed.' " Kerrick felt a chill. His hand was shaking as he finished. "It's signed by Grimwar Bane, King of Suderhold."

"It doesn't say where the treasure is?" Coraltop pressed. "Or even if there's diamonds? I really really hoped there'd be diamonds. . . ."

Kerrick was barely listening. He scrutinized the words again, read the letter a third time to make sure he had made no mistake understanding the message. Then he slumped back against the transom and looked at his companion with a sense of frustration mingled with deep fear.

"What is it?" Coraltop asked. "No diamonds?"

The elf shook his head. "Worse. It means that Moreen and her people are in grave danger." He looked at the sea, dazzling in the new morning, and at the coastline slipping past a few miles to port. He thought of home and thought of Brackenrock. There was no choice—his duty was clear.

"It means," he said bitterly, thoughts of Silvanesti vanishing, "that I have to go back there and warn her."

———◆◆◆———

The wind held fair for three days, and Kerrick slept at the tiller each night. Coraltop Netfisher settled in as if he had never left, and the elf noted—even if Coraltop was imaginary—the little fellow seemed to eat plenty of fish and drink lots of fresh water. As well he frequently sampled the flask of warqat the elf had brought along, loudly smacking his lips and complaining about the stinging burn, the harsh taste, then helping himself to more.

The elf studied the letter, taking it out to read and re-read, wondering about what kind of weapon could level Brackenrock. How would it work? No doubt there was magic at work . . . foul magic worked by this mysterious "alchemist."

Despite the many questions in his mind, Kerrick had no doubt about one thing: The letter described a real threat. The elf would have bet his sailboat and all his gold upon that.

On the last night of his return voyage he awakened with a start to the memory of a haunting dream, a dream of loss and tragedy and lives wasted. There were familiar images, a shipfitter's shop with forge alight, a shining ring held out to Kerrick by a strong hand, and a shadowy presence that vanished before the young elf could speak. He knew, instinctively, this was a dream about his father.

He stayed awake the rest of that brief night, allowing Coraltop to have the bunk in the cabin while he remained on deck and watched the arrival of the clear dawn. As the sun poked into view again, he spied the heights of Brackenrock off the starboard bow. When he went to awaken his shipmate, he half-expected what he found. The kender had vanished and could not be located anywhere on the boat.

He was once again alone as he steered *Cutter* into the harbor, where he wasted no time tossing his lines to the wharf. A crowd of Arktos had gathered as soon as he sailed into sight, and willing hands made the boat fast, while cheerful boatmen greeted him. Kerrick bounded onto the wharf, shoving past the welcoming handclasps.

"Stow the sails for me," he told several eager lads, then looked up the steep road climbing away from the harbor. "I've got to see Moreen."

"Do you believe it?" Moreen fixed an eye on Kerrick, knowing that he couldn't lie to her even if he'd wanted to. "Could it be some kind of trick?"

"I believed it enough to turn around and come back here," he said impatiently. "Long-Swim Greatfin was on a mission for the ogre king—or queen—that much I know. He was wounded badly, fatally as it turned out, and the wounds looked like shark bites. I'm certain that wasn't any ruse. And he was wearing that ornament."

He gestured to the royal collar, shining gold on the table before the chiefwoman. Other Arktos—Bruni and Mouse among them—were in the great hall, standing in a loose ring a few paces away from the table where they talked. The elf pointed at the letter, which Moreen held in her hand. "This was inside an ivory tube, borne by the thanoi on his return toward the island he called 'Dracoheim.' "

"I had hoped for more time to prepare for the next attack on Brackenrock, though I knew it would come someday," the chiefwoman said soberly. "Still, I allowed myself to believe that it would not happen for many, many years. Now it would appear that our time is short, and our need to prepare is immediate. Thank you for bringing this fortuitous warning. Did the thanoi give you any sense of when this attack would occur?"

"Not really," the elf admitted. "It's in the works, I would guess. This year, probably." He was impressed by her coolness, by the detachment and steadiness with which she appeared to shift from peace to war.

She addressed all of them. "With our people scattered across the coast, I don't know how we can stand against a full-strength attack—if they have some new terror to unleash. I'd like to know what that weapon is, how we can prepare for it!"

"I have already cast the bones," declared Dinekki, her voice carrying through the great hall even though she had just entered from the far door. The shaman was stooped, small, and rather far away, but her presence seemed larger than that of anyone else in the room. Kerrick immediately felt better now that she was here.

The elder hobbled slowly across the floor, and the elf saw Moreen bite her lip with impatience, though she stood still and waited for the elder to cross the large room.

"Welcome back," the shaman said to Kerrick, and he was surprised to note the mischievous twinkle in her eye. "It is good to see you here, where you belong."

"What did you learn, Grandmother?" asked Moreen, the urgency of the question underlined by her clipped tone. Kerrick, meanwhile, was strangely moved by her words. His regret and frustration about turning back were gone—he felt that Dinekki was right. This *was* where he belonged, at least now, in this hour of need.

"The danger is real but not imminent. That is, it does not lurk just beyond sunset, or tomorrow's dawn," replied the elder. "Chislev in her mercy revealed much to me, and I know that the ogres have not yet made necessary preparations to depart their stronghold."

"That gives us some time, another week at the very least and hopefully longer," Moreen said quickly. She addressed the gathered Arktos. "Send runners to each village along the coast. Tell the people we need them here, in Brackenrock. They should bring their livestock and move here at once."

She turned and walked away from the table, then abruptly wheeled. Her face was grave, her eyes introspective. When she looked up she spoke, not to Kerrick, but to Dinekki.

"I must send a message to Strongwind Whalebone and arrange an immediate meeting," she said. "I fear we need the help of the Highlander leaders, and he is the only one who can rally the clans." She turned back to the elf. "Kerrick, will you take me across the strait as soon as he can see me?"

He hesitated. His last hope of going home was dashed by her request. And he had not come back to take Moreen to plead for the help of the man who so steadfastly sought an alliance with her by marriage. Her eyes widened, her expression strangely imploring, and he could not deny her.

"Yes, of course," the elf replied firmly, though, inside, he felt a kernel of the old resentment and a growing fear of coming events.

8

Midnight Sun

The king of Suderhold could wander the halls of his great fortress city without escort if he so chose, and on this day he did so choose. He told his wife that he merely wanted some solitude before he performed the Ceremony of the Midnight Sun in the presence of thousands, but Grimwar Bane had another reason to seek some private time, as well.

He emerged from his apartment and stretched his great arms, working out the kinks in his back, allowing a deep growl of contentment to rumble in his chest.

He advanced to the edge of the balcony above the central atrium, looking all the way down through the levels of Winterheim to the placid waters of the enclosed harbor. From the Royal Quarter, many hundreds of feet above sea level, he could view the heart of his great city. The enclosed waters were sunlit now, as the great doors of the anchorage stood open, and the sun, low in the north, spilled directly across the gently rippled surface.

Very little of that illumination reached high into the cavernous city. Instead, the placid waters sparkled like a dazzling mirror, outlining the wharves and the two great galleys in sparkling light. The Royal Quarter, and other midlevels of the palace, had massive windows of transluscent ice, magically protected against melt, exposed to the sky. During the months of summer these admitted enough illumination to diminish the darkness throughout the underground capital.

Even on a bright day such as this, however, great swaths of the halls and chambers were cloaked in semi-darkness, and this suited Grimwar as he departed the balcony and began to walk along the great avenue encircling the atrium. He met many human slaves, all of whom bowed respectfully and halted as he passed, and several braces of Royal Watchmen clapped their halberds to their gold-studded breastplates. They stood at attention, faces blank and tusks gleaming, and the king acknowledged each with a regal nod.

A massive ogre waddled out from a lordly manor, wiping crumbs from his chin, trailing a cloud of red silk as he waved at the king. "Your Majesty! Your Majesty!" He pulled his free arm through the red silk, which turned out to be a dressing gown, and tried to make himself presentable.

"I have completed the viewing assignments for the Ceremony of the Midnight Sun. The baron of Glacierheim and his entourage will have the place of honor, just below the King's Roost. Lord Darsoonian wanted to be there, but I told him that the baron was the queen's uncle and that he had come all this way and I wasn't about to make him stand on some silly lower outcrop. So, I told him, he, Darsoonian that is, would just have to—"

"Yes, fine, Lord Quendip," Grimwar said. "Was there anything else that you wanted?"

"What, well, no . . . just to let you know that I had things under control. There were so many special requests, but I tried to honor them when I could. That is, to put the nobles where I thought you wanted them to be."

"That's very thoughtful," said the king, tilting his head to avoid the noxious waft of garlic tainting the obese ogre's breath. "Now, if you don't mind . . ." He indicated his intent to keep walking.

"Oh, not at all," said the lord, missing the hint entirely as he fell into step beside the king, jowls bouncing as he hurried to keep up. "But say," Quendip added conspiratorially, "I spotted the Lady Thraid along the Promenade. I imagine she would be particularly delighted to see—ouch!"

The pudgy ogre recoiled, hand to his ear, eyes wide as he ducked away in anticipation of a second blow. Instead, Grimwar leaned close and growled into his underling's quivering jowls, "Do watch your tongue, Lord Quendip . . . and have a care with a lady's good name. Do you take my meaning?"

"Er . . . yes, Sire! Of course I do! I meant no insult . . . oh, and I have to go . . . er, my lunch! It awaits!"

The king had already turned away as Quendip, blubbery knees quaking, lumbered back to his apartment. Grimwar continued his tour, walking slowly past a statue of an ogre five times life size. This was King Garren Icetusk, first king of the Tusk Dynasty. The statue was the most imposing of its kind in Winterheim, for King Garren was the monarch who had advanced Suderhold from the small colony established by the Barkon rulers, founders of the kingdom, to the mighty realm it remained today.

Under Garren's leadership the ogres who had journeyed to the Icereach from Ansalon nearly five thousand years ago had expanded beyond Winterheim, establishing strongholds in Glacierheim, Icewall, and Dracoheim, among other places. It was this expansion that for nearly five thousand years had ensured that ogres were the dominant race upon this southern continent. The Tusk founder was now remembered with this towering statue, the likeness of the ogre sheeted in pure gold, looking over his city with an expression of scowling concern.

The king nodded in reflection, feeling vaguely inadequate as he looked up at his great ancestor. There were lessons to be drawn from King Garren Icetusk's reign, though he wasn't entirely certain what those lessons might be. He ought to remember them. His old tutor, Baldruk Dinmaker, had spent weeks, months, drumming this kind of trivial fact into his skull, and it irritated the king that he could no longer recall the details. Somehow, now that Baldruk was gone, it seemed more important that the king know these things. But who was there left to ask?

More to the point, the large statue was good cover, and he had previously visited it for just that purpose. He could only hope that she would remember. . . .

A trace of color caught his eye and he stepped around the base of the monument to see Thraid Dimmarkull standing at the balcony, looking across the atrium from a position of deep shadow between the statue's knees. Wisps of steamy fog had begun to rise from the harbor, and Grimwar had the sudden feeling that he and the ogress were outside, alone in some mountain fastness.

"Hello," he said, stepping to the edge, carefully placing his hands upon the rail of carved whaletusk. He wanted to reach out, to embrace her, but he knew that Stariz had spies even—*especially*—here, in Winterheim. With great restraint he kept his voice low. "You look beautiful . . . ."

She did. From here he looked out the corner of his eye and could see her in profile, the full lips and sensuous, rounded cheeks. She was pleasantly round elsewhere, he noted, as his eyes trailed down the tight-fitting bodice of her ice-blue gown to where her waist narrowed, so unusual in an ogress. Grimwar drew a ragged breath as the ache of desire seized him.

Furtively he looked around. The mist was pale vapor rising and growing thick as the air cooled, obscuring the view from all but the nearest balconies. So far as he could see, those were empty. The huge statue concealed them from the avenue.

In another instant it didn't matter. He couldn't stop himself. He stepped to her side and pulled her to his chest with brute force. She grunted in eager pleasure at the rough contact. He kissed her, fully, heatedly, and felt her melt against him. His growl rumbled unconsciously, and she squealed as he bit, tasted blood.

"My lord—do I please you?" she gasped teasingly.

He smothered her with another embrace, then released her and turned away.

"When can we steal a moment, my king?" she asked, squeezing his arm as she pouted.

"I will come to you—soon!" he promised, "but not until it is safe."

"I understand," Thraid whispered.

Footsteps echoed on the avenue, the booming laughter of young ogres. A party of slaves came past, one young man glancing over to see the king, then hastily averting his eyes. Straightening himself, wanting nothing so much as to stay here, with this woman, the king of Suderhold marched onto the avenue and marked his course toward the mountaintop, and the preparations for the Ceremony of the Midnight Sun.

The advent of the first of the nightless days was a time of rare beauty and profound ceremony throughout the Icereach. In the mountain fortress of the ogre king, the rituals dated back more than five thousand years, remnants of histories written in realms thousands of miles away from here. But in none of those lands, no other corner of the world, Grimwar felt certain, was there the start of a day when the sun would never set. The ritual would occur at midnight, and the sun flickering low on the southern horizon inevitably provided a perfect symbol of light and power when viewed from up here, atop the great, glacier-shrouded peak of Winterheim.

The land fell away to all sides, shades of black rock and stark ice contrasting with the pale green of tundra and meadow. Distant peaks ringed them, and these were haloed in purple and pink as the low-lying sun cast rays across them all. To the north, the waters of Black Ice Bay were shrouded in the mountain's shadow, while the distant White Bear Sea remained shiny in the lingering daylight.

The route to the summit emerged from the Royal Quarter, the upper level of the mountain's hollow core. A massive gate, consisting of two granite slabs hewn from the bedrock of the peak, stood open to admit the summer breeze into the mountain's heart. At the same time, it allowed passage from the cavernous interior onto a lofty shoulder of the massif.

From the gate, a winding trail angled across the steep terrain. Now, in high summer, the ground was alive with wildflowers and copses of lush, low grass. Streams spilled between rocky outcrops, and waterfalls were common. These sparkled like diamonds in the bright sunlight, and Grimwar paused to relish the sight—and catch his breath—before he climbed the last dozen steps up to the mountain's small summit platform.

This was a square clearing no more than three paces on a side. Stones had been carefully fitted to make a smooth floor. Every spring, masons climbed to the top of the mountain to repair damage wrought by the winter snow and ice. These workers only crawled when they came onto the platform, for these stones were hallowed—they would bear no feet except those of the monarchs of Suderhold.

The King's Roost, it was called, and Grimwar treasured this place and this ceremony more perhaps than any other aspect of his kingship. He watched the shadows play across the plaza as the sun, still visible at midnight on the southern horizon, cast its rays horizontally across the platform, highlighting the numerous tiny irregularities. A pebble stretched a shadow as long as his finger. The rim of a tiny crack loomed like a bluff over a plain.

He heard Stariz cry out, "The moment of zenith is now!"

That was his cue. Knowing that the hour was exactly midnight—as accurately as that hour could be identified by his high priestess—the ogre king strode onto the small platform, planted his great fists on his hips, and turned his tusked face southward, squarely facing toward the sun. There was little warmth, for the sun was too low in the sky, but there was undeniable brightness there. He squinted, his eyes pained by the unaccustomed light.

He looked below to see the other nobles of Winterheim moving into their places. The baron of Glacierheim stood with his wife and several companions on a small, smooth clearing a little distance below. The baron was Stariz's uncle, a proud and haughty bull with a thick mane of gray hair, now an honored guest who had come to Winterheim for this ceremony. His eyes were fixed upon the king, and he nodded with great dignity when Grimwar's gaze fell upon him.

Beyond, the monarch saw Lord Quendip, stumbling, leaning on the sturdy arms of two human footmen, struggling to make it to a patch of level ground on a ridge some distance below the king. Queen Stariz stood just below the Roost, her expression invisible behind the huge black mask of Gonnas. The tusked image of the ogre god stared sternly up at Grimwar as his gaze swept across the rest of the crowd.

Thraid was a stone's throw away, amidst a small crowd, resplendent in a dress of metallic gold, the material shimmering like a liquid in the bright sunlight. The king dared to allow his gaze to linger on her voluptuous form for a moment, before his wife's ostentatious cough drew his attention back to the matter at hand. Grimwar straightened, staring at the sun again as Stariz began to intone the ritual benediction.

"Gonnas the Mighty! Willful deity of ogrekind—Lord of Suderhold, and master of tusk and talon! Hear our pledges, and be pleased!

"God of my kings, I hereby pledge to secure your sacred kingdom against all threats," Grimwar chanted, reciting the words he stated every midsummer. "Your enemies are mine. I wage war against them at your will and maintain my mastery over all your realm. Hear my pledge, and be pleased!"

The prayers rippled farther down the mountain, then, as the other noble ogres made their promises of faith. The commoners began soon after, and the noise of thousands of voices merged together into a placid rumble. The king was soothed by that sound, borne upward as if it freed him from the bonds of gravity.

After the stolid resonance of the prayers, Stariz ber Glacierheim ber Bane advanced. All eyes went to the high priestess, who loomed even taller than usual in the great mask of her god. She stalked toward the base of the King's Roost with manifest urgency. Many ogres gasped when it appeared that she would actually set foot upon the sacred stone, but she halted at the last instant and stood motionless, staring up at Grimwar.

"Speak, my queen, priestess of our mighty god!" he declared, eyeing her warily. Would she keep her side of the agreement?

"I may speak for the god on some matters, but in matters of his will you should listen to Gonnas alone." She looked at him pointedly. "It must be you, my king, who beseeches his sign. Only then shall you know if you truly work the will of the god."

"Indeed." The king lifted his head again, then turned back to the south and raised his massive arms. He knew this ritual too. Grimwar considered himself a faithful servant of Gonnas, but he didn't expect the god to speak to him directly, now or ever. Smugly, he began.

His two great hands extended toward that midsummer's beacon, as if he would embrace it. He roared the traditional words in a voice that boomed down the mountainside and echoed from the faces of glacier and cliff.

"Gonnas the Mighty! God of my fathers and my sons! If you are displeased with my loyal efforts to work your will, give me a sign! Show me . . . show my people. We will obey!"

Facing that sparkling sun, the king allowed his delight to spread across his face. He would make the attack on Brackenrock when *he* wished, not when his wife commanded. Indeed, it was Stariz herself who had, all unknowingly, suggested to him the means to prove his god's favor. He closed his eyes, savored the tiny bit of warmth he could extract from those feeble rays. The favor of his god was like a blessing on his skin, and he exerted his strength, holding the pose for a very long time. He knew that he was a masterful figure, that the eyes of all his people were upon him. Gonnas himself would approve.

Someone gasped. "What's happening?"

"The sun—it grows dark!" cried another.

Grimwar opened his eyes and stared in alarm. Surely they were imagining it, old women cackling like frightened chickens! The sun was still bright, painful to look at as it blazed on the horizon.

The mountaintop seemed cloaked in an eerie shadow, and that shade seemed to be growing. Grimwar stared now in disbelief—it was if as something had taken a bite out of the sun, obscuring more and more of the fiery disk. Dumbstruck, the king of Suderhold realized that the sun was being swallowed, darkened and obscured by a black presence of unmistakable might.

"Gonnas?" he croaked weakly. "Are you displeased?"

The answer was clear, even before Stariz articulated the sign for those who might have trouble understanding.

"It is the will of our god!" cried the priestess, sounding awestruck herself. "He has heard your cry, and he sends the sign!"

Grimwar stayed on the King's Roost for a long time, determined not to show his fear as his world was plunged into a chill and artificial night. The weeping and crying of his people, bold warriors as well as women and youngsters, was a cacophony of terror across the whole vast summit of Winterheim. Some turned and fled, while others huddled in misery and fear, looking from the sun to the king and back again.

The king knew when he was defeated. Grimwar bowed his head, and pledged to do the will of his god, muttering the statement, then raising his voice and crying aloud his mission. Very slowly, the daylight brightened, the midnight sun escaping from the grip of the shadow to once again wash Icereach in its pearly light.

Grimwar was the last one through the gates into the city, following right behind Stariz. He watched her, that lofty mask and the wide-shouldered ceremonial robe, and thought again about the darkening sun.

He wondered how his wife had done it.

9

Strongwind Whalebone

The breeze out of the south was strong, and judging from the chill it would get stronger, and colder, sometime during the next few days. Kerrick knew from long experience that squalls, complete with lashing rain, cold winds and violent seas, could strike the White Bear Sea at any time, even in the midst of summer. Now one such storm brewed ominously, dark clouds forming an image like a mountainous horizon far to the south of Brackenrock.

Still, the elf was eager for this mission, sailing with Moreen across the Bluewater Strait, carrying her to a meeting with the Highlander king. His feelings regarding Strongwind Whalebone were far from fond. The strapping, bearded king was a powerful man, handsome and persuasive, and he had been smitten by the chiefwoman of the Arktos eight years before. Now Moreen was going to seek his help, and Kerrick didn't want to speculate on what she might have to give up to gain the Highlanders' aid.

Yet the thought of a half day alone with Moreen as they crossed the strait before the threatening storm was enough to negate all his other concerns. The arrangements for the council had been made quickly by means of carrier pigeons. Strongwind Whalebone would arrive at Tall Cedar Bay today, and by the twin gods of Zivilyn and Chislev the chiefwoman was also determined to get there today. She was the Lady of Brackenrock, and she did not want to keep the proud Strongwind Whalebone waiting.

The elf's fingers tightened on the tiller as he turned the sleek prow slightly to deflect the blow of a looming breaker, bracing himself for the pressure against the hull as if it was a slap against his own skin. As the boat crested the swell and pressed on, he took the same pleasure he would have gained from sloughing off a powerful but misjudged attack. The clouds were dark, but still distant, and he didn't doubt but they would make a fast crossing.

It pleased him that Moreen was here, to see his skill, to ride his ship through this lively sea. As the spray lashed across the chill waters, soaking his oilskin slicker and stinging his eyes, he drank in the sight of the black-haired woman. She looked back at him from her position fore of the cabin, where she balanced on the pitching deck to look over at the elf from the small compartment in the stern cockpit. He loved her wry, half-turned smile, the way her dark eyes flashed when she noticed him watching her.

"Do you want me to take in some sail?" she called, flexing her knees as the bow rose sharply beneath her.

"Yes," he replied, as much because he wanted the trip to last a little longer as to avoid the jarring and bouncing of their wild ride. Even if Strongwind couldn't be expected to wait too long, it wouldn't hurt the king to stand around for an hour or two before the lady got there. This was a time, a moment in his life, that Kerrick wanted to savor.

Moreen adjusted the lines, playing out the boom so that more wind slipped past the main sail. She skirted the cabin to come back and sit beside Kerrick.

"Are you worried?" she asked, after studying his thoughtful expression for a moment. "Do you think we should turn back?"

"Worried? No. Why do you ask?"

"It was the expression on your face . . . like something was wrong."

Kerrick shook his head. "I was thinking about the dream I've been having. I've had it several times now, variations of the same message. It's a dream about my father and my homeland."

She was silent for a moment, gazing across the wind-tossed waters of the strait. "You haven't spoken of Silvanesti since you came back to Brackenrock, but I know you must miss your home, don't you?"

Kerrick shrugged. "Actually, I'm not so sure I miss the place as it is right now. It's more as though I long for the place it was when I was a child, when my father was there."

Her laughter was wry. "You're not the only one to have such longings." Her gaze turned ahead and her eyes narrowed as she peered at the horizon. "You know, you've never told me much about your father—only that he was captain of that galley, *Silvanos Oak*, that sailed to the Icereach."

"He was captured by ogres," the elf declared bluntly. "Grimwar Bane renamed my father's ship, made it *Goldwing*, the ogre flagship. My father suffered—the gods know how he must have suffered!—in the king's dungeon. If he was lucky, he died quickly. At best, he could have survived a year or two. This is all I've been able to find out over the last several years. Only tidbits and rumor. But the notion that he might have escaped and returned home . . . ridiculous! Just ridiculous."

Kerrick sighed. "What's the point in knowing how he died? Or who killed him? There are some revelations better left in the dark."

Moreen shook her head with a slight grimace. "When I saw my father killed by the ogre's spear it was a horror, a nightmare, but at least I was there, I saw it, and I *know* he's gone. There's a comfort in that."

"Maybe it was the same thing for me when I saw the galley under Grimwar Bane's control. Did you know, my father drew the plans for *Silvanos Oak* himself? He helped with every phase of the construction. To see that beautiful vessel corrupted to the ends of the ogre king . . . *that* was proof enough of my father's death."

"If you hadn't come here when you did, that ship in our enemy's hands probably would have been our undoing. The gods work in strange ways," Moreen replied. "I don't know if I ever really thanked you for designing and installing the harbor boom." The chiefwoman changed the subject quietly. She looked at Kerrick with dark eyes, soft and pensive, and he felt a stab of irrational guilt.

"It was little enough," he declared, not very truthfully. "Now you'll get help from the Highlanders, too. Strongwind was eager to meet with you, or he wouldn't have agreed to come to the bay on such short notice."

"No doubt he's worried about the possibility of a new ogre weapon; I warned him about that in the message. He's got his own interests to look out for and will want to know everything we can tell him," she said pensively.

"Yes. Some new horror of unspeakable power." The elf found himself wishing that he had interrogated the thanoi aggressively, had learned more—something useful! But the creature was in such a bad way, and Kerrick had felt only pity for him.

Moreen looked past the cabin, along the bow. "It's possible that Strongwind will already know something about it. He surprises me, sometimes, with his sources of information . . . with . . ."

"Will . . . will your meeting with him take very long, do you think?" asked the elf warily.

"I'd like to get back to Brackenrock by tomorrow night," she replied quickly. "There's so much to do."

"Okay, fine. I'll stay at the bay, probably sleep on the boat. We can go whenever you want to leave in the morning."

All too soon, for the elf, the forested ridges of the strait's eastern shore darkened the horizon. Long familiar with this section of coast, Kerrick needed only a slight course adjustment to bring them sailing directly toward the little cove that in the past eight years had become home to a small but prosperous fishing village.

Tall Cedar Bay was sheltered by the promontories of evergreen-studded cliffs that reached out to enclose the anchorage in protective arms. Only when *Cutter* glided though the gap between those sheltering ridges did Kerrick relax his grip on the tiller and allow Moreen to haul in more sail. The wind and storm, blocked by the flanking heights, dropped away almost to nothing, and the jarring motion of the boat settled into a smooth glide.

As *Cutter* sliced through the calm water, Kerrick looked to the shore and reflected on how much this place had changed. It had been his first landfall when he had reached the Icereach, nine summers ago, though then it was merely a grove of wild evergreens and a rocky, wild shore.

Now he sailed past five fishing curraghs, the sturdy boats anchored just offshore, a stone's throw from the solid rock piers that flanked the small waterfront. On one of the banks a stone fishhouse belched smoke from its squat chimney, while the odor of salmon hung in the air.

Nearer to the anchorage, the wide log façade of the Tall Cedar Inn occupied a commanding position on a small rise of land, overlooking the bay. Several burly Highlanders were lounging about on the veranda, and they came down to the wharf as the sailboat slowed and finally came to a stop. Kerrick glanced at them, then turned his attention to the front door of the inn.

Strongwind Whalebone, king of the Highlanders, stood there, his arms planted on his hips, his straw-bearded face split by a wide grin of welcome. To Kerrick, as he turned the boat to allow the wind to flow past the sail, the day suddenly seemed to get much colder.

Moreen walked up the gentle hill and accepted Strongwind's warm embrace, the bristly kiss on each of her cheeks. She even returned the hug with enough pressure to let him know that she was glad to see him.

Surprisingly enough, she was. There was a sense of competence and strength in his familiar, bearlike presence. Here, with his arms around her, she felt safer than she had in a long time. Here was the only place she where she could let someone else take charge, at least for awhile.

"I see Randall's tent over there," Kerrick said, when she finally broke away to look at the elf. His expression was strangely pinched, and she wondered, again, about the secret pain that lurked within him.

For now she only nodded, looking at Strongwind. "We'll talk at the inn?" Tall Cedar Bay boasted but one sprawling inn, the large cabin on the rise above the waterfront and the bay.

Strongwind nodded. "Yes—Dannard has turned it over to me for as long as we need it." He turned to Kerrick. "Randall was hoping to see you, I know. I daresay I'd rather spend the evening with you men around the fire, drinking and tell tales, than to have to bear these burdens of state." He smiled, but Moreen saw little humor in the expression—it was more the smile of the wolf who has tired his prey and now closes in for the kill.

Kerrick smiled gamely in return, and his humor seemed genuine. "The crown weighs heavy, eh, my lord? Well, we'll save you a draught in case you can slip away."

"No chance of that," said the king, turning and wrapping a lanky arm around Moreen's shoulders. She twisted slightly to break free of his grip, taking his elbow and walking at his side to the inn. Kerrick headed in the opposite direction.

At the door to the inn Strongwind bowed, and extended a hand. "My lady, know that all the hospitality of this little den is available to your merest whim."

"Why, thank you my lord," she said, slightly mocking him as she passed inside. Taking a deep breath, she waited as Strongwind poured several large glasses of warqat. He led her to a pair of comfortable chairs before the hearth, where a low fire burned. Then she began to talk.

She told him of Kerrick's encounter with the dying thanoi, the missive from the ogre king to his mother on mysterious Dracoheim. She said she was convinced of the truth of the threat, that the ogres had some powerful new weapon. Moreen related the results of Dinekki's auguries, indicating they still had some time to prepare their defense. The king listened thoughtfully, drinking slowly from his goblet, until at last Moreen was done talking and ready for his reaction.

"Will you stand with us against this new threat?" she asked. "If you will send warriors to Brackenrock to reinforce our own fighters, we can present a united front—and give the ogres a serious defeat if they do come against us."

Strongwind nodded solemnly, and for a few moments Moreen wondered if he was going to say anything at all. She took a sip of her warqat, feeling the warmth slide down her gullet, surprised to note that her glass was nearly empty. Finally he looked up at her and spoke.

"I remember Dinekki," Strongwind said softly. "It was she who brought our two gods together, caused the very ground to shake—and helped save our lives when the ogres attacked eight years ago. If Dinekki is convinced of the threat, that is enough for me. Added to the elf's story about saving the thanoi, I agree that we are in for some dangerous times. For now, of course we will help," he said, "but I beg you to think of this alliance more for the long term."

"What do you mean?"

"Become my queen!" Strongwind pleaded in a burst of emotion. "Marry me, and unite our peoples in a way that will bind them together through the future. Certainly, I will send warriors to aid you now. I assume you would do the same, if we learned of any threat against us. That is to be expected of old friends, but that is not enough! If we were wed, our descendants would be linked forever, and we would present a front against the ogres they would never shatter!"

"You make a compelling case, politically, at least," Moreen said dryly, feeling more touched by his proposal than she cared to admit—even to herself. "But I had always hoped that, if I married, it would be for a more personal reason. I am my people's leader, but I am also a woman . . . a woman who wants to love and be loved."

"I do love you!" proclaimed the king. He set down his goblet and kneeled beside Moreen's chair, taking one of her hands in both of his. "I've loved you since I first saw you. I only wish I had told you the truth then, rather than speaking in political riddles. Speak, lady chiefwoman: Could there be any glimmer of love in your soul, for me?"

Moreen drew a deep breath. Strongwind's words were seductive, and his blue eyes, so close to hers, were overpowering.

"You are a good man, Your Majesty," she said softly. "Perhaps the best I have ever known." But she felt it was wiser for them to defeat the enemy first, and then talk about marriage afterward. "We have time to talk about these things," she said. "For now, would you fill my glass again and join me in a toast to this summer's alliance?"

———— ◆ ————

"A new weapon, hmm?" Randall speculated. "Something to blow Brackenrock right off the face of Krynn. Of course, if it can destroy that citadel, it could blow up anything else, too. Guess I'll be there with ye to stand against the bastards, if they come."

The Highlander drew from his mug of warqat and instead of swallowing spat a stream into the fire. Blue flames surged upward, and Kerrick relished the feel of the sudden heat against his face. The waters of Tall

Cedar Bay shimmered in the twilight, and the salt smell of the sea mingled with sweet pine smoke. Dry logs crackled as the flames devoured them, mingling with the lapping of waves against the shore—the only sounds in the still summer night.

Furtively, the elf looked up the hill, toward the inn. Subdued lights, like a fire fading low in the hearth, still glowed in the windows. Moreen Bayguard and Strongwind Whalebone were in there, alone, had been for many hours. It was past midnight, though it had never really grown dark.

Randall saw his glance and shook his head. Lars Redbeard, the third of the companionable trio gathered around the fire, sighed sympathetically. "Don't know what they can be talking about for so . . . long," he said without much conviction.

Kerrick could imagine but didn't want to. The king of the Highlanders was unwed, and his desire for the chiefwoman was known to all. For eight years Moreen had stood independent of the king's will, safely distant behind Brackenrock's high walls. If she was really frightened, convinced her tribe was in dire danger, would she weaken?

"Would the ogres be comin' this summer, then?" inquired Redbeard. "That would be a hard blow."

"Yes, but we'll be ready," Kerrick said, surprised at the realization that he had included himself among the Arktos. "Most of the past eight years have been spent building and expanding the fortress, reinforcing walls, putting up new bulwarks. We're ready for war."

"I have some business over in Brackenrock, anyway," Lars said casually. "The men from my clanhold are itching for a ride across the strait. Maybe we'll come over, camp out for awhile. We shan't be any bother."

Kerrick was touched by the offer of support, and he knew that Moreen would be too. "Thanks, and I'm sure your presence would be welcome," he said. Again he looked up at the inn. The lights were even lower now, it seemed.

"Here," the elf said, reaching a hand toward Randall. "Let me have a drink."

She woke up to see the light of dawn brightening the eastern sky, through the unshuttered window. The great, broad swath of the Icereach morning brightened the sky to a rosy coral. Reclining on the cushioned bench, she sleepily looked out the window, between a gap in the tall cedars.

A rattling snore drew her attention to the nearby chair, where the king of the Highlanders slumbered. A goblet lay sideways on the floor, just beneath his dangling hand. Strongwind rustled slightly in his chair, extending one foot. Moreen saw the big toe jutting from a hole in his woolen stocking.

Her own head hurt, and her mouth felt gummy and sour. Grimacing with distaste she rose and crossed to the water pitcher. Her legs were unsteady, and the movement brought the pounding in her head to an uncomfortable crescendo. She drank deeply, felt a little better. Crossing back to the bench and chair, she smiled wryly, then flung the contents of the pitcher into Strongwind's face.

The king came up swinging, almost surprising her before she hopped out of the way. Groggily Strongwind opened his eyes, wringing his long hair in both hands. "What did you do that for?" he demanded, then winced as if the sound of his own voice stung the inside of his skull.

"It's your turn," she said, gesturing to the goblet that lay sideways beside the king's chair, "to make a toast."

He gaped at her, then, grudgingly, chuckled. "You wore me down, didn't you? A little thing like you, and I fell asleep in the chair. I know I can't out-talk you, but by Kradok I was pretty sure I could out-drink you!"

She looked at him, feeling a strange tenderness. "Actually, I was pouring it into the spittoon after the first few rounds."

"Waste of good warqat," the king muttered glumly. "So that's it, then? We talk for half the night, and that's all we do, as usual. You won't be my queen?"

Moreen shook her head. "You're a good man and a good king, but I'm not ready to marry you," she said.

"You never give me a reason," Strongwind pressed. "I hope it is not that the sight of me repulses you?"

She smiled, a wry tilt of her lips. "Hardly. You're right, I didn't give you a reason. I don't intend to give you a reason."

"You're a stern woman, Moreen, Lady of Brackenrock," Strongwind Whalebone admitted, "but I admire you, and I will send three hundred warriors to help defend your fortress, if and when the ogre king comes."

———◆———

"I think you should stay another night," Strongwind persisted. The wind was gusting hard, and another of the periodic cloudbursts was drumming rain. "You too, of course, Kerrick—both of you, my guests. We'll tell some stories, drink some warqat, and you can be on your way when this storm passes."

Kerrick didn't reply, but he concentrated all of his will on Moreen as she squinted in thought. It took all his elven reserve to conceal his elation when she finally spoke.

"Thanks, but if Kerrick's willing, I'd like to try to get across right away—if the weather's not too bad."

"No problem for *Cutter*," Kerrick quickly agreed. "With a wind like this, we'll make it across in a few hours—though it will be a little bumpy."

"Then let's go," said Moreen, though she turned a little green as she stared at the bay, where even the semi-sheltered waters were whipped into whitecaps. She turned to Strongwind. "Thank you again for your hospitality, and for your willingness to help."

The king took Moreen's hand and gazed up at her. "I am grateful for the discussions we were able to share . . . and may Chislev and Kradok together grant that we will lead our people into a new, bright era."

"Yes," the Lady of Brackenrock agreed, sincerely. "I look forward to seeing you and your warriors within the walls of our citadel."

Kerrick offered his help as she started down the steep ladder beside the wharf, but Moreen hiked up her long skirt and hopped nimbly down the metal rungs. Kerrick followed, and soon the boatman was pushing the dinghy back to the moored sailboat.

They crossed back to Brackenrock with the sun barely visible between the scudding clouds. Kerrick was sore from sleeping on the ground, cold from sleeping outside, and queasy from the effects of too much campfire warqat. As Moreen sat beside the transom, wrapped in her own thoughts, her ashen face indicated that she, too, had indulged too much in the bitter but potent brew of the Icereach.

By noon the headland of Brackenrock rose before them. From several miles out they could see the fortress, the smooth walls reflecting the light of the bright sun, the towers and parapet shimmering like jewels in a crown.

Kerrick looked over at Moreen. She had been strangely quiet during the return trip. He guessed that she was steeling herself for the task ahead. The Lady of Brackenrock didn't even notice the elf staring at her. As she studied the strait and the pillar at the mouth of the harbor, the grim look on her face made another kind of fortress.

"You know," Moreen said finally, over her shoulder as she continued to look over the stern, toward Tall Cedar Bay. "He isn't such a bad man. Not so bad at all."

Two days later a veritable parade of curraghs began to cross the strait, and a week after that Strongwind Whalebone himself made the trip, bringing his personal bodyguard of veteran axemen. All told, more than four hundred and thirty Highlander warriors arrived to camp outside and inside the walls of Brackenrock.

10

The Forge

The royal smithy was a huge, vaulted chamber with numerous forges, ovens, anvils, and stout stone tables. Great piles of coal rose like black mountains in the far corners of the room, mingling with the shadows that seemed to creep outward from the walls. A hundred ogres and slaves could work in here at one time, raising a din like an enclosed thunderstorm. Now, however, most of the room was dark, though bright lamps illuminated the one forge where a fire burned and the master smith who worked on the artifact that would destroy Brackenrock.

Grimwar and Stariz stood on a railed platform just above the floor of the smithy. The stones had been swept, and the fans were pumping away, but the king still felt the air of sooty grime against his skin, smelled the acrid stench of the smelting process every time he drew a breath. If the queen noticed these same effects, she gave no indication. Instead, her eyes were alight, bright with the reflected light of the forge, and her thin lips were moist, glistening as she nervously licked them. Her attention never wavered.

The king, with considerable input from his wife, had decided to move ahead on invasion plans by dividing the powder from the Alchemist into two different weapons. One was small, a bell-shaped chalice designed to blast away the gates of Brackenrock and allow the ogre troops to gain entrance to the courtyard and the keep. There, Stariz's spies had confirmed, the Axe of Gonnas was displayed above the great hearth, and she was determined that the hallowed artifact be retrieved.

After that, the main power of the Alchemist's discovery would be brought to bear, enclosed in a round sphere of metal that the Alchemist had dubbed the Golden Orb. This weapon was a large sphere of pure gold, hollowed to contain the powder and a bottle of magic potion. When the orb was pitched into a target by catapult, the container would break, and the mixing of the potion with powder would detonate the full power of destruction.

The chalice intended for the initial attack was a small, trumpet-shaped cup of pure gold, currently gleaming on the smith's anvil. The orb, in two hollow halves, sat nearby. When the two halves were fused together, it would weigh more than one hundred pounds and form a perfectly spherical shape.

Both vessels had been shaped precisely to the specifications laid down by Queen Stariz. The stem of the chalice was molded into a grooved mount upon a block of square granite, the heavy stone forming a solid anchor for the tall, flaring vessel. Right now the object sat on an anvil beside the forge, with the furnace doors open, blue-yellow flames flickering eerily from the coal. The smith, a burly human slave, applied foot pressure to the bellows, and the flames increased to white heat. His face was invisible behind a slit-eyed mask of steel, and his hands and forearms were protected by heavy leather gauntlets.

The dust, the treasure from the Alchemist, was now in both the chalice and the orb. Grimwar had watched his wife barely controlling the excited trembling of her hands as she poured the stuff into the two different vessels. She had taken care not to lose a single flake of the precious dust. The king had said nothing as she described to the smith the procedure for capping the potent powder in the chalice, but now he paid attention as the man carefully followed the queen's instructions. The smith was preparing to seal up the cup, the first of the weapons to be completed.

The smith had a small disk of gold in his hand, a circle of metal with a slotted hole in the center. Now he pressed that plate down into the mouth of the goblet, and Stariz barked sharply. "The wick—don't forget the wick!"

Grimwar knew that tone and bristled. The smith showed no irritation, merely nodded. "Of course, Lady Queen. I am merely checking to see the sizing is correct."

"Very well," she replied.

The man brought the disk out, then turned a valve and opened a small chute. Immediately a point of blue flame sprang up from the middle of the forge. This was a cutting flame, Grimwar knew. The smith held the golden disk in a small pair of tongs, masterfully rotating it so that the cutting flame sliced just a bit off the outer perimeter. Moments later, he pulled the plate aside, then took a slender bar of silver and inserted it through the slotted hole.

"The wick is installed, my queen," the smith declared. "Pure magnesium. It will burn with a fire as hot as the sun."

"Hotter still, when the dust takes light," Stariz replied, with another lick of her lips. She almost smiled.

Quickly the smith pressed the disk down into the

chalice, compressing the dust in the bottom. With practiced gestures the man took a small cup of molten gold and poured it carefully into the chalice, sealing the disk in place as the metal cooled. Finally he slammed the door to his furnace, immediately cooling the large chamber, and lifted his mask to regard the queen with a blank expression.

"It is finished, Lady Queen. The chalice may lay on its side or even upside down, and the dust is contained in the base. It is penetrated by the shaft of magnesium, and when that wick is ignited the fire will inevitably take its course. The granite gives it plenty of heft, of course, so that once the weapon is placed it will remain stationary."

"To the orb, then," the queen declared curtly. She produced a clear bottle that Grimwar saw was full of a cloudy liquid, the magic potion that would interact with the powder.

"Careful!" she snapped, as the smith took the vial, inspected the stopper—which was waxed in place—then carefully set it into the shell of half the orb.

Following Stariz's instructions, the smith lifted the second half of the sphere into place, and used an oil torch to carefully fuse the two halves together with a bead of molten gold. When it was finished, Grimwar saw an object that looked almost innocently like a large child's ball.

"You have done well," Stariz said. The smith bowed and departed. He was a man with rare skills and a unique status among the slaves of Winterheim. He knew that he would collect a reward later. The queen turned to her husband.

"The weapons are prepared. We must depart for Brackenrock immediately."

"One more day," growled Grimwar Bane, in such a tone that his wife had to bite her tongue. "There are still preparations to be made, but the galleys will sail on the morning tide."

"Very well," she said, regarding him with that gaze that seemed to bore into the center of his being. "I will prepare for a departure on the morrow."

The king nodded. He was not happy that his wife would accompany him on this campaign—she rarely journeyed onto the sea, and when she did she was invariably ill-tempered and demanding. All the same, he was glad to have her aboard the ship, for there was another reason, even more compelling, that he didn't want to leave her behind when he embarked for war.

———◆———

"How—how long will you be gone?"

Thraid was still pale from her spell of sickness, though she had smeared some rouge upon her round cheeks. The effect was rather garish, Grimwar thought, though he made no remark. Instead, he patted her hand and tried to answer her question.

"Maybe a month. It's hard to say, with these things. I will return in plenty of time for the Harvest Festival."

"That's not terribly long, then," said the ogress, trying bravely, albeit unsuccessfully, to control her sniffling. "Not like when you campaign over the whole summer."

"No," he agreed, not sure what else he could say. "How are you feeling?" he asked lamely.

"It's passing, I think," she said bravely. "The purgatives of the royal physician seem to have made a difference."

"Good." He wanted to tell her about his arrangement with Stariz, the queen's pledge of safety, but somehow he feared even the mention of the other ogress, as if her name was a toxin that would weaken, perhaps kill, his cherished mistress.

"I wish . . . I wish that I was able to send you off with a proper farewell," the ogress said, with just a hint of her old sexiness. He felt the familiar flush, and though he tried to remain silent his chest rumbled to an unconscious growl. Thraid smiled. "However, I will be waiting for you here, my king, when you return."

"And I, my lover, will find my way back to you soonest," he pledged.

Whatever the cost, he vowed to himself. He rose, bent over to kiss her cheek, and turned to the door. The golden orb was ready, and Brackenrock awaited.

Sunlight spilled through as the great harbor doors rumbled open. Hundreds of slaves labored, straining against their lines, as the huge capstans rotated and the gap between the massive slabs grew wider and wider. Open water beckoned, shimmering in the sunlight, and the two great ships moved forward, like eager creatures ready to emerge from a long winter's hibernation.

Goldwing was in the lead, the king standing at the rail, accepting the cheers of the thousand ogres gathered on the waterfront to wish the warriors well. Light swelled around him as the harbor shadows fell behind, and the salt breeze was sweet in his nostrils. He let the accolades wash over him, bearing him into that light, and he tried to convince himself that he embarked upon an epic mission.

At the edge of the prow he saw Stariz, impassive in her great mask. She was holding a long pole, with several smoldering pots swinging from the tip of the shaft. The odor of the sacred incense wafted past the monarch's nostrils as the galley slid into the open air of Black Ice Bay.

The twin summits of the Ice Gates, lofty peaks marking the watery passage into Winterheim, loomed tall and dazzling, sunlight glittering from the many glaciers and ice fields rimming their flanks. Looking to the stern, the king admired the great massif of Winterheim rising above, even higher than the Gates. Great cliffs were draped with ice, and streams and waterfalls sparkled on the lower slopes as the huge mountain shone with midsummer vitality.

Hornet, slightly smaller and lower than the great flagship, came behind, and Grimwar watched the steady strokes of the oars move that galley past the wharf, out through the great arch into the light of the full summer sun. The king felt a thrill of pride, knowing that the second ship had been built at his order. The Alchemist had provided the design, of course, but ogre skills had shaped the vessel. Now it glided along as tangible proof of Grimwar Bane's greatness, a seafaring majesty no ogre monarch of Suderhold could claim over the past three thousand years.

For the current mission, each galley was being rowed by ogres instead of the normal complement of slaves. Although the brutish warriors were less adept at propelling the ship than humans, they would serve to swell the ranks of the king's army after they landed below Brackenrock. In this fashion he would be able to amass nearly a thousand of his veteran ogre troops against the human citadel.

The two ships, one following the other, crossed Black Ice Bay and made their way through the narrow fjord, flanked by the lofty peaks known as the Ice Gates. Soon the king saw whitecaps streaking the water before him, and he felt the wind of the open sea. The big ship was stable, pitching only slightly as she emerged from the narrow way to forge through deep, choppy waters.

Grimwar's thoughts turned to the strongbox locked in his cabin amidships. The golden orb was in there, while the heavy catapult that would ultimately launch it rested on the rear deck. The chalice, primed by the smith, was also resting in the strongbox. Stariz had created several small flares, any one of which, when ignited, would burn hot enough to ignite the magnesium fuse. The orb, of course, was fused by the bottle of potion inside of it. The ogre king tried to imagine the coming devastation, to picture the power of the strange new explosive, but after only a few moments his thoughts drifted.

"Pick up the pace," the king declared, knowing the message would be quickly borne to the helmsman. "I want us to reach Brackenrock in five days." And be done with this war and return as soon as possible, he added to himself.

"Very good, Majesty," came the reply, even as the rhythmic pounding of the cadence drum accelerated. Very slowly, the galley surged forward. The western coast of the White Bear Sea slid past. The course had already been laid—they would stay as close to that shore as possible, to minimize the chance of discovery. He pictured the scene. They would erupt upon the human citadel with surprise as their ally, blast the gate from its hinges, seize the Axe of Gonnas, and proceed to blow the place off the face of Krynn.

11

Dragon Ships

Work on the terraces had been suspended, and all the Arktos set about carrying provisions into the citadel. Fletchers went to work swiftly making arrows, while the few smiths among the humans—Highlanders, most of them—got busy making arrowheads, sharpening swords, repairing armor. Word had been carried to the outlying villages, and within days more Arktos arrived at Brackenrock—fathers in bearskins, carrying spears and harpoons, sturdy mothers carrying heavy packs, while children pulled light sledges of their own. At last, the fortress was fully garrisoned, as ready for war as it could be.

"Why don't they just *come*?" demanded Moreen impatiently. She paced back and forth in her bedroom, while Dinekki clucked disapprovingly.

"Be careful what you wish for, child. There's always more thinking and preparation to be done."

The chiefwoman nodded, even smiled slightly. There was no one else in the world who would dare to call her 'child,' yet when the old shaman said it the word immediately lightened Moreen's spirits. She was able to ask the question that had been burning since the shaman had climbed to the platform a few minutes earlier.

"What did you see when you cast the bones this morning?"

Dinekki sniffed, then shook her head. "Dark omens, I saw . . . there are forces gathering against us now. The threat is imminent, more so than when I cast the auguries last week."

Moreen looked across the green fields of the terraces, thinking how deceptively peaceful everything looked, even though the planting had been delayed and the sheep, goats, pigs, as well as the few precious dairy cows, had been brought from all the pastures, herded into the citadel. Already the courtyard was a makeshift corral, a crowded mingling of bleating, mooing, and snorting as the last few animals were herded through the gate.

"I was thinking about something," the chiefwoman said. "We would be planting now, fishing along the shore, tanning hides, just like eight years ago, before the ogres came. Because Kerrick chose to leave here when he did, because he encountered a dying walrus-man and came back, we have a chance to defend ourselves."

"Thanoi. For generations they have been our enemies," the shaman noted.

"I know. Ironic, isn't it?"

Dinekki chuckled. "Yes. The gods like irony, in my observation. I imagine they are highly entertained by this spectacle."

"It's too bad the bones didn't say anything about this new weapon we have to face," murmured Moreen. Dinekki had no answer, and the chiefwoman looked again at the peaceful fields, the dazzling ocean.

She wrestled with her impatience, wanting the fight to start right now. Silently, she wondered, are we truly ready?

Kerrick and Mouse raised the mainsail and drifted away from the wharf. They planned one more quick run across the strait to Tall Cedar Bay to load up a dozen barrels of oil that Strongwind Whalebone was donating to the cause. The wind was out of the west, so they turned south as soon as they left the harbor, commencing one leg of a long tack across the Bluewater narrows. Kerrick was distracted and didn't really want to leave Brackenrock. He knew the oil would be useful, however, and there was no faster way to fetch it than with his sailboat. But he couldn't shake his misgivings.

"Look—there!" Mouse cried, pointing south.

He saw the prow of the first ogre galley coming around the point, barely three miles away, and immediately he felt that stomach-clenching thrill of terror and excitement that for him always preceded battle. The trip to Tall Cedar Bay was forgotten. He made to turn his boat—Brackenrock would have to live or die with the oil currently on hand.

The tall prow of the lead vessel boasted the curling head of a gold dragon, skillfully rendered by the Silvanesti woodcarvers of his homeland. The twin ramps, raised now to flank that figurehead, were later additions, designed to facilitate the landing of raiders. Kerrick had long thought these ramps the marred the ship's once graceful lines. Long banks of oars stroked the water on either side of the ship, propelling the great hull with rhythmic force.

"Come about!" Kerrick called, and Mouse threw his athletic body to the deck as the boom swept past. *Cutter* heeled through a sharp turn, and by the time the huge raiding ship came fully into view the nimble sailboat had wheeled around to mark a straight line back toward the harbor mouth, three or four miles distant. Mouse dashed to the bow, unleashed a fresh roll of canvas, smoothly hoisting the jib into the freshening air.

The sail instantly caught the wind, bulging over the prow and pulling the vessel forward with lurching acceleration. Kerrick kept his hand on the tiller, exerting all his strength to keep them on a course. At the same time, the wind, like a capricious force, tried to push them past, steering them toward the blue waters of the Courrain Ocean, dazzling in the summer sunlight beyond the strait.

Together, elf and human forced the keen hull to slice through the waters, keeping the boat aimed toward the Signpost and the harbor, coaxing her away from the great ocean.

"Is it *Goldwing*?" Kerrick asked, concentrating on holding their bearing while Mouse looked towards the stern.

"Yes. With *Hornet* right behind. She's not as fast—*Goldwing* seems to be pulling away."

Already they were so close to Brackenrock that the view of the battlements and towers of the great fortress was blocked by the looming promontory of the nearest ridge.

"The boom! Has the watchman seen the galleys yet?" cried Mouse.

As if in answer, a long horn blast, followed by a second, brayed across the sea. Fortunately, the wind—for all its capriciousness—was now aiding them by filling the sail with relentless power. The galleys, propelled only by oars, rapidly dwindled astern, even as the spire of the Signpost rock loomed ahead. The lookout had already run up the warning flag, and continued to blow his warning horn. Kerrick imagined that he could hear the braying of other, louder trumpets from the mountain-top fortress. He knew Moreen's people would be racing to close the gates, to move weapons, fire, and oil into position.

Moreen Bayguard, the Lady of Brackenrock would be the least flustered of all her people. Her orders would be direct and unambiguous, and the Arktos—and those Highlanders who had come to help—would hasten to obey.

Kerrick turned the tiller, and Mouse trimmed the sail, as *Cutter* went gliding through the narrow gap between the Signpost and the opposite sheer cliff. Barely a hundred feet of water spanned that entrance.

He saw with satisfaction that a few men, Highlanders who had been learning the craft of the boatwright in Brackenrock's yard alongside a couple of young Arktos apprentices, were gathered around the boom winch, working on the crank. They were gesturing frantically, however, and when the elf looked closely he saw they were pulling loose links of a broken chain from around the capstan.

"The winch broke!" Kerrick cried. "They'll never be able to free the catch-lever by hand!"

"Can we do it with the boat, from this side of the bay?" Mouse asked, echoing the elf's thoughts.

"The boom! Get over to it—we'll certainly try. We've got ten minutes at most!" shouted the elf, steering the sailboat toward the end of the sturdy construct. With a sharp turn, he brought the boat to an easy stop, as Mouse leaned over the gunwale to seize the lead rope.

The boatmen were too far away to lend assistance. The ogre ships, by keeping close to the shoreline on their northward sortie from Winterheim, had indeed burst upon Brackenrock with more surprise than the Arktos had anticipated. Now all the plans, all the work that had gone into this untried harbor defense, seemed doomed— unless they could free the heavy boom with the help of this brisk wind.

The wind ruffled canvas, and *Cutter* started to slide past the shore, into the harbor. Mouse secured the line fast to a deck clamp. Beside them loomed the end of the beam, supported in a cradle of heavy chain, floating just below the surface of the water, against the rocks of the shoreline. It was secured in place by a heavy lever that was designed to be released by the winch across the harbor mouth. When the chain was released, the heavy beam would float freely in the water, and men hauling on the other side of the entrance could pull the boom across the opening, where it was intended to block access to any vessel trying to pass.

There were simply not enough men now, not with the winch broken and the boom firmly locked in place. They would not be able to release the heavy catch or pull the massive weight across the narrow gap. And they required a wind gust of such power that it seemed hopeless.

Mouse was working hard. He looped a second, then a third line over the end of the boom until the sailboat was lashed with enough rope to support a monstrous load. Kerrick looked at the big, rust-covered lever and made a decision. He ducked into the cabin, quickly went to his sea chest and tossed his clothes out of the way, fumbling to open the little wooden box. Without thinking—because thinking could lead to doubt—he slipped the circle of gold, his father's ring, over his finger and returned to the cockpit.

He could feel the magic, the warm pleasure of pure strength permeating his flesh, tingling his nerves, stiff-ening resolve. Mouse was at the boom, ready to release the sail to catch the wind. Kerrick pointed at the lever, and the young man nodded.

"I'll take the tiller as soon as you go!"

Feeling a surge of power, the elf leaped toward the rocky shore, making a balanced landing on a flat-crested rock, dry and sunlit above the surging breakers. Another spring took him to the nest of chains that bracketed the end of the boom in its cradle.

Behind him the mainsail snapped taut, and Mouse clutched the tiller, as the boat strained against the multiple lines connected to the boom.

Kerrick grabbed the lever, the metal cold and rough under the skin of his palm. He pulled and strained, feeling the metal, creaking and reluctant, begin to move. His flesh, stiffened by the power of the ring, was corded wire, his will a furnace of determination.

Slowly, the mechanism began to open. Chain spilled through the sprocket, at first one link and then a breathtaking pause before the next. He heard another sharp clack, then another, finally a steady cadence of moving chain. Faster, then, like the pounding of his heart, the metal links tumbled past until the gear was spinning free and the boom lunged outward eagerly, free from anchor.

A great splash of water rose across the stern, drenching Mouse and releasing *Cutter*. The boat sprang forward, pushed by the wind, dragging the massive weight of the boom through the seas swelling into the narrow harbor mouth. Across the harbor, Mouse saw the tower watchmen waiting to lash the boom in place. The sailboat strained and moved slowly closer, as some of the men waded into the cold water, reaching with gaff hooks to haul the heavy barrier into its socket. The boom stretched fully across the anchorage now, steel spikes here and there jutting above the surface of the water, a menacing line vaguely suggesting a formation of underwater pikemen.

Kerrick looked to sea then, saw the looming prows of the two galleys, each cutting a white swath through the rolling swells. A momentary hatred seized him, making him tremble. He wanted to hurl himself against those ships, his weapon being his own flesh. It took all of his will to check the impulse and keep his feet planted on the slippery rocks.

The ogre king, Grimwar Bane himself, judging by his golden breastplate, stood on the deck and glared at the harbor. The elf grinned fiercely, imagining his enemy's displeasure. Would the galleys try to charge through? If they did, would the boom hold? It *had* to hold! Furiously, he thought of leaping into the sea and reinforcing the boom with his own enhanced strength.

Only then did he realize his foolishness and immediately pulled off the ring. It was cold and deceptively light in his hand, yet it had almost overcome him with its seductive power. He felt immeasurably weak now, sapped by a depression that tempted him to collapse, to rest and sleep. All his body called out for him to lie here on these rocks.

At last his mind took over, reminding him that there was plenty more work to be done. Stumbling, taking great care with his balance lest his enfeebled legs betray him on this rough ground, he made his way along the shore, past the great stone mount where the boom was secured, and into the fragile security of Brackenrock's port.

"Sire! We must turn!" Argus Darkand shouted over the din of the rowing drums, as the galley surged forward.

"By Gonnas, we will not!" roared Grimwar Bane, glaring at his helmsman until that veteran ogre sailor nodded his acquiescence. "Take us forward, through that toothpick of a barrier!"

The king squinted for a better look, not entirely sure what the elf and the humans had just done. He saw a long shaft floating in the water, sensed that it had been pulled across like a gate. Surely there was no threat in that, nothing that could harm his mighty flagship!

He stood above the great gap running along the center of the deck, looked down onto the shoulders and backs of his straining oarsmen.

"Row, you louts!" he bellowed. "Row like the wind— show these humans the power of ogre brawn!"

The ship made another surge, but once again Argus Darkand found his way to the king's side. The helmsman was nervous, his normally florid flesh now grown pale. Angrily the king pushed him away, strode back to the bow.

"My husband, consider." He recognized his wife's voice, but was so preoccupied he didn't turn to acknowledge her. "Have patience, Sire. We can win this fight in good time—we do not need to take a rash risk now, in the opening movement."

He saw the metal barbs, waves lapping just over the tips. They were arrayed with their points jutting toward his ship. Possibly *Goldwing* could smash through that boom with only a few scratches, but what if he was wrong and one of those stout shafts punched through the hull?

"Slow!" he roared, and immediately Argus Darkand echoed the command to the rowers. The cadence of the drums fell off. "Stand off!"

Grimwar Bane scowled at the vast hooked timber that floated, just below water level, across the mouth of the bay. He had scuffed his ship on a rock, once, and it had taken a whole summer to repair the hull—he could vividly imagine what damage those barbed links might wreak on the planks of *Goldwing*'s hull.

"Come around the point. We anchor off the beaches below the citadel farms and attack by land," he ordered. "The humans have bought themselves another few hours. I hope they enjoy them, for they will be their last hours upon Krynn."

———◆———

The lookout on the high tower blew his trumpet, three long, braying notes that meant the best news Moreen could hope for, under the circumstances.

"They're quitting the harbor!" she cried.

Once again the Lady of Brackenrock stood atop the highest tower of her citadel's gatehouse. She looked down into the great courtyard, where her people were running back and forth in well-ordered chaos. "Archers, bring the extra arrows up to the walls!"

She spotted a lithe farmwife coming through the gate directly beneath her. "Martine, start bringing the people up from the lower terraces. We're closing the gates, but we'll leave the sortie door open until the last minute. Tell everyone they have to get up here now!"

"Yes, m'lady!" called Martine, and immediately raced off on her errand.

"They're coming for real?"

Moreen recognized Bruni's voice and turned around with relief. The big woman emerged from the stairwell. "Yes, the signals say 'two ships,' but also that the boom stopped them at the harbor mouth. So they'll be coming by land—which gives us a little time. Are the Highlanders ready?"

"All six hundred, including Strongwind's heavy axemen. That's fifty more strong, big men. Gustav the White was here with a load of gold from his mine, and dozens more came in his caravan. They're anxious for the chance to fight some ogres."

Moreen smiled grimly. "That will come to pass soon enough," she said. "If we're lucky, we match them in numbers now, but that counts our women, children, and elders, while they are seasoned warriors and brutes under a king who will not tolerate defeat. What about their secret weapon? Do we know anything more about it?"

"Not yet," admitted Bruni, "but Dinekki continues to cast her bones."

Moreen looked to the north, toward the deceptively peaceful waters of the Courrain Ocean. Sunlight reflected from the waves in shimmering patterns, and the blue sky mocked her with its promise of a beautiful day ahead. It had been a day like this, eight years before, when the ogres had attacked her village with disastrous results. Now all of these people were gathered in this cherished place, and all she could think was that the stakes were so much higher and it was her responsibility to command. If she lost this fight, it would not be just a small tribe that suffered. She was keenly aware that the stakes were nothing less than the future of all humans in the Icereach.

12

Attack on Brackenrock

Kerrick stumbled up the road. Mouse lingered behind to secure the boat in the anchorage. The elf barely noticed the fact that the ogre galleys had sailed on, past the mouth of Brackenrock Harbor. Weariness tore at his limbs, his feet felt like stone. When he looked up, the fortress seemed impossibly far ahead. He swayed dizzily, then fell onto his back.

For an interminable moment he couldn't seem to draw a breath. He stared up at the white sky as darkness closed in. His vision narrowed to a pinprick before, finally, air rushed into his lungs and the face of someone vaguely familiar appeared overhead. He noted the Highlander accent.

"Nice bit of work out there, closing the boom," Strongwind Whalebone said. "There'll be more to do up at the fortress. Lean on me, and we'll go up there together."

"What . . . why are you here?" asked the elf, confused.

"Came down to help block the harbor," replied the king. "I would have been too late, but it turns out you and Mouse did the job just fine."

Kerrick remembered the ring, now safe in his pocket. He owed that feat to the magic of the golden circlet. He thought how easy it would be, how pleasant and warm, to just slide his finger through the ring again. Stubbornly, he shook his head.

The elf climbed to one knee, then allowed the king to lift him, half-draping Kerrick over one broad shoulder. Together they started up the road, which no longer seemed as though it climbed to the heights of infinity.

The two galleys, with *Goldwing* still in the lead, emerged from the Bluewater Strait into the full sweep of the Courrain Ocean swells. The powerful, deep waves surprised Grimwar Bane and in fact frightened him a little, but he didn't let his concern show. Instead, he kept his stern, tusked composure and stared at the rocky headland.

Stariz stood at his side, holding her mask in the crook of her arm as she inspected the landscape with a critical glare. As they came around the point, turning broadside to the waves, there seemed to be no good place to land. The entire shore was a rough headland, broken sheets of rock slashing down straight into the deep, churning water.

"Ahead, a few miles around there," Argus Darkand pointed, as the deck pitched and yawed beneath the helmsman's feet. "There's a long stretch of flat beaches, with a nice hillside rising all the way to the citadel."

"I remember," the king declared. "I noticed the place years ago, marked it for just such a situation." He turned to his wife. "Does Captain Broadnose have the Shield-Breakers ready? I want them to be first ashore."

The queen nodded to the foredeck, where a hundred heavily armored ogres, each carrying a monstrous double-bladed axe, had hunkered down in various states of seasickness, clinging to rails. "I daresay they will waste no time stepping onto solid land," she said dryly.

The rowers held a strong pace, and as the mouth of the strait slipped astern the precipitous coastline dwindled into rocky spurs and narrow coves. Now the king saw the green slopes of the terraces, rising like gigantic steps from the shore of a shallow bay. This approach, he thought, could not be guarded by any contraption of sticks and chain!

"Mark a course for the middle beach, and ground us there," the king called back to Argus, as the drummer slowed the rowers to an easy, gentle glide.

There were no defenders in sight, the humans obviously having decided to cower behind the lofty walls of the fortress. Grimwar allowed himself a low chuckle, as he thought of the potent chalice and the orb. Those walls, that sturdy gate, would not give his army any trouble.

Many kayaks dotted the shore, above the reach of the high tide, while numerous shacks gathered around the base of a long pier a short distance down the beach. The galley continued to slow as it approached the gravelly shoreline. A steady surf pounded, waves that would have capsized a lesser boat, but Grimwar Bane's galley smoothly cut through the foaming crests. There was a scuffing of the pebbled seabed under the hull, then the ship gave a huge lurch as it grounded. Stariz stumbled, and the king caught her elbow before she fell to her knees. A hundred paces to the left *Hornet* drove similarly into the shallows.

The great ramps, one to either side of the prow, creaked downward as the ogre king scanned the beach.

Warriors moved into position, feet tromping on the deck.

"Take the buildings and boats at once," ordered Grimwar Bane. "Bring any livestock you capture back to the boat. Any humans put to the axe!"

As soon as the ramps were grounded the Shield-Breakers stormed ashore, roaring the name of Suderhold in unison, hammering their axes against their shields with a thunderous din. Wading awkwardly onto the dry, flat gravel above the breaking waves, they spread into a double-rank line and charged inland, scrambling up a low sea wall and rushing across the first of the terraced fields.

The great hatches on the mid-deck slammed open and more ogres came rushing up from below, charging straight down the ramps into the shallows and gathering into twenty-warrior raiding parties just in front of the galley. These were the Grenadiers, another of the king's elite companies. Each was armed with a sword and a bundle of javelins. Once formed, they swarmed toward the huts and piers, using their blades and heavy, iron-studded boots to quickly shatter the wooden structures into kindling.

One detachment of the Shield-Breakers rambled along the high water line. Tearing into the kayaks with their axes, they swiftly destroyed two score of the boats. By then the king had swaggered down the ramp and waded onto the beach. Stariz, with Broadnose and a dozen ogres as her bodyguard, followed just behind. The ogres who had manned the oars were gathering their gear, emerging from hatches and filing off the deck. These were light troops, protected by stiff leather shirts, armed with short swords and spears. A score of them hauled heavy ropes, easing the wheeled catapult down the ramp, through the surf, and up onto the beach. Leaving two dozen heavily armed warriors to guard each of his prized galleys, Grimwar started to organize the rest of his troops along the wide, flat beach.

"Spread out there, you oafs!" he roared, as the last of the rowers trundled ashore. "Look smart, all of you!" He turned to Argus Darkand, who, as usual, was not far from his king's side. "Take four warriors you trust and go into my cabin. Have them carry out the lockbox. You'll fall in at the rear of the army, and I want you to keep that box under your eye at all times!"

"Yes, Sire—your will is mine!" declared the loyal helmsman. He turned to shout at several of the Grenadiers. "Scarnose, bring those three—come here!"

A few minutes later Argus emerged from the cabin with the crate containing the two golden weapons. The chest was borne on a pair of long poles supporting the crate. By then the formations on the beach had established regular lines, with the heavily armored Shield-Breakers in the center and the relatively light troops on the flanks. One group of Grenadiers formed a tight ring around the king, and another surrounded the four ogres carrying the crate.

"Remember, we must breach the walls and enter the keep to recover the Axe of Gonnas!" Stariz reminded her husband, as the front ranks started across a field of young barley. The plants, ankle high and frail, were trampled into pulp by the heavy ogre feet. The queen and her retinue of bodyguards lingered behind the others with the catapult, which rumbled slowly at the rear of the army.

"I have not forgotten," the king replied cheerfully, tasting the great victory ahead. "Our first rush will plant the chalice beside the gate, where the fuse will be lit."

Smoke tickled Grimwar's nostrils as the first little fishing village yielded to flame. He scowled impatiently at his axemen, who were busy in the shallows chopping away the pilings of the sturdy pier. With a groan and snap of breaking timbers, the dock wobbled and collapsed.

"No animals in the sheds or pastures down here, Your Majesty," reported one sooty warrior. "Nor humans. Lots of fodder and tools, though, which we have put to the torch."

"Tools and fodder, but no men?" snorted the monarch, irritated. Given the hours it had taken the galleys to journey around the point so they could land on this shore, it was no wonder that the humans had made some safety preparations.

"No matter—there will be plenty of blood to be had up there," he growled, looking up the slope at the far lofty citadel. "And livestock enough to fill our holds!" He started to laugh, then stopped, struck by a thought.

"That is, if the golden orb doesn't blow everything inside that place clear off the face of the Icereach," he added under his breath, in wonder.

Moreen stood atop one of the two tall gatehouse towers, watching the ogre ships come ashore. She clenched her teeth as the raiders destroyed the kayaks, broke apart the houses, and wrecked the pier of the nascent village. The sight of the two enemy galleys, but especially the gilt-trimmed *Goldwing*, caused an almost physical ache—even now, after eight years, she remembered her first sight of that vessel—the day her parents and all the warriors of her village had been slain by the brutish invaders.

But, she reminded herself, this time she was ready for the ogre attack—as ready as she could possibly be. A look into the citadel courtyard reassured her. Hundreds of Highlanders milled about. They would remain out of sight for now. She would not sacrifice valuable lives in a fruitless defense of the grounds outside Brackenrock's walls. She looked along the trail leading toward the harbor, knowing Strongwind and many of his warriors had disappeared over the bluff a half hour earlier.

Watching the ogre raiders as they started climbing the terraces, heading toward the lofty citadel, Moreen felt another stab of fear. Each little hut on the farm terraces, home to an Arktos family now sheltered within the fortress, sprang into flames as the ogres passed, their heavy boots making muddy waste of each carefully tended field. With every indignity, each insult and offense to her peoples' homes, her fear coalesced into deep, abiding rage.

But she was not foolish enough to send her warriors, brave though they might be, out to defend the surrounding land against the ogre horde. It was the walls of Brackenrock that were her peoples' best hope. Farms could be rebuilt, crops replanted. She would be patient, conserving her army and resources for the fight ahead.

Finally Strongwind and Kerrick came up the path from the harbor, appearing at the top of the long, steep climb. Moreen breathed a sigh of relief—before frowning with the realization that the elf was all but stumbling as though he was wounded, helped along by the Highlander king.

There was no sign of blood, and as they passed through the narrow sortie door—the only remaining access to the fortress now that the great gates were closed—Moreen turned her attention back to the attackers.

The rank of ogres was moving through the second terrace now, churning up fields, knocking down irrigation dikes, barns, and corrals. The enemy moved in a broad line, a few ranks deep, spread out for more than a mile. She spotted the ogre king, identified by his great golden breastplate, in the center of the formation. A wheeled catapult lumbered along behind. Just beyond that center came a small party of ogres, four strapping fellows bearing poles from which was suspended a heavy chest.

She felt instantly certain that the chest contained the awful weapon of which she had been warned. Ideas, all of them impractical, came to her: They should send a sortie out, break through the ogre line, and capture the weapon! But that line was solid, with a whole company—a hundred or more ogres—clustered around the center.

As the ogres climbed the steep slope toward the third, highest terrace, Moreen kept her eyes fixed on the small group clustered around the secret weapon, but no matter how many options she considered, she could think of no way to strike first. She summoned her archers to be ready when the enemy moved within arrow range.

"My men are ready," Strongwind said, arriving at the top of the tower to give his report. "Shall we keep them in the courtyard until we know where they're needed?"

"Yes," the chiefwoman agreed, noticing that the king looked distracted. "What?" she asked.

"The elf—he seems to be ill."

Moreen saw that Kerrick, too, had climbed to the platform atop the gate tower, emerging through the trapdoor. Pale, he paused to lean against the parapet. Moreen dismissed Strongwind and went up to the elf.

"What's the matter? Are you sick, or injured?"

Kerrick shook his head and blinked, making an effort to focus. "I'm sorry." His hand went to the hilt of his sword, and she was taken aback by the way his fingers shook. Suddenly she understood what had happened.

"The ring of your father? Did you put it on?" she demanded, knowing the risk, the debilitating cost of the magical talisman.

"I had to—there was no other way to secure the boom." He sagged against the wall, gazing out in dismay at the attackers, easily a thousand strong, who could be seen pillaging and smashing the last cluster of farmhouses.

"You have to get down from here!" Moreen snapped, irritated that he had resorted to the magic ring. "If you try to fight in this condition, you'll only get yourself killed!"

"I'll be all right!" Kerrick insisted. He stood straight and looked her in the eye. "Where do you want me?"

"Stay with the Highlanders in the courtyard," the chiefwoman ordered. "If the ogres breach the gate, you know how important it will be to hold them in the gatehouse." And if you fall over, you won't have as far to fall, she added to herself, half annoyed and half concerned.

She recalled the toll on Kerrick when he used his father's ring, once, four years earlier, to steer *Cutter* into port against the fury of an early autumn squall. Afterward he had lain in bed for days, wan and listless and wracked with chills. Today, he wouldn't have the luxury of such a long recovery.

"Leave nothing standing!" roared the king, his nostrils tingling to the scent of burning. He was frustrated, angry that his great army had encountered no living resistance, not even a stray calf. These were hollow prizes, these crude huts that collapsed after a few whacks of an axe.

Before him loomed the citadel of Brackenrock, its walls and towers rising higher even than the summit of the mountain. His ogres had reached the top of the long slope, and the humans had withdrawn. They would not contest his advance but instead would wage the fight from behind their walls.

Good, thought the ogre king. In fact, that was just about perfect for what he had planned. Grimwar looked around for his lieutenant, Argus Darkand, and curtly gestured to him. "Get the chest open and prepare to advance. It is time we unleashed the golden chalice."

"Aye, Sire," declared Darkand. "It shall be done."

"You have the flares, to light the fuse?" pressed Grimwar Bane.

"Indeed, four of them, safe in my pouch."

"Good. Bring the chalice forward and wait for my command. At my signal, you will do as we planned. Light the weapon—and the gates will fall!" He turned to Stariz, who was gazing at the fortress, licking her lips while her eyes blazed with fervor. "My queen."

"Yes, Sire?"

"Remain with the catapult and the golden orb. As we rush the gates, have the men get the thing ready to fire. Load the orb as we charge inside, and as soon as we rush out—with the axe—I want you to fire over our heads. One blast, and Gonnas willing, our enemies will be gone."

———◆◆◆———

Moreen watched as the ogres massed in the trampled fields, just beyond archery range from the walls. Many had leather shields the size of barn doors, and they raised these overhead to create a vast, rippling roof over their heads. Roaring in unison, they started forward at a fast march.

"They're coming, the whole lot of them, charging the gate," the chiefwoman mused. "I would rather have expected them to try for the walls at the same time."

"They don't seem to have any kind of ram," Bruni noted.

"Maybe they hope to chop through with axes." The chiefwoman glanced at the huge vats of oil, two here and two ready on the opposite tower, each resting on a bed of glowing charcoal, heated to deadly temperature. "I think we can make them regret that strategy. I wish I could figure out how they intend to use their secret weapon."

Her trepidation mounted as she went to the edge of the rampart and leaned out, watching as the archers along the fortress wall sent out a volley. The arrows rose high, glittering in the bright sun, before swooshing into the swath of upraised shields. Most stuck there, a bristling nest of quivering shafts, with only a precious few of the missiles darting through gaps to prick ogre flesh. She heard a few howls of pain, but the tide of advance never wavered, as a second and third volley of arrows peppered the ogre attackers. The enemy formation surged against the base of the wall and around the gate, like a wave crashing futilely onto cliffs. The solid ranks cracked open, wide gaps in the shield-roof. Archers poured arrows into the openings. More ogres roared in pain and fury, and for a moment it seemed as though the enemy would break and flee.

Moreen was confident of the gate, a double slab of solid oak beams strapped with heavy iron. The wood was treated in salt, tremendously resistant to fire. The hinges were anchored six feet deep in the bedrock of the mountain, and as the ogre army wavered she looked in vain for any sign of a battering ram or other special war machine.

There *was* something—a flash of gold, an object clutched to the chest of a single ogre. This ogre wended his way through the formation, discreetly carrying his burden, sheltered by the shields. The ogre had worked his way close to where the cobblestone roadway met the outer wall.

"Shoot him—stop him!" cried Moreen, even as her archers noticed the ogre's maneuver and aimed a volley of short, steel-tipped arrows at the gold bearer. Two struck his shoulders, with others thunking into the many shields.

The ogre was cloaked in heavy armor, however, and seemed uninjured. He continued to edge forward. Arrows clattered off of the metal plates half-blocking him from view. The ogre bulled ahead, staggering now, still carrying an unusual object of shining gold. More arrows showered down, and the ogre flinched as several found gaps in his plate mail, jutting from the flesh of his shoulders and hips.

He pulled something from the folds of his uniform and Moreen saw a flash, a small flame sparking brightly in the ogre's burly fist. He reached down and touched the mouth of the object, which looked like a large goblet of pure gold. The flame turned white, as bright as the sun. Even in full daylight Moreen blinked against the painful brilliance and threw up a hand to shade her eyes.

She could see what it was now: a chalice of gold, a great cup with fire spilling out of its mouth, onto the gravel and dust of the road, streaming slowly toward the gate.

The ogre army halted and began to withdraw, and Moreen knew with a sickening feeling why they did so. She stared at the cup with its oozing gold liquid, almost beautiful. It was hard to imagine that this was a terrible secret weapon, but that hissing, sparking fire convinced her.

"Get off the towers!" she shouted, waving to the warriors on the opposite rampart. "Get away from the gate! Hurry—*move*!" Immediately the garrisons started down the winding stairs. She raced to the inner parapet and waved frantically, repeated the command to the Highlanders in the courtyard. Those defenders, Kerrick among them, quickly shifted back from the gatehouse.

Except for one. The Highlander Lars Redbeard suddenly pushed open the sortie door, a small hatch located in the citadel's main gate, and stepped through. He stood there, alone outside the walls, brilliantly lit by the white fire of the fuse. Moreen saw him reach down to seize the lip of the heavy chalice and then, very slowly, drag it a short distance away, so that it was no longer aimed directly at the gate but obliquely, toward one of the gatehouse towers.

Lars was still straining to move the chalice when Moreen's feet, of their own will, compelled her to take flight. The chiefwoman was the last one off the rampart, bounding down the stairs after Bruni. The big woman reached the first exit, the door leading to the top of the first wall, and dashed through it, into bright sunlight.

Moreen was just about to follow her friend to safety, when the world shook, and she felt herself flying sideways through the air. Stones crashed past, and darkness fell.

13

Wrath

Kerrick saw the chiefwoman's frantic wave and understood that some terrible danger menaced the gate and that the citadel's defenders in the courtyard had to flee as swiftly as possible. He saw Lars Redbeard charge out the small door, but everything else was confusion. His mind was still thick and lethargic from using the magic ring.

He joined the Highlanders scattering out of the open courtyard, racing for doors and niches, barracks and stables and sheds along the fortress's inner wall. A glance over his shoulder showed the gatehouse defenders spilling down from the parapets, pouring from the doors onto the top of the great wall. He could hear lookouts shouting that the ogre attackers had abruptly fallen back from the portal. Guided by instinct, he found a narrow, deep doorway in the side wall of the keep and ducked inside. There he crouched, momentarily, hand on the hilt of his sword.

Terrible fatigue threatened to overcome him. Every movement was a great effort, and he slumped against the cold stone, longing only for sleep or for even deeper oblivion. His surroundings, the attack and the fortress and the human fighters, all seemed vague and unreal.

The explosion ripped through the courtyard like surreal thunder. He glimpsed a blast of dust and debris, a massive, tumbling slab—one of the gates—and he was blinded by the stinging soot and heat. He lay stunned on the ground for an eerie span of time that seemed to last for hours but actually passed in a matter of seconds. At first his muscles seemed beyond the control of his will. Gradually, his body obeyed him, and he pushed himself upward to sit and blink, wiping dust and grime from his face.

Gasping and choking, he groped to his feet and lurched into the great courtyard of Brackenrock. He was too numb to feel horror. He only registered disbelief as he gaped at the splintered remains of several wooden structures near the gate, saw the spreading aperture where once the heavy barrier had rested on iron hinges. The sky, cloudy and obscured by black, roiling smoke, was all he could see where once stood a stout and protective barrier.

The walls of Brackenrock were breached.

———◆●◆———

The ogre king's ears still rang from the echoes of the blast, but he shouted exultantly, his thunderous voice oddly muffled in his own hearing. Still he roared with delight, lifting his royal sword and circling it over his head.

"Up, you louts! Up, and behold the power of Gonnas!"

That power was obvious to all. The gap in the walls of Brackenrock was a breach such as even Grimwar had scarcely dared to imagine. True, one of the towers still stood, leaning precipitously, stones breaking free from the gash along the gate side, tumbling and clattering into the rubble-strewn gap, but the gate and other tower and a section of the wall beyond had been simply blown to bits.

All around, the ogres were rising from crouches, gaping in shock, blinking in disbelief. A hardy few were the first to take up the king's cries, then more, and soon the entire company of Grenadiers was bellowing in joy. Grimwar turned, saw his wife's face alight with battle-fury.

"The axe!" Stariz demanded.

"We go, now!" he replied fervently. "Prepare the catapult—ready the golden orb!"

Broadnose and his squad wheeled the great weapon around, aligning the lever so that it would launch its load over the fortress wall, into the keep itself. Already they were cocking back the arm of the catapult, while the queen herself gingerly lifted the heavy metallic sphere, cradling the orb against her belly as she waited for the basket to be lowered.

The Grenadiers moved forward with a fierce will, with so much eagerness that it took the sergeant-major's use of his whip to dress the lines. The king approved of the discipline. This was a great opportunity, and his warriors must keep to the plan.

Grimwar Bane himself strode forward with the Shield-Breakers, bravely showing himself in the second rank of the line. He looked between the brawny forms, saw the smoke and dust blowing out of the gap, and felt the thrill of battle, a killing frenzy such as he had not known in years. A few humans were visible, one small-ish fellow rushing forward in a completely irrational manner, others forming a pathetically thin line across the breach

As if these puny humans could stop the might of Suderhold, when Gonnas the Strong was with his king!

———◆◆◆———

The gate was gone, and one of the two towers had been completely obliterated! Kerrick was stunned to note that the very hinges had been bent and twisted by the force of the blast, and both the gate and the portcullis had been tossed into the courtyard, so much splintered wreckage. Then he saw shapes forming, advancing through the murk.

An ogre charge! The realization barely seemed to seep through his stunned consciousness. He shuffled, forced his feet into a trot, his sword awkward in his hands.

"Here they come!" cried Strongwind Whalebone, urging his men to form a line. "Meet them with Highlander steel!"

The king charged and waved, exhorting his men. From a stone-walled storeroom a dozen shaken Highlanders spilled forth, while a few more stumbled out of various shelters. A score at least had perished instantly in each of the structures nearest the shattered gate . . . how many others were dead? The swiftness of the carnage was unthinkable, but Stronghold was rallying his warriors, and they roared for vengeance as they rushed to block the gate.

Kerrick had a sickening thought. The missing gatehouse—Moreen had been atop that parapet! There was nothing left of her previous perch. Stone and lumber had been blasted to oblivion. Surely there was no way mere flesh could have survived! Furiously he pushed his fears aside. She couldn't be gone! The very idea was impossible, and he took faint comfort in that impossibility.

Through the smoke and settling dust cloud, the horde of dark shapes advanced on the breach, hulking shapes marching shoulder to shoulder, bristling with great spears. Besides his enormous fatigue Kerrick felt a sudden overpowering sense of hopelessness. Surely there was no way for the Arktos and Highlanders to stop such an attack.

Others must have felt the same, as, crying in pain or shouting in panic a few turned and ran. Kerrick felt a sob well up. It was too much! He had no strength left!

"Stand and fight—it's our only hope!" Kerrick tried to shout, croaking the words as he waved his sword at one of the frightened survivors. The fellow, eyes wide but unseeing, stumbled past the elf, shouting inarticulately.

One man drew the attention of many others, racing toward the gate in a frenzy. The elf's hopes flared at the inspiring sight of Mad Randall. The berserker's mouth was open, a rictus of fury. His voice swirled through the chaos like a banshee's song, and he held his axe upraised. Mad Randall charged as though he could turn back the entire army alone, hurling himself into the path of the ogres.

"Follow Randall! For Kradok and the Lady of Brackenrock!" Strongwind roared, and his men took up the cry.

Even the surging army of ogres seemed to hesitate in the face of this clearly deranged foe, screaming with laughter as he taunted their front ranks. The other Highlanders and Kerrick as well took heart from the berserker's courage, rushing after, enough of them materializing to form a ragged line, a gate made of flesh and steel, standing shoulder to shoulder across the entrance.

Before the ogre charge struck, the voice of an old woman, brittle and sharp as an angry bird's, rose above the din.

"*Chislev Wilder, born of flood—render bedrock into mud!*"

Dinekki! The old shaman was casting a spell from somewhere just behind the rank of defenders, who cheered a hurrah as the front rank of ogres suddenly tripped and flailed. Their boots sank into ooze, a soft patch that quickly spread to cover all the ground in front of shattered gate. Mud sucked at feet, slurped around stout knees. The next rank of ogres spilled forward, tumbling over their fellows, and for several moments the enemy front dissolved into a chaotic tangle of infuriated warriors, some drowning, others hacking their own companions in their struggles.

One finally broke free, climbing from the slimy pit, roaring in rage as he lifted arms draped with mud. As he strode forward Mad Randall howled and charged him with his axe whirling. The ogre flailed wildly, wielding a weapon clotted with soil. The berserker ducked underneath the blow and swung his axe like a lumberjack. The steel edge slashed through armor plate and scored a deep wound across the bulging belly. With a moan, the ogre fell backward and sank into the muck. The humans cheered.

Others struggled forward now, but the humans sprang to meet them. Steel clashed with steel at the edge of the mud pit. A few ogres still clutched their spears and thrust these long weapons into the rank of lightly armored human defenders. A Highlander next to Kerrick went down, bleeding heavily. Another doubled over, clutching his gut, resisting only weakly as the spearbearer jerked his barbed weapon backward and dragged the hapless human away.

Kerrick's weariness still hampered him. It felt like slow motion as he slashed with his sword, and his keen steel edge sliced past one ogre buckler to draw blood from a thick forearm. The hammer blow of the attacker's fist slammed the elf backward, and he barely hung onto his weapon as he smashed to his back and lay gasping for breath. Somehow he managed to push himself up back in line.

The mud pit was now choked with ogre bodies, and the attackers had to climb and kick their way across the corpses of their fellows to join the fight. More Highlanders went down, slashed by cruel axes or crushed by blows of massive war hammers. Other humans stepped in to take the places of the fallen, but there were fewer and fewer reserves. As the attackers pressed, the line was depleted and bent until the defenders were stretched thin.

Abruptly a cloud of smoke billowed in the melee , and the howls of pain-maddened ogres rose above the din of battle. A mist of liquid spilled from the high wall, from the tower that still stood, and the elf knew that some of the gatehouse defenders were pouring hot oil onto the attacking army. Infuriated ogres fanned out to all sides, frantic to escape, while the defenders knew where to step to avoid the searing rain. The humans were heartened and stood firm, knocking ogres away into the spattering, blistering deluge.

Another fresh company of ogres charged forward, however, shields over their heads as they lumbered through the bodies of their compatriots. A desultory splash of oil hit the first of these, burning through gauntlets and armor, but then the trickle ceased, as the precious liquid was expended. A few arrows pelted down from the walls, some of them causing painful wounds, but that barrage was too diffuse to have any effect on the large number of enemies.

Kerrick fell to one knee, too weak even to stand as an armored ogre, tusked face leering grotesquely, loomed overhead. The elf raised his sword, knowing he didn't have the strength to block the ogre thrust. In the instant before the strike, however, Mad Randall whirled into view, slashing the ogre's hamstring with his own axe, then cutting the brute's throat with a blow from the opposite direction. The berserker was gone before Kerrick could thank him—and the elf doubted that the infuriated warrior would even have heard him. Once again, he somehow pushed himself to his feet and strained to raise his sword.

Another Highlander fell, pierced by an ogre spear, and an ogre lunged toward the gap. Strongwind himself sent the brute tumbling back, with a slash across his face. The charge was relentless, however, and the Highlanders couldn't keep up. Now the defenders to the elf's left were falling back, and still Kerrick could barely lift his sword.

Without pausing to consider the consequences, he reached into his pocket and slipped his finger through the cold circle of his magic ring. Immediately the strength suffused him, and his sword seemed to grow lighter in his hand. He lashed out with renewed fury, piercing the breastplate of a monstrous ogre halberdier. A white rage consumed him as he swung again and again at other attackers. Randall, cackling nearby, gave him a nod, and the two of them together rushed against the group of ogres leading the others in their furious attack.

The elf parried a blow from a heavy battle-axe, and the ogre warrior in front of him gaped stupidly as the haft of his massive weapon snapped, broken on the slender blade of elven steel. That expression remained on his face as the raider died, transfixed by a lightning thrust of that same deadly metal. Kerrick wrenched his weapon free, ignoring the gore that trailed from his blade as he pushed after another brutal attacker. That one stumbled back but not fast enough to escape a swift slash of that blade. With a horrified howl the ogre fell back, struggling to contain his spilling guts.

Randall's singsong shriek came from somewhere on his right as Kerrick fought exultantly. More of the attackers fell, and then the two comrades were fighting back to back, surrounded by hulking bodies, yet stabbing and parrying so quickly that none of the brutish attackers dared to move in close. The elf felt no fatigue, no fear . . . only a growing hatred and fury that denied any frailty in either his flesh or his will. The magic of the ring conquered his weakness even as it buried his normal restraint and conscience.

Through a gap in the enemy line he espied a great ogre, brutish face contorted in fury. Some glimmer of recognition pierced his battle haze. This was Grimwar Bane himself, Kerrick suddenly realized—the same cruel monarch who had destroyed Moreen's village and who had driven the humans behind the walls of Brackenrock years before. Now the king carried a heavy sword and stood several feet away, waging war with his own hands.

The elf twisted, sidestepping a crushing blow that left an ogre axe blade lodged in the ground next to him. He smashed a blow into the axer's temple, punching sideways with his sword, using the metal hilt. The supernatural force of the ring added to his blow, and the ogre dropped like a felled tree. Immediately the elf leaped forward, as if his blade magically drew him toward the nearby monarch.

Grimwar Bane brought his sword up with startling alacrity, holding the weapon in both hands, swiping it sideways to knock away the charging elf. Kerrick was aware of ogres flocking to their king, saw armored bodyguards on his flanks, but he pressed forward as if immune to the lethal blades slashing at him from all sides.

Perhaps it was his audacity that protected him, or else his speed—like his strength, enhanced by the ring—was just too much for these hulking creatures. In any event, several blows missed, one ogre even hacked into a comrade's arm as he slashed wildly at the elf. Kerrick tried to shove between two guards and once more stabbed at the king, who gaped in astonishment at the frenzied attack.

The massive bodies guarded the king like pillars, even as Kerrick thrust his silvery elven blade between them. The tip of it carved through the king's golden breastplate, and the elf lunged closer, twisting, drawing a sudden gout of blood from the wound. Ogres roared in shock and rage as their leader fell back, and only then did the elf treat his own safety. He knocked away one bodyguard with a stab to the throat, sent the other stumbling off with a slashed knee. Now Randall was beside him, and once again the two warriors stood back to back, encircled by murderous ogres.

"A good enough way to die," stated the berserker, his voice surprisingly calm as it emerged from the frenzied grimace of his face. Kerrick merely nodded, his own expression a grim smile. Death was nothing to him at the moment—there was no future, no past, merely this savage melee.

Flames crackled through the air, and the ring of ogres parted. Suddenly, they were three. Suddenly Bruni was above them, standing on a low wall, holding a long-hafted axe in both hands. The big woman swung the weapon and fire trailed from the enchanted metal, white sparks cascading down and across the courtyard ground.

"The Axe! The Axe of Gonnas!" ogres cried, their voices shrill with dismay. Bruni jumped down and waded forward, laying waste to right and left, and all around the attackers gaped and groaned at the sight of the artifact. The Axe of Gonnas was their hallowed icon, treasured by generations of Suderhold's kings and high priests. Now the appearance of the sacred blade, at the same time as their king lay bleeding and as this human and elf fought them with such tireless intensity, proved cruelly disheartening.

Some of the ogres edged back away from the yawning gate, then turned to flee the citadel, ignoring the impassioned cries of their captains—who waited with fresh warriors just beyond arrow range of the walls. A small knot of attackers remained, protecting their fallen ruler, but now they were squeezed from three sides. The elf paused, blinking the haze of sweat and smoke from his eyes as Strongwind came up beside him. The Highlander king joined Kerrick, Randall, and Bruni, as the ogres retreated, some carrying the wounded monarch, others turning to give their lives so Grimwar Bane could be brought to safety.

"There!" warned Strongwind, clapping Kerrick on the shoulder and pointing toward the edge of the clearing. Through a gap he saw the ogre catapult, cocked and poised.

"Let's get it," agreed the elf, suddenly focused on the big weapon.

Bruni and Randall nodded, and the four made a dash through the scattered ogres toward the wheeled machine.

A strangely garbed, impressive-looking ogress stood next to the catapult. Kerrick recognized the queen he had met in battle eight years earlier, wresting the Axe of Gonnas from her hands. Now this ogre queen screeched a command, but the nearby warriors ignored her, flocking to surround their stricken monarch. She looked in panic at the machine but couldn't trigger it herself, and at the last moment she turned and fled with the panicked troops of her army, lumbering down the slope, leaving the catapult undefended.

"Help me turn it!" cried Bruni, putting her shoulder to one of the great wheels as Strongwind and Randall knocked the chocks away. Kerrick, still filled with magical strength, sheathed his sword so he could help. His sinews strained, and the elf grunted, pushing and pushing, gradually wheeling the catapult around toward the fleeing ogres. He saw something gold and round in the load basket but had barely registered the sight when Strongwind Whalebone chopped downward, slashing the trigger. With a loud *snap*, the catapult's arm whipped upward, hurling the sphere into the air, far, far toward the seashore below the fortress.

Immediately Kerrick turned to the ogres, drawing his sword, sprinting with murderous intensity toward the stricken king.

"Chislev Wilder, see defeat! Hold the hasty warrior's feet!"

The magic chant came from behind him, but Kerrick didn't even hear the words. Instead, he flailed furiously as his boots became stuck fast to the ground. He cried out in grief and rage as the shaman's magic robbed him of his chance to pursue the retreating enemy with a final killing frenzy that would have borne him into the enemy ranks.

Kerrick sobbed in frustration as he felt Bruni's strong arms encircle him, somehow plucking the sword from his clutching fingers. He sagged, fatigue suddenly sapping him, and when she slipped the ring off of his finger he collapsed into her embrace.

The sky turned a brilliant searing white, and the ground heaved and writhed under his feet. A blast of sound chopped through the air, deafening all who heard it, and the elf felt as though an angry god had picked him up, them slammed him to the ground with immortal fury.

Finally he lay in a place of utter, consuming darkness.

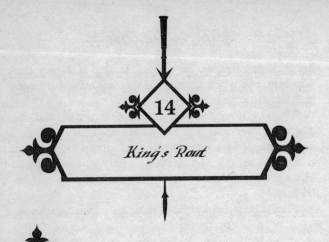

14

King's Rout

A curtain of red, pulsing and fiery, filled the view of Grimwar Bane. He could hardly breathe, and it was impossible to move. He strained to clench a fist, even to wiggle his toes within the heavy, whaleskin boot. The king was vaguely aware of being borne on a makeshift litter, hauled down the hill and onto the terraced fields, away from Brackenrock. He tried to object, to order these craven cowards to turn back, to pour through the breach, swarm across those walls, and raze the entire cursed citadel.

Someone cried out something about the catapult, and he wanted to repeat his orders even louder—shoot the orb! Blast Brackenrock into dust! Damn the Axe of Gonnas and every other trivial complication—blow that wretched place off the face of Krynn!

No words came. Instead, there was crushing pain in his chest, and each bubbling breath required a monstrous effort. Wetness spilled down his flanks, sticky within the confines of his leather shirt and punctured breastplate, and he realized that he was leaking blood. Cold fear rose within him—for the first time in his life he confronted the possibility that he was mortal, that he might die. The very notion seemed monstrously unfair, incomprehensible.

"I refuse!" He wanted to bellow the denial but instead merely coughed an inarticulate word, tasting blood in his throat. No! He couldn't imagine that his life had come to this, to a dirty retreat from a band of ragged human rabble.

That red sheet blocking his vision thinned slightly, cleared enough that he could see the sky above and the ocean below. Frantically he struggled to rise, to strike these disobedient ogres who carried him away from the fight, but he fell back in agony, watching as his quarry, that nightmare citadel, receded in his hazy vision. He smelled salty air, saw his beautiful ships so far below, drawn onto the beach where they had landed. Not there . . . not yet . . .

Something sparkled in his line of sight, a golden flicker of brightness, and again he remembered the orb.

Stariz stumbled down the slope toward the second terrace, falling onto her face in the trampled mud of a ruined field. The ogre queen lay still, hoping she was unseen, fearing the thrust of human steel into her back, but there were no footsteps, no obvious signs of pursuit.

She was still lying there when she heard the spring-snap noise of the catapult triggering its heavy load. Numb with disbelief, she understood only that the golden orb was not supposed to be launched until she had the Axe of Gonnas in her hands. Bitter fury blinded her, but she choked back the screams of rage. Instead she hissed to herself, "The humans will suffer for this—they and whoever has aided them will *die* in pain and misery and subjugation!"

She pushed herself up to her knees, and only then did she recognize the orb arcing over her head, soaring outward and downward, toward the shore. In a moment it had plummeted from her field of vision, falling beyond the rim of the terrace. With a gasp, she rose to her feet and started forward at a lumbering run. Before she reached the edge of the flat, muddy grange, everything turned white, as if she had crashed into the sun. She felt the ground heave under her feet, and the brilliance became a hole in the center of her vision. She staggered on, reaching the lip of the terrace, staring dizzily down the steep hill at the beach. The sea had erupted into a mountainous fountaining wave.

No, it was a series of waves rippling toward the beach. Wood and sticks blew past in the furious wind, and she vaguely understood that one of the galleys had been shattered. Bodies flew by and rolled around on the shore, and she was vaguely aware these were ogre bodies—though they looked insignificant, almost toylike, from her vantage.

The blast of waves took longer to strike the other galley, *Goldwing*, and in bright, flickering flashes the ogre queen now saw the royal ship heel violently, spin sideways and skid through the shallows parallel to the shoreline—blown as though it was a leaf. She was still watching, mesmerized, when an invisible force hit her in the face. The huge ogress was thrown backward as though she had been slapped by a dragon's tail. Flattened on her back, gasping for air, she offered a mute prayer to her mighty god, a plea for survival and vengeance.

After a short time she could breathe again, and slowly she sat up, then pushed herself laboriously to her feet, looking at the shore below her. *Hornet* was gone—utterly gone—and *Goldwing* had been heaved sideways, tossed down the shore upon sand. None of the two score ogres left to guard the beach were visible.

"O my wrathful god!" she groaned. "How did we fail you?" Though unable to deny the evidence of her eyes, Stariz was unwilling to accept the fantastic scope of the disaster.

She started forward at a jog, her mind whirling, filled with chaotic images and hateful thoughts. Her trunklike legs pumped, carrying her down the hill. She passed the trudging Shield-Breakers who were picking themselves up, plodding dazedly onto the beach. Some distance away, still coming down the hill, Stariz saw a party of ogre warriors bearing a litter and recognized the golden breastplate.

The king! What further disasters could this day bring? Now pure fear choked her throat, apprehension that Grimwar Bane would die and she would become a mere priestess again, would lose the status and power that she had worked so hard to attain. She lumbered along the shore, and she saw the figure on the litter thrashing, rejoiced to think her husband still lived. Perhaps the power of her god might aid her to heal him, as long as he breathed, no matter how grievously injured he might be.

Exhaustion forced her to slow. She looked around, saw a vast gaping hole in the ground and the seawall made by the wasted explosion of the golden orb.

Stariz crossed the beach, meeting the party bearing the fallen king. Already a hundred of the Grenadiers were heaving at the beached hull of the royal galley, dragging it across the sand and into shallow water, from there out to where it could float, while a ramp was lowered for the survivors and the king. Thankfully, the *Goldwing,* for all that it had experienced, seemed remarkably undamaged.

"My queen!" called Argus Darkand, reliably close by Grimwar's side. "The king is sorely hurt!"

"Take him onto the deck and into his cabin!" Stariz cried, pointing imperiously. The ogres hastened to obey, and she felt she had recovered some measure of dignity and satisfaction as she stalked up the ramp and onto the galley's deck.

She had thought of a new plan.

Grimwar Bane sensed walls and a ceiling—a darkened room. He smelled the sea and weathered timbers. It was a cabin. He was in a cabin on his ship, he deduced, and somehow he was still alive—though it still seemed that his chest was all pain and his breathing was torturous. Argus Darkand stood over him, the ogre's face contorted by worry.

"Take me out of here, onto the deck!" The king's words were croaked, so great was the fire in his lungs, but he flailed a hand and was able to make himself understood. The helmsman looked reluctant.

"It was the queen's order, Sire," Argus Darkand declared, "to place you in the cabin. She will be here in a moment, said she needed to retrieve some unguents and a talisman from her sea-chest . . . ."

"No!" groaned the king. "I want to see the water, the sky." He felt a stark fear that he might never behold those sights again, and he desperately wanted to feast on their natural glory before he perished.

"I am here, Husband," Stariz declared, stepping forward

to loom over him, her square bulk blocking out the little daylight streaming through the door. "Stand back!" she cried to the gaping helmsman, her voice an almost hysterical screech. "Leave me alone with the king, and I shall bring the power of Gonnas to bear on his wounds!"

Argus fled, joining Broadnose and some of the Grenadiers who had clustered on the deck, nervously peeking through the open door. The ogre monarch was touched when his wife knelt at his feet and bowed her head, wailing great sobs that echoed back and forth in the small cabin. The audience outside the cabin jostled for view, dumbstruck and wide-eyed, as the queen's grief rose to a crescendo.

Abruptly Stariz lifted her head, her tiny eyes blazing, her mouth twisted by a grimace, more of outrage than mourning. "My Lord King! Who dared to strike you? May Gonnas drag him into an eternity of torment for his impudence!"

Grimwar drew a ragged breath, wincing against the iron grip of pain in his chest. He made no answer, had no voice at the moment and didn't himself know for certain who had struck him. Still kneeling, his wife reached forward and placed one massive hand across his bandaged chest, gently caressing his wound.

"O Willful One, show us thy mercy!" Grimwar's wife and queen cried, leaning her head back, squeezing her eyes shut as she aimed her voice upward, a powerful and penetrating bray. It was easy for the king to imagine her plea piercing the sky itself, rising all the way to wherever it was that gods might dwell. "Grant your healing power unto the flesh of your faithful king!"

She looked at him with a penetrating gaze and spoke quietly. "Be strong, Husband, for the flesh-knitting power of the Willful One is not without a cost in pain."

He was afraid of that—almost as afraid as of death—but never did he have more hope and trust in his priestess wife. Abruptly these thoughts were cut off by a fiery agony that clamped Grimwar's chest, constricting his ribs, burning through his lungs and throat. He opened his mouth but still no sound emerged, and the effort only doubled, tripled, the level of his pain. Desperation gripped him. Was he dying, slain by his god's—or his wife's—displeasure?

Flesh twisted and stretched within his rib cage, organs seethed and churned in his torso, and the vise around his lungs closed even tighter. There seemed no air, none at all to breathe—just a blazing fire which seared through his flesh, slowly drawing a smothering cloak over his awareness. The power of Gonnas had seized him by the entrails, crushing with immortal might, and all the king could do was sit upright, open-mouthed, mute, trembling.

Over what seemed an eternity of time, the agony began to pass. Through his tear-blurred vision Grimwar met his wife's eyes fixed upon his own. Her mouth was taut, the thin line of her lips marking something between a smile and a grimace. When at last the monarch drew a ragged breath she raised her voice in a joyful shout.

"The Willful One has healed the king!" Stariz cried. "Glory be to Gonnas the Strong!"

Stariz had triumphed. Gonnas had not forsaken him. Grimwar felt the power of the god fuse his torn flesh and restore his fitness. Gradually his strength returned. He was sore and limp with fatigue, wringing wet from the sweat that had soaked his skin, his hair, his garments. Shaking his head, the ogre king reached a trembling hand and wiped the sheen of perspiration from his forehead and jowls.

But when he looked at the triumphant sneer on the queen's face, he knew there would be a cost for this healing. There was always a cost for her favors—and the good will of Gonnas. Let it be so, he thought grimly.

His brow furrowed, Grimwar thought of the fanatic defenders of Brackenrock. The humans had fought like demons. That slender, golden-haired warrior with the shining sword—that was the elf, Grimwar remembered, the Messenger who had been such a bane to his existence. He was the one who stabbed him, yes. How had that small, almost delicate swordsman, fought with such ferocity? The king remembered his disbelief as the fellow had hurled himself between two monstrous bodyguards, striking out for the king as if that deadly blade had a will of its own.

He pushed himself groggily to his feet. Stariz watched breathlessly. "Is there pain, Sire?" she asked, narrowing her eyes.

"No. Not any more," he replied, amazed that he felt so whole, so intact. The memory of approaching death, the cold, clammy memory, was still fresh and terrifying.

"Thank you," he said quietly, surprising himself with the depths of his sincerity. "You saved my life."

"It was no more than my duty, and the will of Gonnas," she replied humbly, speaking to his ears alone. She looked at him with a curious expression. "Now, I beg, we must talk."

"What is it?" he asked, already with an edge of suspiciousness.

"It is the orb!" she hissed, her little eyes suddenly alight. "The humans wasted it, sent it down the hill—but I saw it explode. The power was beyond belief—if it had fallen into the citadel, Brackenrock would have vanished in an instant! The force of the weapon was as the very fist of Gonnas, a might both beautiful and awesome to behold!"

"Uh . . . oh," said Grimwar, recognition dawning about all that had happened. "Did we suffer many casualties?"

"Listen, you fool," the queen said impatiently, "I'm talking about the orb—"

"It was wasted, you said." The king was suddenly very weary. He longed to escape his wife and return to Winterheim. He pictured the comfort he might find there, when he was back in his royal quarters and could slip away into the arms of Thraid, telling his beloved all about this disaster.

"Yes, *this* orb was wasted. Indeed, you should know that it destroyed the other galley when it erupted and tore a huge hole in the land itself."

"Not *Hornet*?" Grimwar gasped. "The pride of my shipyard—"

"I tell you, it is gone," Stariz retorted sharply. "You must look toward the future, move forward!"

"I suppose you know how I should do this!" he growled.

"Please, Sire—listen to me! Yes, I believe we should sail from here to Dracoheim, and there require the Alchemist to make us more of his powder, so that we can create a new orb. Sail there, and sail back, while the humans are deluded into thinking they have won. They will not expect another attack this summer. We will surprise them with our return and destroy them once and for all."

Grimwar was at once dismayed and intrigued by this suggestion. Winterheim—and Thraid—seemed very far away now. Yet the thought of destroying the human citadel began to gleam like a distinct possibility. In truth, until now he had had a hard time imagining the true might of the golden orb, but the Alchemist's weapon had worked! Why, it had blown up one of his ships, killed who knows how many of his men, and nearly robbed him of his own life!

"We could take the Shield-Breakers," he mused aloud, "and half the oarsmen, in *Goldwing*, but there are too many of us, now, to go in one ship."

"Our numbers are reduced," Stariz noted, "but those who are left behind—surely they can serve as a diversion to keep the humans busy, ignorant of our real purpose."

"I begin to share your idea," the king agreed. He pushed himself to his feet, pleased that his legs seemed wobbly but sturdy. Grimwar strode through the cabin door and stood as tall as he could, allowing the ogres clustered on the deck and on the beach below to cheer lustily.

"These lands on the coast," the king said, gesturing to the shoreline west of Brackenrock as his wife came up to his side. He grimaced in momentary irritation, wishing he'd studied his maps better. "That is a human realm, is it not?"

"Indeed, sire. The humans call the place Whitemoor," Stariz replied.

"Very well. I will send a fierce raiding party across that moor to let these humans know that the ogres of Winterheim are not to be trifled with."

"Yes, Your Majesty!" declared Stariz. "A splendid idea!"

Grimwar selected Broadnose ber Glacierheim to command the raiding party and clapped him on the shoulder. "I want you to take the Grenadiers and the ogres of *Hornet's* rowing company. That should give you a few hundred veteran warriors. You are to march inland from here," the king commanded. "Make war on the humans wherever you can find them—destroy their villages, kill them and their livestock. Strike terror into their craven hearts!"

"It shall be as you command, Majesty!" Broadnose stepped back and clapped a burly arm to his chest in salute.

The king drew a deep breath, relishing the feel of his whole, healthy lungs, fixing his lieutenant with a baleful glare. "This is important," he grunted. "You must distract the humans, keep them afraid, even let them send their fighters after you. Kill them, if you can. Keep raiding until near summer's end and return here. Meet us on the shores below Brackenrock." He looked at his wife. "How long will it take the Alchemist to prepare another orb?"

"We must allow at least a month for the work," she replied. "Thirty days. It may take less than that, but I cannot say for sure."

The king nodded and tried to mentally calculate the time he needed. Frustrated, he turned to Argus Darkand. "How long will it take us to reach Dracoheim?"

"The voyage can be done in seven or eight days, if Gonnas wills it," the helmsman replied. "Call it ten to get there and ten to come back, allowing for safety."

"Very well. Meet us here in thirty and ten and ten days from now!"

"Fifty!" Stariz clarified.

"Er, yes, Sire," the raider captain agreed. "I will return to this place in fifty days."

The king turned to Argus. "In the meantime, we will set our course to Dracoheim."

It didn't take long for Broadnose to pick and assemble his raiders. Grimwar stood at the rail, watching the formation march down the ramp and start across the beach. They would head west along the shore, beyond sight of the humans in the fortress, then turn inland toward the rolling ridge of hills that blocked the view of the moors.

Only when that battle column had disappeared did the rest of the ogres row the galley out to sea, where Argus Darkand barked out the drummer's pace, and the great warship turned westward, toward the frigid waters of the Dracoheim Sea.

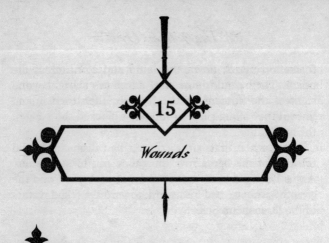

15

Wounds

T here was mist all around. Kerrick could hear the sounds of water slapping against a hull and a more distant wash of noise . . . waves breaking onto a shore. The damp timbers had the familiar chill of his small cabin, and he smelled the pine-caulk and tar that sealed the hull.

Strange, though. The boat wasn't moving, not even the gentle rocking of an anchorage in a placid harbor. The waves were strangely muted, more of a steady hiss than a rhythm of ebb and flow. The water was hot, hot and dry. He had a vague sense that he was safe, that there would be no drowning in this sea, yet at the same time, he found the very idea of safety improbable and troubling.

A furnace door opened, and an elf turned toward him, holding a tongs with a red-hot piece of metal, a sword blade, extended. There was no menace in the image—merely intrigue and wonder. The smith dropped the raw weapon to an anvil, picked up a hammer, and began to stroke the metal. The sound of the hammer blows was loud, thunderously loud, but like the waves it became a constant din rather than a series of individual impacts. As the smith pounded, the blade curled into an arc, then a full circle—a ring. The color brightened, from red to yellow to gold.

The hammer rang louder, a surreal noise beyond imagination.

He opened his eyes and absorbed the vista from a lofty tower. The hills of Silvanesti, the sun-speckled river, the myriad gardens, pools, and fountains, greeted him with such unexpected force that his heart nearly broke. The dazzling towers and manors of the city were living crystal and cultivated wood. Delicate bridges, like lofty webs of spun silk, spanned the gulfs between towers and hilltops.

A tall elf stood beside him, and he took great pleasure in the elf's vague and strangely aloof presence. There was the Tower of the Stars, piercing the heavens with majestic pride, rising into a sky so yellow . . . but wait! He looked, squinted, wondered. Yes, the sky was yellow, a yellow as pure and warm and pleasant as the sun itself.

He knew the yellow sky was wrong and that he must be dreaming. In the easy way of dreaming he decided to visit the king and found himself in the palace. All the courtiers and ladies looked askance at him, but there was still that regal elf at his side, protecting him, so he strode forward without concern. The king was there in person, heir to the line of Silvanos, a golden visage surrounded by the reflected light of a thousand mirrors. His blessing fell upon the tall elf and spilled off of his shoulders, cascaded down to envelop Kerrick as well.

With terrifying quickness, darkness closed in, an awful, suffocating darkness that tried to drown him but did not have the mercy to let him die. His efforts to cry out were muted by a cottony thickness in his throat, and his attempts to thrash and kick were defeated by the weariness that left him limp, drained of all energy. The darkness was a smothering blanket and for a while it seemed an eternal funeral shroud. All the goodness and light was gone, except for one imagined pinprick, a perfect circle of gold.

Very slowly the cloak lifted, and with desperate, straining gasps he filled his lungs and breathed and fell into fitful sleep. He dreamed fitfully, with tantalizingly brief glimpses into a Silvanesti pure, clean, and warm. For a precious time, he felt weightless, careless, and content.

Inevitably the dream was broken, and the nightmare of despair and longing once more dragged him down. Sometimes he saw the golden ring, just out of reach, a taunting reminder of his anguish, his need. The precious magic was available if only he could touch it, could draw upon it. He knew that power would cure him—it was the only thing that could possibly soothe his hurts.

If he had known where the ring was, he would have clawed his way out of bed, crawled across the floor, anything to obtain it. But the ring was gone, and there was no antidote to the pain and despair, so he lay wretched and shaking, sweating and crying, until at last the darkness began to lighten and, once more, he returned to the real world.

He awoke to a grayness that made him think the summer had passed in Icereach. Someone sat beside his bed, and he asked for a candle. The person replied in a woman's voice that sunlight was pouring in the window and a candle would cast no noticeable light.

So the grayness rested in his own eyes, then. The window was near his bed and yes, he could detect the brightness, angled rays from the sun that never climbed very high into the sky over the Icereach. But the sun was high enough—Kerrick knew that it was still summertime. Slowly, other physical details came to him: stone walls . . . heavy timbers in the ceiling . . . bedsheets. He guessed that he was in Brackenrock, probably lying in a small bedchamber somewhere in the fortress, high enough to catch the sunlight streaming over the walls. The person watching over him, that gentle woman, was still there.

"Feathertail?" He finally made out the shy smile of the pretty girl sitting near the bed. She was looking at him hopefully, and when he lifted his hand she reached out to take it.

"Kerrick! You're going to be all right, aren't you? I knew it, and Dinekki knew it—she asked me to keep an eye on you, so that you didn't hurt yourself. You . . ." Her eyes dropped. "Sometimes it seemed as if you were suffering terribly."

The elf felt a chill of longing, a hollow void that he could never fill, but he shook his head stubbornly and tightened his grip on her fingers. "That's all in the past. It's over. Tell me, what happened." He strained to recall. "The last thing I knew I was fighting at the gate with Randall and a few dozen of his men, but the ogres had us outnumbered. They came in a tight formation! I . . . I put on the ring . . . ."

At least that part was a vivid memory, slipping his finger through the golden ring, feeling the magic suffuse his flesh in a sensuous rush. He clenched his teeth. Everything after was a blank. "We won? The ogres were turned away?"

"You fought like a madman!" Feathertail exclaimed, her cheeks flushed. "Even Randall stood back and let you carry the charge. You slew a dozen ogres in as many minutes. You even struck down their king—we raised a great cheer, when we saw that from the walls. When Bruni charged out with the ogre axe, and it started on fire, the ogres fell back.

"That's when you raced out to the catapult and turned it around," she continued. "The catapult shot the golden orb down the mountainside. It blew up one of the galleys on the shore." She drew a breath, suddenly very somber. "Surely it would have blown up all of Brackenrock if it had come down inside the walls."

"A brilliant flash of light." Kerrick vaguely remembered now. "How long ago was that?"

"You've been . . . sleeping, for eight days," the young woman replied softly.

"What of the ogres? Is the king dead?" The elf turned his head, tightened his grip on her hand.

Feathertail shook her head. "I don't think so—they got him back on the ship, and we saw him stand up before they rowed away. That is, some of them marched away—Mouse counted about three hundred. They headed south, across the Whitemoor."

Kerrick winced. "There must be twenty or thirty villages in that direction!"

"Yes. We sent runners to warn them, as much as possible. A few days ago, after they made the citadel as safe as they could, Strongwind Whalebone and Mouse left with five hundred men to try and catch up with them."

"The galley that rowed away—did it turn back to the White Bear Sea?"

"I don't know. I don't think so. It sailed off to the west. That's the last time anyone saw them."

A chilling thought struck him, as he recalled the blast of magical fire and the sight of the gatehouse tower teetering, crumbling. "Moreen? Is she . . . where is she?"

Again Feathertail cast her eyes downward, and Kerrick saw tears glistening.

"She lives! Tell me she lives!" he cried, lurching upward, reaching toward her with both hands.

"Yes, she lives," said the lass, clutching both of the elf's fists in her own. "But she was grievously injured. She lost one eye. Dinekki says that we can only pray that she will be able to see out of the other one, when the bandage is removed."

"Take me to her!" Kerrick declared, throwing back the covers. His muscles were weak, his nerves shaky, but he felt he must do something. "Please, Feather—give me my trousers and tunic."

"Can you even walk? You've been so weak," she demurred. "You should have something to eat, start to get your strength back."

"I need to go now," he said impatiently, determined to see the chiefwoman.

It took several minutes to get him dressed, which didn't encourage a fretful Feathertail. "I'll take you to her room, but it'll be up to Dinekki if you can see her or not."

They followed a sun-washed corridor, great arching open-air windows on one side and a wall of black slate on the other. He felt a rubbery weakness in his knees and had to be supported by Feathertail. The stones had been soaking up heat through the early weeks of the nightless summer, and now they radiated a comforting warmth.

Kerrick stopped halfway so that he could lean against one of the windowsills and catch his breath. They were high in the keep, with a commanding view of the courtyard. The first thing he noticed was the absence of the gatehouse tower. There was a gaping hole in the wall and shattered stones stained with blood all around the gate area.

Beyond, he saw the Courrain Ocean, blue and pristine, extending to the north. The lower terraces could be glimpsed, and Kerrick sadly noted the trampled fields, burned houses, and wrecked buildings dotting the view.

Another dozen steps brought them to Moreen's room. Feathertail knocked quietly and led the elf into the comfortable anteroom. Dinekki was sitting at a table, mixing something brown and gooey in a large bowl. The elder shaman looked up from from her poultice, uttering a snort of surprise when she spotted Kerrick. "I wondered when you'd be comin' round here," she remarked curtly. "Finally got those shivers out of your system, did you?"

Kerrick felt a flush of shame. He said nothing.

"He wanted to . . . that is, he wondered if he could see her," Feathertail explained, after an awkward silence.

"Yes. Probably just what she needs." The elder shaman squinted appraisingly at Kerrick. "That is, if you're sure you're up to it."

"I am," he said levelly.

Dinekki nodded toward the sleeping chamber, and Feathertail watched anxiously as the elf crossed the antechamber, knocked softly, and opened the door.

"Hello?" Moreen turned toward the entrance and Kerrick suppressed a gasp. Her eyes were wrapped in a white gauze bandage that wound around her head. One cheek had been scraped raw, was now covered with a red scab. Her body, always petite, looked like a child's now, buried in a great mound of down quilts. Yet somehow in spite of those hurts, she managed to twist her mouth into her familiar ironic smile, one corner of her mouth tilting up while the opposite curved down.

"Kerrick? It's you, isn't it?"

"Yes," he said, coming to the edge of the bed, kneeling. "How . . . how did you know?"

"I didn't know," Moreen replied, with a tiny shrug, "but I'm glad you're finally up. They told me what you did, and I know how you suffered for donning the ring a second time in one day. It nearly killed you, it seems."

"That's nothing now—but you! Are you in pain? How do you fare?"

"No broken bones," she said flatly. "Just had my face smashed by a half ton of gravel. And no, it doesn't hurt very much any more. When Dinekki takes this bandage off, by Chislev, I promise you that I will be able to see!"

"Your goddess's, and Zivilyn Greentree's blessings as well." The elf invoked the deity of his sailor's clan.

"The floor is cold, is it not?" asked the chiefwoman, as Kerrick shifted his weight uncomfortably from one knee to the other.

"No, not at all, not in this warm summer air."

"Well, still, you should get a chair, anyway," Moreen declared. "I mean, stay here awhile, won't you? Let's talk."

———◆———

For a week he kept to her side, taking his food and drink in the chair, talking to her whenever the chiefwoman was awake, and holding her hand gently during her long hours of sleep. The long slumbering seemed to do her immense good. She began to eat more gustily, and the skin of her cheek healed so cleanly that Dinekki pronounced there would be no trace of a scar. As to her remaining eye, they could only pray to all the gods that it would be intact when the bandage was removed. The shaman sternly warned that the poultice must be allowed to do its work and that the healing required a full fortnight of insulation from light or air. So the gauzy cloth remained in place, even as Moreen spoke enthusiastically about all of the things she would do as soon as she was back on her feet.

Bruni visited several times each day, bringing reports of the ogre marauders, news of the progress of repairs and of prospects for the upcoming fall harvest. "It will be a lean winter, again," Bruni warned, "but there'll be enough in the larder so that no one has to worry about starving."

"That's all we can ask for," Moreen agreed, fidgeting under her covers, twisting her hands in her lap. Kerrick knew she was tempted to pull off some of her bandaging.

At last, one day, Dinekki came through the door with a bowl of steaming water. Feathertail brought a stack of clean cloths, and the shaman sat beside the injured woman. Kerrick leaned over her shoulder to watch, but she clucked him away.

"We'll both want all the light we can get," the old woman declared. "Now, you sit up in bed, Lady Chiefwoman, and let's see how your face is healing up."

Dinekki's bony fingers were steady as they touched the bandage, gently tugging at a knot behind Moreen's ear. The shaman elder painstakingly unwound the strands of gauze, until the last coils of the bandage fell away.

Moreen immediately turned toward the window with a smile on her face. "The daylight—I can see it!"

Kerrick tried not to show the shock he felt. Moreen's right eyelid was swollen shut and surrounded by a purple bruise. Her left eye gleamed beneath wounded skin.

But Moreen was laughing, turning from the window to the old woman. "I see you Dinekki—you saved my eye! Feather, and Kerrick! You've never looked so good, any of you!"

"That's what we need to know. Now, close up and let me wash you off, then a little more of the poultice and a few more days with the bandage.

Moreen nodded, and the shaman dipped a sponge in the steaming water and started, very gently, to wash the chiefwoman's ravaged face. An hour later a fresh bandage was in place, and—aided by a draught of Dinekki's spirits—Moreen slept deeply, without movement or dreaming.

Kerrick went to get a loaf of bread from the kitchen and brought the meager sustenance back to her room. He took his place beside the bed and watched her sleep through the pale daylight of the midnight sun.

Moreen felt a bizarre contentment as she slowly recovered. Her strength seemed to increase every day, as did the clarity of her vision. She took a certain amount of pleasure from the black eye patch, a piece of soft sealskin, that she had taken to wearing over her scarred eye socket.

A week after her bandaging was removed she rose from the bed, took Kerrick's arm, clutched it tightly as he led her through the room and down the hallway. It was the sight of the shattered gatehouse that brought back her memory of helplessness, the horror and doom of the ogre attack. She stood with Kerrick on one of the high ramparts of the keep and looked across the courtyard to the place where her citadel had been so cruelly invaded and nearly conquered.

The gap between the towers had been mostly sealed off with a pile of stones, leaving only a path wide enough for a single file of people to pass into and out of Brackenrock. She knew that Bruni had dispatched work parties to the timber groves to the east of the citadel, along the shore of the White Bear Sea. They were using oxen to haul lumber up the mountain, and by the end of the summer there would be more than enough to repair the gates

She had been reassured, countless times, that her instinctive order to evacuate had saved at least fifty men and women in the towers and on the walls, as well as many Highlanders and Kerrick. Those in the courtyard had been spared the full brunt of the horrific explosion wrought by the ogres.

Though one tower still stood, it was neither occupied nor functional. The explosion had ripped out stairways and doors, cracking support beams and loosing cornerstones. Both towers would have to be rebuilt from the ground up.

"We need to be vigilant, more vigilant even than before," Kerrick told her, but she could tell by the look in his eyes that he shared her apprehension about any future attack. "I don't know . . ." he concluded weakly.

They were wending their way around the citadel wall, looking over the damage. They descended to a low wall that marked off a quarter of barracks and exercise yards, then climbed a steep stairway overlooking the courtyard. Moreen still had not regained her strength, but she was determined to keep active, to show her people that she was recovering, that she was the Lady of Brackenrock again.

She found herself back where she had been injured, looking over a drop of eight or ten feet into a tangled well of rocks and splintered timbers. Her vision was now almost flat, but even she could perceive the menacing depths of this black hole. She couldn't imagine being trapped down there, buried by debris. "Such terrible force. . . ."

"Your goddess was watching over you. There's no other explanation," Kerrick said sincerely.

"What if they come back?" Moreen said, gazing out at the blue sea. With an irritated sigh, she adjusted the patch that covered her empty socket. Moreen still wasn't used to wearing the leather flap, and Kerrick too was getting accustomed to Moreen's permanent eye patch.

"Why, if they come back, we'll fight them again," declared the elf boldly, "and defeat them again. "We know that they hold the Axe of Gonnas in awe—we can use that to our advantage."

"Unless they blow the axe, and all of Brackenrock, to pieces," Moreen replied bitterly. "No, we need some better plan."

"What?" Kerrick asked hopefully.

"I don't know. I just don't know."

16

Fires on the Heath

The ogre captain Broadnose stepped cautiously across the marshy bottomland. From concealment atop a nearby elevation, he had watched sheep crossing here earlier in the day and knew that, while wet, the ground was traversible.

A day earlier, the ogres had spotted the village from the crest of the ridge on the opposite side of the stream. It was a typical village of the Whitemoor, barely two dozen huts, surrounded by a few ragged corrals, with a tangle of drying racks stretching upstream and down. The racks were draped with skins, and a small fish house across a tributary creek belched smoke and smelled of trout. The ogres had studied the place and waited until now, when the hour was after midnight and most of the humans were asleep.

Light still suffused the valley, and thus the raiders had been happy to discover this swampy approach route. They were concealed by an overhang of the riverbank. A bend in the stream blocked their view of the settlement—at least, until the attackers crept up behind the first drying racks.

"We spread out, remember. Hit fast. Every man you see gets killed, cut his head off. We'll pile up the bodies later. If a woman shows some spunk, kill her too. Some of these Arktos females are real fighters. And kill the babies—that's important, that'll make a statement. If a few of the kids and women manage to run off . . . well, chase 'em a bit for show, but then let 'em get away and spread the word."

The ogres nodded. They had been following the same plan for several weeks, raiding other villages, so they were primed.

"Spears first—then we get to hacking and slashing," the burly commander reminded his raiders. They looked at him, tusks bared, broad faces dour and fierce. Satisfied, Broadnose uttered a roar that split the peace of the pastoral vale like an axe blade slicing through a loaf of bread.

His warriors bellowed in kind, and the mass of ogres burst upon the village at a full run, sweeping the racks aside, trampling the partially cured pelts. A large guard dog came charging toward Broadnose, barking, fangs bared, and the ogre leader felled the creature with a powerful thrust of his spear. Next he drew his great sword, swinging it into a bunch of racks, smashing them into kindling.

A human emerged from one of the huts and threw a javelin, the barbed point piercing the thigh of a young ogre. The stricken raider went down with a howl, and Broadnose smashed through a line of racks to confront the brazen human. The man now held a steel-bladed tomahawk, and he slashed the weapon hard enough that the ogre had to pull up short. A single crushing down-swipe of his great sword put an end to the skirmish, however, and the sub-captain moved on. He sought living targets—he would leave the mess of decapitation to his less imaginative followers.

Another Arktos man, a warrior dressed in a heavy leather shirt, carrying a shield and sword, darted from a hut to stab a passing ogre in the flank. Strangely, there were very few humans rushing out of the other dwellings, and all those they encountered seemed to be well-armed warriors. A quick glance showed three ogres lying dying or already dead around the central plaza. Broadnose frowned—this was two more than they had lost in their past five raids combined, and this raid, it seemed, was far from over.

Indeed, a score of Arktos fighters had rallied on a low platform in the middle of the town. Each man held a shield and sword or axe. Although they had cast spears when they first burst from the huts, now they fought in melee order, lining the sides of the little rise and facing outward. The platform was deceptively high, and the ogres were exposed to hacks and stabs from the defenders. The raider captain was trying to think of a plan as an ogre staggered back blindly, blood gushing from his gashed forehead.

"This one is empty!" shouted a young ogre off to the side, emerging from a hut and knocking the frail sealskin structure down behind him. Broadnose saw other raiders kick apart more of the human domiciles, unsuccessfully seeking the victims who should have been cowering within.

"They're all empty!" A big ogre roared in frustration, cleaving his sword right through one of the Arktos abodes.

Suddenly that warrior toppled forward, and Broadnose was startled to see three arrows jutting from the fellow's back. Another volley of arrows drew the captain's attention to the ridge on the far side of the village. The slope was swarming with humans, hundreds of them racing downhill while an equal number stood above and launched a shower of dark missiles into the sky. The arrows rained down on the hapless raiders, and even as Broadnose knelt to pull a dart from his leg he was aware that the archers were skilled marksmen and weren't hitting their own people. Arrows showered across the ogres, for the most part causing pricks of pain more maddening than life-threatening.

"Rally, my warriors!" cried Broadnose. "Form a line across—"

He never finished, as another arrow lanced him in the right eye. He stumbled, then fell on his back. Kicking and thrashing, Broadnose seized the missile and pulled it out, flailing in blind agony as blood streamed across his face, his vision reduced to a film of angry, viscous red.

He heard the clash of steel against steel, the thudding and stomping of frantic footsteps. A heavy body collapsed across Broadnose, driving the breath from his lungs. Something warm washed across his face, and he recognized the wet stench of fresh blood. He pushed at whoever had fallen upon him, but the lump of flesh was very heavy and utterly lifeless. Weakened by his own wounds, Broadnose could not budge the corpse. He panted in exhaustion and pain.

He was vaguely aware of ogres shouting everywhere, but he longed to hear a clarion battle cry, a lustful summons to attack, not these strangled barks of fear, shouts of confusion, even one case of pathetic blubbering. An ogre weeping! He sensed the sounds of battle moving away, the clashing and violence fading, scattering to the winds.

Trying to collect his thoughts, Broadnose began to understand that his raiding party had been trapped. The humans had baited him into this village, then struck with a superior force concealed on the opposite heights. Such trickery infuriated him, but as the pain from his bleeding eye socket seemed to spread through his entire skull he found that he had a hard time concentrating, that his fury and indignation was drowned beneath a rising swell of agony and despair. His awareness became a murky numbness, and Broadnose wondered if he was dying.

But the dying lasted too long, and after a time he heard more sounds, the soft thudding of dead flesh being moved around. Coins rattled, weapons were stacked—scavengers undoubtedly were pillaging the purses of slain raiders.

The wounded ogre felt a sudden sense of relief as the corpse of his comrade was rolled off him. He saw blobs of light, though his unwounded eye did not work well either, failing to provide him with any meaningful shapes. He flinched, grunting, as a sharp tip of steel prodded him.

His ears functioned fine, and he heard the sword wielder speak in a thick Arktos accent.

"This one here is alive. Ya wouldn't know it for all the blood on 'im, though."

"Alive's good enough," said another. "Tie him up real tight. Let's take him back to Brackenrock.

Seeing the world with only one good eye took adjustment. Moreen's vision lacked dimensionality, acuity, and color, when she looked at objects more than a stone's throw away. When she discussed these difficulties with the old shaman woman, Dinekki could only cluck sympathetically and suggest perhaps the chief-woman should consider herself lucky that she could see at all.

Surprisingly enough, Moreen did consider herself lucky. She really didn't have time to dwell on her problems. There had been many reports of ogre raids against the villages on the Whitemoor, and she could only hope Strongwind and Mouse, with their hundreds of brave warriors, would be able to hamper or stop the depredations. She rubbed her swollen eyelid—the swelling hardly diminished, and it never seemed to stop itching—and turned to the schematic diagrams spread across her work table.

The sketches showed the outline for the new towers and a gate, as well as a reinforced section of stone wall that would be raised to repair the breach. Fortunately, there were good quarries located on the rocky dells just behind the fortress, and hundreds of Arktos and Highlanders were already busy cutting and hauling the needed stone.

The quarries had been there for centuries and in fact probably were among the reasons the citadel was originally built in this location. Thanks to a clever rail-and-cart system devised by Kerrick, the rock was being moved from the excavation to the work site faster than ever. Even so, Moreen felt a sense of urgency. She rose from her table and walked to the window, looking across the courtyard, blinking to clear her blurred vision as best she could.

Something was moving toward the gap, Moreen saw, squinting to make out a long column of men marching in from the western trail. A few lights sparkled above the file, undoubtedly sun glinting off of speartips, so she guessed these were her warriors, returning home.

Moments later there came a knock on the door, and

Feathertail entered. "It's Mouse—I mean, Strongwind and the warriors, returning from Whitemoor!" the younger woman exclaimed. "And they've captured an ogre—they have him chained, marching in the middle of the column!"

"Good," the chiefwoman replied. "Let's see what the brute has to say."

A few minutes later they greeted the returning warriors in the great hall of the keep. The ogre captive was held outside while Strongwind and Mouse entered, both crying out with delight as they saw Moreen awaiting them. She grinned, enjoying the Highlander's consternation as he gaped at her eyepatch, then tried to recover his manners.

"My lady!" he said, rushing forward, gently kissing both of her cheeks, then pressing his lips to hers in sudden exuberance. She kissed him back, actually enjoying the embrace for a second, before disengaging. Still he held her by the shoulders, looked into her eyes with genuine joy. "I feared I would never see your smile again! How are you—"

"I'm well enough," she said, breaking away to bring Mouse into the conversation. "I understand that you two have been doing good work—you have brought us a prisoner?"

"Yes, one prisoner. A captain."

"How much damage did they do before you caught them?" asked the chiefwoman.

Mouse replied. "They had wrecked at least five villages by the time we caught up to them. Generally they were moving up the valley of the Whitemoor River, so we got ahead of them, warned the Arkos at Lone Elk Creek, one of the tributaries farther back in the moors. The women and little ones took flight into the hills, and the warriors joined ranks with us. When the ogres came, we were ready for them and caught them by surprise."

"How many escaped?" asked the chiefwoman.

"Not many," Strongwind said. "They were running south, away from the nearest villages."

Mouse nodded. "We killed half of them in the village and chased the rest when they scattered. Most of those we caught and killed. I think a few of them evaded our patrols and vanished into the Glacier Peaks. I presume they'll make their way back to Winterheim from there. We posted scouts along the foothills to keep an eye out for them coming this way, but I think we've had the last trouble from these ogres, at least for this year."

"This prisoner—what does he know?"

"He has been reluctant to talk much, my lady," the young Arktos man explained. "He was the captain of the raiding party and knows more than he will say. Shall we bring him in?"

Moreen glanced to one side, saw that Kerrick had come into the hall and now stood nearby with Dinekki and Bruni. The Axe of Gonnas hung on the wall behind them.

"Yes," she said. "I will talk to this ogre."

Moreen was momentarily blinded as the outer door opened, then the sunlight was blocked by a large shape that filled the portal. She heard the tromping of feet and finally made out the hulking image of the ogre standing heavily guarded about twenty feet away from her.

Moreen's first impression was that the creature did not look exceptionally frightening. Undoubtedly the four chains, each secured to a ring around the prisoner's neck and held by a stout warrior, served to reduce any sense of menace. But it was more than that. This ogre's shoulders slumped, and though he was much taller than she, the foul creature seemed somehow to be looking *up* at her, confused and frightened. One of his eyes was covered by a blood-crusted patch. There were other cuts in his leather tunic and dried blood all over him, on his clothing and limbs.

"What is your name?" she asked curtly.

"I am called Broadnose, captain of the Shield-Breakers." His voice was deep, but more of a rasp than a rumble, and his accent was guttural.

"You were the leader of these killers?' Moreen demanded. "You must be a great warrior to kill mothers and the babes at their breasts. And old grandfathers, who could barely lift a cane against you!"

She was surprised to note a look of injured pride on the tusked, jowly face. "I followed orders of king," the ogre captain said. "He bade me to cause fear."

"To cause fear? Not to steal or take captives?"

Now the ogre looked a little shamefaced. "I failed. Your Mouse-Warrior caught me in a trap."

Moreen was perplexed. The ogres had raided human settlements for generations, but the objective had invariably been plunder, treasure, and slaves. Why would they change their tactics now?

"Why did the king want to cause fear?" Kerrick asked, drawing attention to himself. The ogre prisoner's eyes widened slightly at the sight of the slender, golden-hair figure.

"Why, to make the humans afraid, Lord Elf," Broadnose replied. "To . . ." He looked down at the floor. "Just that. To make you afraid."

"Your king is a mighty lord, is he not?" Dinekki clucked the question as she hobbled forward, holding a finger to her lips. The ogre's one eye narrowed suspiciously, as he warily watched the old woman.

Abruptly the shaman waved her nimble fingers, and the ogre's jaw fell slack.

"Mighty king!" he declared, looking at a place over the old woman's head. "I beg your forgiveness for my failures! What is your command?"

Moreen realized that Dinekki had cast some kind of spell, an illusion or charm that had abruptly transported the ogre—in his own mind—to a different, imaginary council.

"Do you know where I am?" asked Dinekki, her voice somehow booming out of her frail chest. Even the chiefwoman blinked, looked close to make sure this was still the thin, grandmotherly cleric.

"Yes, lord—you sail to Dracoheim!" Broadnose replied.

"Do you know why I sent you inland, told you to cause fear?"

"Indeed, Your Majesty. You wanted me to distract the humans, so that you could see . . ." Broadnose blinked suddenly, shook his head as if trying to clear his thoughts.

"Ogre!" thundered Dinekki. "Your king asks you a question!"

"Your Majesty—forgive me!" gasped the prisoner, his face growing pale. "You would see the Alchemist . . . give him thirty days to work!"

"Explain to me. When will I return from Dracoheim?" Still the old cleric projected, somehow, the aura of a bull ogre. Broadnose nodded, eager to please his imagined liege.

"You have promised that you will return for me, here at the citadel, in fifty days."

"But that will not happen. I have changed my mind," said Dinekki, waving her hand dismissively. "Instead I desire that you cease making war upon the humans. In truth, you are tired, are you not? You need to sleep. Your hosts will show you to a bed, where you will rest and heal."

Moreen watched as Broadnose wavered, his chin drooping forward to his chest. His eyes closed and he let loose a deep, ragged snore.

"Bruni, will you lead the ogre to the deep cell? You men, make sure the door is reinforced," she instructed the brawny warriors holding the chains. "He is to be given the same rations as everyone else."

The big woman took charge of escorts and the drowsy ogre, who sleepwalked along at his shuffling gait, while the others watched Dinekki, impressed. Kerrick grinned, and Moreen couldn't help but smile.

"It seemed the best way to get him to open up," the shaman said genially, waving a hand dismissively.

"Nice work," the chiefwoman agreed, then grew serious. "But this Dracoheim! Again we hear of that place. Clearly, that is where this terrible weapon is crafted."

"This Alchemist was also mentioned by Long-Swim Greatfin, the thanoi," Kerrick noted. "I wouldn't be surprised to learn that he is some kind of lord in that place. Undoubtedly he is the one who created this awful weapon."

"The Alchemist will make another weapon, I fear, and the ogres will return here before summer's end," Moreen stated grimly. "We cannot count on being so fortunate again."

"I agree," Kerrick said, "but there is some hope, in that Grimwar Bane will not return here for fifty days. That gives me some idea of how far away Dracoheim is and how long it will take the Alchemist to complete his task."

She peered at him him, knowing how important he was to her, to all Brackenrock, and yet she had to ask the question. "Do you think you could find this Dracoheim?"

"I'm not sure. According to the thanoi, it's west across that sea—that same body of water he called the 'Dracoheim Sea.' That suggests that the island is fairly large, but I don't know how big the sea is. We might find it right away, and we might look until the Sturmfrost catches us."

She nodded, thinking of the dangers. Clearly, she couldn't ask him to risk his life alone.

"Can you take me there?" Moreen asked.

The elf smiled thinly, with as much confidence as he could muster.

"I can try," was all he said.

⬥

"It's madness!" Strongwind Whalebone declared, pacing around the room in agitation. At the chief-woman's request the others had left, leaving the Highlander king here alone with Moreen and Kerrick. "You're still injured—you can hardly see! You don't know what you'll find on this island, Dracoheim! Why, it's sure to be a stronghold of ogres, as well as whatever dark magic this Alchemist fellow has worked." The king glared at Kerrick, who had been observing the one-sided conversation without taking sides. "You tell her!" Strongwind implored.

The elf shrugged. "Can you think of one time that I, or anyone else, has changed her mind after she decided to do something?"

The Highlander king snorted and stalked a few steps away before whirling back to point a finger at Moreen.

"Then, by Kradok, I'm coming with you—and a half dozen of my best warriors!"

Kerrick shook his head and held up a placating hand. "We're taking *Cutter*, remember, and it will be a voyage of many days. We can't take that many people."

"That's not the only reason," Moreen said, surprising the elf—Strongwind, too, judging from the look on his face—with her calm demeanor. She gazed at both of them earnestly. "I know we can't treat this mission as invasion. Stealth is our greatest ally, and a small group is our best chance of being stealthy."

"I will leave my warriors—but I insist on accompanying you!" The king stared at Kerrick. "Surely you can take three in that boat!"

The elf nodded. "Three, or even four, yes, we can manage that."

"But the third cannot be you," Moreen declared sternly, then softened her tone. "Think about the risk. You, the king of all your people, in all their strongholds, perhaps lost forever."

"The risk is as great for you!" Strongwind retorted. "Your people depend on you! You should be the one to stay—let the elf and me take a pair of veteran warriors and go look for this Alchemist! What if you don't come back? What happens to Brackenrock?"

"I won't send any of my people to do something too dangerous for me to try myself," she replied. "If I don't come back, my tribe is safer here than they have ever been, and for the first time in generations, we have allies." She gazed at Strongwind so intensely that the king fidgeted, and ran his fingers through his coarse beard. "*Loyal*, true allies, who will see that even if Brackenrock falls, the ogres will ultimately not gain mastery over all the Icereach."

"But, Lady—you are no assassin!"

Moreen lowered her eyes. "I hope this mission doesn't call for that, but if it does, if this Alchemist must die so that my people can live, I will do what must be done."

The king looked defeated. He went to the chief-woman, placed his hands on her shoulders, and looked down into her eyes. "May Kradok, and Chislev Wilder, and Zivilyn, and all the gods watch over you. But I insist that I come along—you must not leave me behind!"

She sighed, then smiled grimly. "All right—I guess you're as stubborn as I am. You will come with us." She hugged him, and he looked over her head, met Kerrick's eyes. "We need a fourth. Who is to be the fourth, then?" he asked.

"I should like to go." Mad Randall spoke from the doorway, then took a few tentative steps into the room. The berserker was almost shy in his manner, and as always Kerrick was struck by the incongruity of his neat appearance, his calm demeanor—when not engaged in battle. "That is, if you'd have me?" he asked, hesitantly.

"I think we need someone exactly like you," Kerrick said, and the crew of the *Cutter* was set.

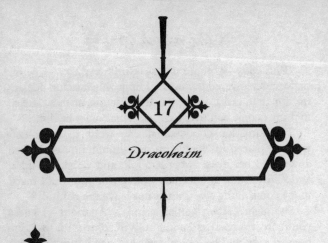

17

Dracoheim

The prow of the dark galley sliced the water of the Dracoheim Sea, a knife cutting through the ripples of a silk sheet, curling away two slender wakes that quickly vanished into the roiling, choppy surface. Two hundred oars dipped and drove, propelling the narrow hull with steady power, onward, westward. It had been several days since they had last glimpsed land, and the ogre rowers were worn from the long voyage. Now all of them tilted ears and eyes toward the lone figure standing in the prow, the king who remained immobile as he watched the western horizon. For now, there was only the gray sea, water stretching to all horizons. The drummer maintained his insistent pace, Argus Darkand standing beside him, marking the cadence as *Goldwing* pushed through the cold brine.

Stariz watched the activity all across *Goldwing* with a sense of satisfaction. She stood on the square observation platform that rose like a small house above the flat, long deck. From here she could look down onto the benches within the hull, at the sweaty backs, the strapping sinews of ogres flexing and pulling in unison. For six days now they had rowed relentlessly, through the ghostly bright nights and sparkling, sunlit mornings. They had persevered in the afternoons when capricious rainstorms often lashed them.

Now, at last, when the queen raised her eyes and looked past the bow, across the rippled surface of the Dracoheim Sea, she detected a tiny blemish on the horizon. Stariz ber Glacierheim ber Bane smiled in private satisfaction.

"Within this day we shall arrive at Dracoheim," the queen declared loudly, her voice reaching the ear of every oarsman. She was also heard by her husband, who turned halfway around from his position to nod to her. He fought the impulse to come to her—she enjoyed watching the conflict in his posture—but finally gave in and strolled along the deck until he stood below the platform. She started down the ladder, her bulk awkward on the steep steps.

"You sound very confident, my queen," he said, helping her to ease off the last few rungs. "That would make for a very fast crossing of this cold sea."

"Your helmsman knows his work, and the rowers—your own warriors, brawny and loyal ogres every one—put more admirable effort into their work than human galley slaves," she noted. "Look to the horizon. I predict that the island of Dracoheim will soon be in sight."

"So you say," replied the king, scratching his chin. In silence they went together to the bow and looked across the sea, the waters rippled by the steady, criss-crossing winds that had accompanied the galley all the way from Brackenrock.

Within another hour a land mass darkened the horizon. The king nodded in confirmation, as if he had expected this all along. Stariz savored her moment of triumph behind a blank and impassive expression.

"Argus," Grimwar called to his helmsman. "I want a good pace for the run into the harbor. You rowers, put your backs into it and earn yourself a keg of warqat and a warm fire tonight!"

"Yes, Sire," declared Argus, with a bare-tusked grin. "You heard His Highness!" he barked to the stoop-shouldered drummer. That ogre lifted his batons high and boomed one, then the other, down upon the head of his drum. With a barely a pause he picked up the pace, and the ship surged forward under the labors of the ogres at the oars. The rowers worked well in regular rhythm, propelling the vessel steadily closer to the looming island.

"You look impatient, Sire," Stariz said, coming up close behind Grimwar and almost startling him "It has been many years since you have seen your mother. You must be eager for the meeting."

"I am eager to see the Alchemist, to get on with the work of killing humans. As to my mother, she knows she can come home any time she wants to," Grimwar said sharply. "Do not try to blame me for her exile!"

"Certainly I would not," replied the queen. "I merely wondered—"

"Keep your wonderings to yourself!" snapped the king. "I will return to my cabin and prepare for landfall." He stalked away without turning back, so he did not see the queen's lips crease into an amused and slightly contemptuous smile.

As they approached the remote outpost, Stariz remained at her place in the bow, standing tall, staring into the horizon. The waters had brightened, now looked golden in this constant sun. The island of Dracoheim rose proudly from that bright sea, a flinty spearhead thrusting skyward. Cliffs of dark slate and lofty summits of knife-edged granite stood tall and forbidding. Cornices of snow draped the heights, and the bare teeth of hanging glaciers gleamed from many a lofty vale. The hour was midnight by the time they drew close, but the overcast skies were gray-white with an arctic brilliance that cast no shadows but illuminated every detail of the ship, the sea, and the stone-shanked island.

Goldwing was a fast, nimble ship but now her rowers exerted their skill to slow the steady glide as she passed through the mouth of the bay. Jagged cliffs, faces of dark rock so smooth they glimmered like smoky mirrors, rose to the right and left, guarding the entrance to a small, deep anchorage. Smoke smeared the air in a shallow valley, a haze hanging low over the shacks and smelters of a mining town. Other buildings sprawled along the shore, haphazard and temporary-looking against the grandeur of mountain and vale.

Cutting a graceful turn around the point of a black stone breakwater, the galley eased across the cove, through water as still and dark as shadowed glass. All was shadow here, and not just because the midnight sun lay low across the sea and was filtered by that slate blanket of cloud. No, the chill darkness here had a more peculiar cause: The cove, the shoreline, the entire slope of the island's steep terrain, all lay beneath the stark, ominous framework of a lofty castle. Turrets and bridges arced like spiderwebs through the air, and high ramparts overlooked steep cliff and knife-crested ridge. Walls plunged like faces of lofty precipice, and slender parapets twisted and curled across every vantage.

Queen Stariz inspected the island and the massive castle—and surreptitiously studied her husband. Grimwar's dark brows glowered. Aloft, the citadel seemed to enfold itself, concealing myriad corners with impenetrable shadow. Great winged birds, hawkish in appearance but in size more like horse or kine, curled and soared above the highest turrets. The mighty ogre, king of Suderhold, rubbed his right tusk with a quick, nervous gesture and unconsciously licked his lips.

The queen's attention turned to the shore, the barren land sloping into the sea so close before her now. A file of ogres hurried down from the castle, and human slaves spilled from the buildings of the small town at the base of the bluff. An honor guard of armored ogre troops formed a line near the shore.

The keel scuffed the gravel bottom, and a moment later the narrow hull was firmly grounded. There came from the hold a rattle of timbers as the ogre rowers shipped their oars. Argus Darkand barked orders, while several burly sailors dropped into the frigid, calf-deep water. They bore stout cables ashore, and soon the vessel was securely anchored to a pair of massive pilings planted well above the tidemark.

With a rattle of chains, the broad ramp descended from the bow of the ship to rest on graveled ground. For this occasion Queen Stariz donned her ceremonial mask, the obsidian image of Gonnas, the bull ogre-god of her people. Her robe, spreading regally to the sides under the span of her shoulder boards, hung straight and umoving as she accompanied her husband down the ramp and onto the beach.

The king had donned full ceremonial regalia as well. His golden breastplate gleamed, and the cloak of black bearskin—his prized trophy from the raids against the Arktos—was a sheen of inky shadow around his shoulders. He walked down the ramp with what he hoped was immense dignity, accepting the salutes of the guards who formed a long aisle leading upward from the beach. His eyes searched the shoreline, looking for one ogress in particular.

Only then did a figure emerge from among the party on the shore, advancing to stride toward King Grimwar and Queen Stariz. The Dowager Queen wore a heavy cloak of white bearskin, and diamonds winked from the great coil of her white hair. She was short and round for one of her race but walked with a solid gait. Her tusks were blunt and small, barely protruding from behind her lower lip. She regarded her visitors with an expression of interest, of welcome combined with surprise.

"My son and my king, welcome to Dracoheim," declared Hannareit ber Bane, with a shallow curtsy. "Welcome to your gracious Queen Stariz, as well. This is an unexpected surprise and pleasure."

"We come on a mission of some urgency, Mother," Grimwar declared. "There was no time to send word announcing our arrival."

"Nor is such word necessary," replied the elder queen. "As I said, welcome to you both."

Grimwar stepped forward and kissed his mother on both cheeks, then looked past her, up at the formidable castle on its black stone summit. His every gesture spoke of impatience.

"My Dowager Queen Hannareit," declared Stariz, pausing to remove the heavy mask. Even without the impressive guise, she stood nearly a foot taller than the other ogress. Stariz regarded the elder, studied the visage that was strong, square, and stern—exhibiting the same characteristics that were the best features of the younger queen's face, as well. "I see that you have borne these long years in Dracoheim with the grace of a true monarch," she said graciously.

Hanna snorted, but reached up a great hand to touch the cottony threads of her hair. "I do what I can . . . what I must. I have my household here, and gold mines aplenty. The Alchemist provides me with productive distraction. It is true, though, there are things in Winterheim that I miss." She darted a sharp glance at Grimwar.

"The Alchemist is a valuable tool, indeed," Grimwar commented dryly. "He is the reason for our visit. I wish to see him, as soon as possible."

"Of course, my son and lord king. Even now he awaits you in the great hall of the castle."

The monarch turned to his wife. "Let us go there now and waste no time. I want the Alchemist to begin at once." He raised his voice to bark commands to Argus Darkand, who had remained on deck. "Make arrangements to bring my belongings to the royal suite. Then report to me in the castle."

The helmsman saluted and turned to organize the unloading.

"May I come too, Sire?" asked Stariz, with a slight, mocking bow.

Grimwar ignored her. He knew she would do what she willed. Without another word, he started toward the road leading up to the great fortress, accompanied by a dozen of his loyal guards. Shrugging at each other over his impetuousness, the two queens followed behind.

Grimwar Bane was astonished at the frail appearance of the person who greeted him in the great hall. He had not laid eyes on the Alchemist for five or six years, since his last visit to Dracoheim. At that time, as he always did, he had found the place cold and forbidding and had vowed not to return until he had a good reason for the trip. Nor had he cared to hurry any next visit with the strange Alchemist.

At the time of their last meeting, the Alchemist had looked slender, perhaps even frail. Now he was positively cadaverous. Hair that had once been the color of straw was now bleached to a pallid white and in some places seemed to have been torn from his scalp in great clumps. His slender hands trembled as with palsy, and his legs were so sticklike that the king wondered if they might not break when the man feebly rose upon Grimwar's entrance, then awkwardly genuflected.

The room itself was high, with musty beams arching across the ceiling, and several large tables and benches occupying the middle of the vaulted chamber. A fire burned in a large hearth, spreading welcome warmth, and whale oil lamps flared on each table. Around the edges of the hall, the light cast served to ease the sense of gloom.

"Your Majesty," said the Alchemist. "This is indeed an honor. I only hope that you deem my meager efforts on your behalf worthy of acceptance." He nodded at the pair of ogresses who had entered behind the king. "Worthy of the approval of the two great queens, as well."

"Your discovery, the explosive powder, proved to be useful," the king replied formally. "It was quite destructive, if I do say so myself. Yes, the golden orb turned out to be a mighty weapon, though flawed. I am hopeful that we can create a means of improving it. It is for that purpose that I come to you, now."

"Please, shall we be seated?" The withered figure indicated chairs near the fire. "Tell me what you need. I exist to serve the crown, the royal family in all its forms."

"So long as we see to his needs," declared Queen Hanna, archly.

The Alchemist stiffened, his narrow face becoming even more pinched as he looked at the Dowager Queen, his mistress.

"My needs are simple, and straightforward," he said, with a humble bow. "My Lady Queen has good cause to trust in my skills . . . when those *needs*, as you call them, are met."

"You shall have whatever you desire," declared the king, surprised and a little disturbed by the sudden gleam in the fellow's eyes. "I need more of this powder, and I need it quickly. You must get to work right away."

"The king is very wise and forceful," the Alchemist agreed with a humble bow. "The hand of Gonnas is indeed mighty, but it remains the task of his followers and their loyal servants to put the proper tool in that immortal fist. I shall make the powder as soon as the ingredients can be collected. That task has already been begun."

Stariz smiled tightly, looking down at the small man in the concealing cloak. "Excellent. Are you so eager to serve, that you do not even ask why?"

"Indeed, Your Highness. I do my utmost, working within the restrictions imposed by the barren nature of our remote outpost. I can only assume a wise purpose, from this wise king, and I obey. I am resourceful and can do much to hasten re-creation of the powder you desire. The Dowager Queen herself has provided me with the holy ash, and I can gather cinders from the summit of Mount Dracoheim itself—there is a whole mountainside of black, powdery stone. Of course, the admixture requires a catalyst, a liquid to trigger the reaction." His eyes, downcast during his speech, suddenly rose to fasten, hungrily, on the face of the Dowager Queen.

"I understand what you want," Hanna said tersely, betraying her scorn with a curl of her lip. "Rest assured that you shall have another cask of your elixir. Indeed, I shall create a potion that will aid you in the task at hand."

The Dowager Queen stepped forward and gestured to the door on the far side of the hall, addressing the king and his wife. "Now, perhaps, you should be shown to your quarters. I ordered the royal apartments cleaned as soon as the approach of your ship was noted. They should be ready for you. The crossing from Winterheim is never pleasant, though I hope that your winds were fair."

"They were capricious," Stariz replied, "but you speak the truth. The sea is an unfriendly host, and I desire to clean and rest."

"Very well," said the king. "I would rest from the voyage too, but I repeat that I wish the Alchemist to commence at once. I do not wish to tarry in Dracoheim."

"At once, indeed! As soon as my Dowager Queen can provide for my humble needs," replied the Alchemist, with a sly look at the elder ogress.

"It shall be done," Hanna agreed. "I will prepare a potion immediately and have the cask brought to his laboratory."

A short time later the king and queen of Suderhold were shown by several human slave women into a sprawling suite of rooms high on one of the castle's turreted towers. From here *Goldwing* appeared a mere sliver in the gray anchorage, surrounded by lofty summits and icy ridges that were as inhospitable as they looked.

"We have hot water running through the vaults of the castle," one of the slave women said to the queen. "Would Your Highness care for a bath?"

"Yes, at once," Stariz replied, clearly pleased.

A steaming bath was quickly filled, and the slaves withdrew. The queen relished the warmth, but the king ignored the water, striding out onto the encircling balcony, the parapet that surrounded this lofty suite. He paced around, thinking, his eyes riveted by the forbidding vista of sea, glaciers, and mountains.

Cutter danced on the crests of the waves, skipping from one to the next like a dancer garbed in a shroud of white silk. Kerrick, Moreen, Strongwind Whalebone, and Randall were all aboard, following the glacial coast to the west of Brackenrock, virtually retracing the route that had brought the elf into his fateful encounter with the thanoi Long-Swim Greatfin, some two months before.

"Did you see much more of this coastline during your mapping voyages of the past two years?" Moreen asked. She was leaning back against the transom, the tiller resting easily under her arm as Kerrick stood atop the cabin, hand braced on an overhead line. He squinted to the south, watching the mainland that was barely visible. Randall slept in the cabin, resting for a turn at the watch during the night. Strongwind sat near the bow keeping a lookout.

"Yes, all the way beyond the western glacier," he replied, swinging down from his perch to settle on the bench near Moreen. "I drew the features on the chart— I have the map in the cabin, if you'd like to see."

"Yes—but not till we're in calm water again." She pointed at the bank of darkness that had spread across the whole southern horizon. "How bad does that look?"

"Solid and black, but the main blow seems to be moving west, not north," Kerrick assessed. He looked astern, where the eastern sea was a low, dark line on the horizon. "But we'll be stuck in the wind and rain—ten or twelve hours of rough riding, unless you want to change course, look for smoother seas."

"Turn aside already? I don't think so." Moreen smiled at him, a bold twinkle in her eye. "I didn't eat anything too greasy today. Did you?"

Kerrick chuckled, acknowledging that her resistance to seasickness was extraordinary compared to most humans. "We'd best be putting the rain gear on," he suggested. He went into the cabin, sidling past the bunk where Randall snored noisily. The elf opened his sea chest and gathered up a pair of oilskins, supple but protective garments made from the tanned pelts of seals.

In the chest was the box that held his father's ring, and Kerrick suppressed a thrill of longing as he thought of it. It would be so easy to take it, to slide his finger through. He reached out, almost touched it, then snatched his hand away as if burned. Shivering, he realized that his body was wet with perspiration.

He also saw the thin, wreathlike object Dinekki had made for him when he had embarked on his intended journey to Silvanesti. He had kept it safe here in case he needed it, though he didn't know exactly what it was or how it worked. It comforted him to know that the protection of the ancient shaman was with him here and now.

Closing the lid, he noticed that Randall had ceased snoring. He looked up to see the Highlander regarding him with a quiet, studious expression.

"Sorry—didn't mean to wake you," the elf apologized.

"No worry, you didn't," replied the man, closing his eyes and immediately lapsing back into deep slumber.

Kerrick emerged, and soon he and Moreen were comfortably ensconced on the transom bench, insulated by their heavy oilskins, close enough that through his garments Kerrick could feel the heat of her nearness.

"What of the ogres? Did you see lots of signs of them along this . . . what did you call it? The Dracoheim Sea?" Moreen asked.

"That's what the thanoi called it. No, not a lot of ogre presence—just a few remote outposts. There were some watchtowers on promontories and a small fortress at the terminus of the glacier, where it looked like the ice had receded quite a bit since the place was built. I saw smoke from the chimneys, though I didn't care to get too close. That was three years ago."

"So it seems that they have these outposts spread all across the southern Icereach, doesn't it?"

"Places in the shadow of the Icewall, mostly, leaving the humans, you Arktos and the Highlanders, to the north. Where you have trees, hot springs, gold mines, and fertile fields. I should say you have the best of the arrangement."

"Yes, so long as we can keep things that way.

Moreen watched the approaching clouds roiling in the south. Kerrick continued to guide his boat between the swells.

"You have been paid again for helping the Highlanders build a whole fleet of curraghs, haven't you?" asked the chiefwoman. "You must have collected quite a hoard of gold by now."

Kerrick nodded, guilty and a little uncomfortable with the thought of his accumulating wealth. Of course, the humans paid him willingly and seemed to find the fees he charged more than fair in exchange for the skills he had taught them and the frequent short trips he made, ferrying passengers or goods back and forth across the White Bear Sea. A Highlander thane would think nothing of paying him twenty or thirty gold pieces for such a jaunt, a service which would have fetched only three coins in Silvanesti.

"Yes. I will be considered a wealthy elf when I return to my homeland. I have three chests of gold here in *Cutter*'s hold."

"You could turn for home whenever you want . . . start over as a rich man," Moreen mused. She narrowed her eyes, turning from the looming storm to study him shrewdly. A blast of spray came across the gunwale, and she blinked away the brine, then shook her head. "Yet still you stay here among us human barbarians," she said, with wry sarcasm. "You risk your life to carry us into Chislev knows what kind of danger. Why?"

Kerrick squirmed. "I like it here. I like your people. I like *you*," he finally stated. "Believe it or not, I'm going to miss you when I finally leave."

"Oh, you'll come back and visit, won't you?"

"I imagine I will. Someone will have to show the elves how to find Brackenrock."

"You really think they'll come to trade?"

"I'm certain of it. Elven merchants will bring goods such as you've never seen—silks, and spices, horses, dyes, and exotic fruits." He paused, looked at her earnestly. "I'd love to see you get your first taste of an orange."

"Tell me, when you return to Silvanesti will you take a wife?"

Kerrick was startled by the blunt question, asked with a forthrightness that no elf would have tolerated from one of his own kind. Yet he had grown more comfortable among humans, and so he took no offense, merely drew a deep breath while he pondered his reply.

"I don't see why," he said slowly. "In Silvanesti marriages are mostly matters of alliance, of status and position. Often parents arrange the weddings, and you know that my parents are dead."

"Yes, but perhaps some patriarch will eye you as a prize for his daughter's hand," Moreen said, again with that twinkle in her eye.

"Hmph!" Kerrick snorted, suddenly uncomfortable with the turn in the conversation. No, he vowed silently, he wouldn't be a pawn in some noble's power scheme. He would never be a part of that world again.

"I don't know why I should want to take a wife—I never lacked for lovers," he said defensively, then regretted the words when he saw the frown momentarily darken Moreen's expression.

"Did the wind change?" He raised his head and immediately saw that she had observed an important swing in the wind. Strongwind had noticed too. He came back to the cockpit, easing sideways past the cabin.

"Looks like it's bearing right out of the south now. I guess we're in for it," the king of the Highlanders said, looking at both of them with narrowed eyes.

Indeed, the storm was blowing harder, wind lashing from port, needles of spray sweeping across them at intervals. Kerrick took a moment to steer along a trough between two rising crests. When one wave broke over the gunwale he, Strongwind and Moreen ducked their heads and held on as the chilly brine swept past, soaking their boots and leggings.

"You two go below," offered the elf. "I'll stay here and keep us afloat."

"I'll keep you company," Moreen said cheerfully. Strongwind, looking glum, gamely declared that he, too, would stay out in the "fresh air".

Another wave loomed high, and crashed down upon the boat. Kerrick gave the tiller to Moreen, tied a safety line around his waist, and moved forward to take in more sail. When he returned to the cockpit, Strongwind was retching over the side while the chiefwoman clung to the steering bar, wrestling against the force of the sea.

Kerrick sat beside her, and together they held the sailboat on course. "Why don't you go into the cabin and start the fire—warm up and get dry," the elf urged the Highlander, and this time the king—his face with a decidedly greenish cast—agreed with visible relief.

For several hours the elf and the chiefwoman struggled to maintain their westward course against the power of the storm. At last, as yet another wave slammed into *Cutter*, soaking them and sloshing around their feet in the cockpit, Kerrick announced that they must yield.

"We'll run with the wind for awhile, wait for it to blow out," he explained. turning the tiller, moving them onto a northward course. "It's too dangerous to keep following the shoreline."

"So we'll be carried into the ocean, off course?" Moreen asked, with a flicker of irritation. Not fear, he noticed, impressed.

"Yes. We'll sail back when the storm passes. With luck, we'll get in sight of the mainland tomorrow or the day after. At least we won't sink."

"Well, then that sounds like the way to go," she said. "What do you want me to do?"

"We'll need to take in more sail," he said. "Use a lifeline, then check the hatches."

Soon Moreen was edging her way past the cabin, an anchoring rope tied around her waist. Kerrick held the tiller, guiding them along the waves. The ride was rough but more predictable now that they were racing along with the wind full astern.

The chiefwoman pulled in the sail until no more than a blanket-sized swath of canvas caught the sweeping gale. She secured the latches over the hold and the cabin and finally settled in beside Kerrick in the stern. Strong-wind opened the hatch to weakly offer his relief, and Kerrick saw that Mad Randall still snored lustily in the bunk, below.

"Try and get some rest," the elf urged the Highlander king. "I'll be okay out here for some time yet."

The midnight sun was invisible behind the storm, but the sea was suffused with an eerie light. Massive crests rose like ghosts bedecked with foaming manes, rolling past, carrying *Cutter* and her four passengers into deep, uncharted waters. The mainland fell behind quickly as the boat made its headlong rush.

Kerrick took Moreen's hand, and together they held the tiller. He saw the brightness of her eyes, the flush of her cheek, and he was awed. On they sailed, into the nothingness of the Courrain Ocean.

The Alchemist took the ladle, swilled eagerly from the potion barrel, then laid the large utensil down on the bench. Energy and vitality suffused him, a keen exhilaration . . . but not enough. Not yet. After a moment's pause he picked the dipper up again, scooped deeply, and drank, uncaring of the trickle overflowing his lips, spilling down his chin.

When he again put the ladle down he moved so quickly that the gesture was completed before the small stream of liquid falling from his face spattered onto the workbench. He watched as the globules of potion touched the flat surface. In his perception they slowly bulged, then separated into miniature drops that started to drift outward in all directions from the point of impact.

Amused, he reached out and plucked these droplets, one by one, out of the air, gathering them all before the spatter was finished and licking them off his fingers.

He went to work, piling grains of cinder neatly in the mortar. He filtered a large pile of gold dust, screening the finest metallic flakes. The potion in the barrel, the new gift the Dowager Queen had provided for him, ran through his veins. He remained visible and corporeal, for this elixir had a new effect, a magic that would actually aid his work.

The Dowager Queen had made for him a potion of haste, so he completed the first two hours' worth of preparation, mixing, measuring and sorting, in only ten minutes' time.

"Daltic!" he shouted, calling for the slave assigned to attend to his needs. "I want you to bring me two pitchers of clean water. And tell Queen Hannareit I need another box of gold dust. This one is too coarse!"

It seemed to take forever for the man to show up, and when he opened the door the motion itself was interminable. When Daltic spoke, it was as though his words were dragged through thick mud—the Alchemist wanted to reach out and twist the man's tongue to make him talk faster.

"I beg the Lord Alchemist's forgiveness," Daltic said, looking down at the floor. "But you speak too fast—I cannot make out the words."

Of course! The potion was accelerating his sense of time, while the rest of these pathetic mortals went through their day as if in a thick, constricting haze.

Instead of answering the man, the Alchemist only threw back his head and laughed.

18

Quarry on the Sea

For a week the king and queen made themselves at home in and around Castle Dracoheim. There were shallow streams fished by massive ice bears along the nearby shore, and Grimwar made several outings to hunt the great creatures. On one occasion he killed a big male with a single cast of his spear. That night he hosted a great feast for his mother and all the ogres of her court, including his own crew. Warqat was swilled through the long night, and the celebration rang through the keep of the remote outpost.

Stariz confined her expeditions to more civilized locales, traveling with Hanna to several of the nearby gold mines, touring the walled villages wherein dwelt the many human slaves sharing the island with the ogres. The queen was particularly impressed by the glassy smoothness of one place, where Hanna told her a human village had once stood.

"This is the place where the first orb was tested," explained the elder queen with a tight smile.

"Impressive," Stariz agreed enthusiastically. "Soon, Gonnas willing, Brackenrock itself will look like this!"

The younger queen was not surprised to find that she preferred the company of her husband's mother to the companionship of the king himself. Indeed, the two priestesses shared much, including a profound devotion to their god and to the kingdom. They spent many enjoyable hours engaged in discussion as to how they could best serve the former and ensure the advancement of the latter.

It suited Stariz, in fact, that her husband avoided these outings—where he would suffer the combined influence of the two ogresses. Stariz was content with the gradual progress made by the Alchemist, whom she checked on daily. He was a blur of activity and invariably took her breath away with his deft gestures, quick dashes around his laboratory, and startlingly quick comments. She thought Hanna's selection of elixir—giving him a potion of haste—was a clever, even inspired idea. Stariz had no doubts that the fellow would complete his preparations in time for *Goldwing* to return to Brackenrock by summer's end.

Eight days after arriving on the island, however, she found herself bored. Grimwar was gone on another of his tedious bear hunts, and the Alchemist was making drawings for the smith. Hanna, too, was off somewhere.

One of the nicer features of Castle Dracoheim was the system of pressurized water the slaves had shown her, much of it drawn directly from hot springs beneath the fortress. Momentarily without something to do, Stariz had her slaves draw a deep bath, and the ogress settled into the great tub with a grunt of pleasure. As she lay there, peacefully, her thoughts slowly focused on her husband.

What a king Grimwar Bane, proud ruler of Suderhold, could be! If he would only heed her advice. As strapping and powerful as any ogre bull in all the land, by his mere presence he commanded the respect and devotion of his people. He was ruthless enough to be a great leader. He had proved that when he had slain his own father, more than eight years before. All Grimwar needed was a sense of his own destiny, a sense that his wife, the wise and powerful queen, could and, justly, tried to provide.

But his character flaws—how could she correct those and guide him to his full potential? There was his childish dalliance with Thraid, a mirror of his father's weakness. Oh, yes, she knew about Thraid. Though she was disgusted by his lust, until now she had tolerated it as a harmless diversion. Thraid was one of his capricious whims, just like these ridiculous bear hunts, which hampered him from focusing on more important tasks.

Though, in truth, she admitted that he had impressed her with his determination to have a second orb created. He had been decisive in bringing his ship directly to Dracoheim. Perhaps, finally, he was starting to grow wise.

Her bath-time reverie was interrupted by a slave woman, knocking hesitantly, entering the chamber only after the queen angrily raised her voice to call her in.

"It is the Dowager Queen, Your Highness," said the quavering human. "She says it is vital that you and the king come as soon as you can, to meet her in the Ice Chamber."

"The king is gone hunting bears," Stariz replied with some annoyance.

"Begging Your Highness's pardon, but his party is coming up the road even now. He will reach the main gate within twenty minutes."

"Very well," grunted the queen. "Bring my towels—I will come."

Half an hour later Stariz met Grimwar in the main courtyard and brought him down the steps to the chilly vault in the castle's most sacred temple. This was a cavern bored deep into the bedrock, well below the main walls and keep. A sheet of ice shimmered in one niche in the black chamber, while icicles draped the walls and the ogres' breath frosted in the air. Thunder echoed in the distance, vague and fading, as if lingering from an earlier storm.

Queen Hannareit was already there, her eyes closed, hands outstretched in the trance of seeing. She lowered her arms, relaxed, and turned to welcome the royal pair, at least one of whom—her son—didn't appear overly pleased at the prospect of this summit meeting. Behind her, the wall of ice swirled with flashes of light and roiling images of black cloud.

"I think you both must see this," declared the Dowager Queen, gesturing to the strange sheet of ice. "I will focus the power of the Willful One."

Once again the elder queen closed her eyes and raised her broad hands. She murmured a prayer to Gonnas—a prayer Stariz mouthed silently—and once again drew upon the might of the god to illuminate the sacred ice.

Thunder rumbled, the sound emanating from within the depths of the world. Lightning flashed in the slick surface, flashes brightening a mass of roiling, dark cloud.

Grimwar stared worriedly. Stariz looked too, as slowly the gray brightness devolved into flickering images. The clouds parted, the lightning faded. They noted the shape of a slender sailboat, which appeared to be tossing in the midst of a storm-lashed sea.

Grimwar's eyes widened, as he pointed in fury.

"That's the elf's sailboat!" declared the king.

As usual, Stariz thought, he stated the obvious.

"Where do you see this?" the queen asked, already knowing the answer. "Where is the elf?"

"On the Sea of Dracoheim," replied the elder queen Hannareit. "No more than two or three days away from here."

In a matter of an hour ogres were hauling casks of fresh water up *Goldwing*'s ramps, while slaves packed dried fish and flatbread into the huge storage lockers. Grimwar had decreed they needed provisions for a week, though they hoped to find the elven sailboat quickly and destroy it in just an easy couple of days.

"I hope we can catch him in light winds," groused the ogre monarch. "Too often he has spread those sails and vanished over the horizon faster than my oarsmen can row. But if we get a stretch of calm, I vow he will be mine!"

"Please allow me to accompany you, my king," said Stariz sweetly. "It may be that through my flesh the power of Gonnas will come to your aid."

Grimwar scowled. He had resisted her entreaties, thus far. Having endured two long journeys with his wife aboard, he had looked forward to a voyage of relative independence. Even so, he knew the might of his god and could not deny that the power of a high priestess could prove very useful. Grudgingly he assented.

They carried the full complement of ogre rowers, as well as two dozen armored warriors, veterans culled from the ranks of the Grenadiers. Very soon all were aboard, and the galley pushed off from the beach, glided through the harbor, and broke from the protected anchorage into the expanse of the Dracoheim Sea.

"Turn northward—make a course for the ocean," Grimwar Bane declared. A storm was rolling out from the land onto the gray sea across their intended course.

"No, we must go straight!" Stariz protested, pointing north of due west. "The elf comes from that way!"

Grimwar grimaced. His wife was already interfering. The king pointed to the clouds fleeing along the horizon. "That will blow past in a few hours, but for now it stands in our path," he said sharply. "If we sail into the storm, it will put us off track to meet the Messenger and his boat."

The king derived satisfaction from the chagrin on his wife's face. She lacked his experience on the sea, which certainly aggravated her, but she could see the evidence of his words. Stariz grunted and went below, while the ogre king felt the icy raindrops begin to spatter against his skin. He looked north toward the black clouds and was pleased with himself.

Goldwing glided through the water steadily, leaving a white wake foaming at her stern. The warriors maintained the beat of Argus Darkand's drumming, and in the clear light of the constant day the king of Suderhold could allow himself to believe that he really was the master of his world.

The gray waves rolled and pitched relentlessly, a legion of watery warriors marching against their speck of a foe, *Cutter*. Kerrick's steadfast vessel had taken the attacks of these warriors, one by one, and defeated them.

Now the swells evidenced the rhythm of deep ocean currents, and though the waves towered higher than before, the briny summits did not break with extreme violence or frequency. The wind had settled enough to allow the mainsail almost full spread, and the elf smoothly steered his boat along the vast slopes of these watery ridges, while Moreen, Strongwind, and Randall played out the sail to its full capacity. The gray clouds lingered overhead, but off to the south they broke to reveal patches of pale blue. From the cabin top, however, there was no sign of land.

"I think it would be safe to mark a course west by southwest," Kerrick said, seeing in the opening sky proof that the storm had exhausted itself.

"How far north are we?" asked Moreen.

"We might be eighty miles, even a hundred, from the Icereach. We'll probably have to tack some to get back on course, but we're not more than a day away from land, at the very most."

"Then let's do as you say," said the chiefwoman.

Kerrick made the turn as they started up the slope of one of the mountainous swells, levering the tiller to move the boat through a gradual arc. Moreen pulled the line and ducked as the boom swung past her head, and *Cutter* heeled across the rising sea. In another moment they were racing back to the south, down the wave, up the steeper water beyond, and slicing through the narrowed crest.

Wind pressed the sail, and the boat shot forward. The sun poked between ragged shreds of cloud, lighting the deck, dazzling the flying drops of spray and turning them into liquid gemstones, and in the magical brilliance of the sunshine the gray waters became a deep, vivid blue.

After eight or ten hours, the gray coastline took shape, and they changed course to run to the west. The icy face of the mainland quickly faded to the stern, and the wide, gray swells of the Dracoheim Sea now opened up before them.

Randall joined the elf in the cockpit, while Moreen and Strongwind talked quietly in the cabin. The berserker whistled breezily, leaning back against the transom for a few minutes before abruptly sitting up straight and fixing Kerrick with an intense look.

"They say you wear a ring into battle," said the Highlander with forced casualness. "That it brings a madness of war upon you. I have seen the madness but confess to wondering about the ring."

Kerrick shrugged. He had not talked of his ring with anyone but Moreen. Still, the humans knew of it, certainly. He thought about how to reply.

"Not a madness of war. More of a madness of need or desire, I would say. I know that when I take the ring off, there are times when I would almost kill someone just to be able to put it on again. I don't use the ring very often. I can't let myself. It has too much power."

"I know that feeling," said the berserker. "When the spell of war and fighting comes upon me, it's as though I then—and only then—truly come to life. All the rest of existence is just some pale charade."

"But you enjoy the peaceful side of life too, don't you?" pressed the elf, disturbed by the conversation. Randall had always struck him as one of the most serenely contented people he knew—a boon companion around a campfire—eerily transformed by the battle madness.

"Endure more than enjoy," said the Highlander frankly. "I know that when I die, I want to die with the madness upon me, in my eyes, ruling my mind."

The elf nodded, acutely conscious of the ring in his sea chest, feeling the desire to get it and put it on right now. Despite the longing, he stayed where he was, fighting off the almost physical urge of temptation. "May the gods see that day a long way off," he said.

"Aye. Or perhaps it will be soon," Randall replied, with apparent good cheer. Again he leaned back and started to whistle, forgetting all about Kerrick.

The cabin door opened, and Moreen emerged to stretch in the small cockpit. "I'll go forward and have a look around," she offered. With lithe grace she scrambled up the ladder to the cabin roof, flexing her knees to keep her balance as the sailboat coursed over the rough water.

"What's that?" the chiefwoman asked suddenly, pointing.

"What?" asked the elf, seeing nothing unusual.

"Something floating on the top of a waves . . . like a boat. At least, I don't think it was a rock, or an island."

"What direction?" Kerrick queried, standing and looking past the cabin as they came over the next crest.

"Just to port," Moreen said. "I don't see it now."

"That doesn't mean there's nothing there," Kerrick replied, alertly. "In a sea like this, you'll only see another boat when you're both on top of the waves at the same time. Keep looking."

He took the tiller and used it to slowly adjust the course, bringing them directly into line with Moreen's sighting. A minute later she cried out. "There it is again—it's something, for sure. Not a boat, though . . . wait, it's a ship! The ogre galley, and it's heading straight toward us!"

"Close on them—crush them!" Grimwar howled, in a frenzy of exultation. He gestured madly, exhorting more strength from the muscles of his oarsmen. "Row like the wind, you dogs!"

He paced back and forth on the observation platform, clapping one fist into his other palm. He gazed forward, saw the elf's sailboat bobbing plainly several miles ahead among the tossing waves.

Already the cursed elf was turning, using the full sail to catch the wind, propelling the little boat into birdlike speed.

"Gonnas curse him and all his children—he's getting away!" roared the monarch.

"Have faith, Husband," chided Stariz, scrambling awkwardly up the ladder to the platform. She took a magisterial stance beside the king, glaring into the distance as Grimwar stalked impotently back and forth.

"Now—may the power of Gonnas strike this wind from the sky!" This was Stariz the high priestess speaking, booming out a full-throated prayer that resounded over the wave-lashed sea. Her arms were spread wide. "Smite the very air, O Willful One, and cripple the flight of your enemies!"

As Grimwar watched her dubiously, Stariz whipped her arms upward and swirled them over her head. The ogre king felt a chill down his spine that had nothing to do with the weather. He heard an ominous muffling of noise, as if the very hand of Gonnas had come down to cup them, to cover the whole of the sea under its protective dome.

Within that invisible and immortal shelter, to Grimwar's astonishment, the wind died away to nothing.

———◆———

"They must be coming from Dracoheim—I'd bet my gold on it!" Kerrick said excitedly. "We must outrun them, then backtrack their course—that should lead us directly to the island. In this wind, we can escape without a problem."

The great ogre ship, maybe five miles away now, came on steadily but was clearly no match for the sailboat's nimble fleetness. Randall and Strongwind had gone to the high gunwale, where they added their weight as ballast, leaning outward to keep the sailboat racing through the choppy seas, countering the straining sails as the boat pulled along sharply with the powerful force of air.

All of a sudden the boat heeled violently, almost throwing the two men into the water. They scrambled onto the deck, pulled themselves up as *Cutter* lurched and slowed. In seconds the boat was rocking listlessly. The frothy whitecaps had vanished, and the sails now hung limply, like so many useless sheets drying on a line.

"What happened?" asked the amazed Highlander king.

"The wind has died!" Kerrick declared. He glanced around, saw that waves were still rolling, but that the air had grown utterly still. "But how—it's not possible!"

"No, not possible," Moreen agreed worriedly, making her way to the top of the cabin and gazing at the galley bearing in on them. "Unless it is magic of some kind."

Kerrick's heart pounded in his chest as he peered at the sky. "Well, we'd better hope the magic wanes and the wind starts up again, or we're doomed," he said hoarsely, holding up a hand, groping for the touch of even a faint gust.

But there was no wind.

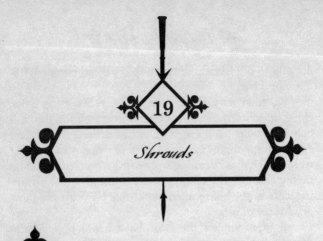

19

Shrouds

At last that blasted elf they call the Messenger is mine!" cried the ogre king, exultant as he saw that his oar-powered galley was closing upon the wind-powered craft. "Row faster!" he called to his oarsmen, even as the wooden blades slapped the water with increasing speed. "Give them all your strength, my brutes, and victory will be ours!"

Goldwing surged like a great, water-borne predator, closing on helpless prey. It seemed as though the ship reflected the ogre impulse in its hull, keel, and deck and leaped ahead in response to the eagerness of her master.

"Yes, Sire—we will crush them!" cried Stariz enthusiastically, still standing with her arms outspread. Her eyes were open and glazed in a religious trance. Near the stern Argus Darkand shouted out a frenzied cadence, and the drummer pounded his drum. The ogres pulling the oars maintained their impressive pace with strong strokes, the hull sliding even faster through the smooth and windless waves.

"Straight ahead!" Grimwar ordered. He stared at the sailboat, every feature of which he hated—the teak deck, the smooth hull, the low cabin and the vast sheets of white canvas. He was thrilled to see those sails hanging utterly limp, useless. The boat looked crippled, like a duck that had fallen, broken-winged, into a pond.

"Full speed! Make for the middle of the hull—we'll smash the boat to kindling and haul the elf aboard as a captive of the crown!"

The king's mind whirled, savoring the tortures and torments he could inflict upon this prisoner, the troublesome outlander who had made himself an enemy of the throne. There would be pokers to heat, barbed hooks to sharpen that would, very slowly, rend the elven flesh.

"This is a prisoner who must be put to death—at once!" snapped the queen. "We dare not leave him alive. I myself will cut his head from his scrawny neck!"

Grimwar shook his head in irritation, turned to glare at his wife.

"This fellow has come out of nowhere to vex me for eight years," he retorted. "I will learn a few things from him, then I will select the manner of his punishment. There will be plenty of time to kill him, and I don't intend to be hasty about it. Rather, his will be a death to relish."

"No, he must die at once!" cried Stariz, her voice shrill. "Too often has he challenged us and thwarted the clear will of Gonnas! Consider the danger, Sire! Promise that you will slay him as soon as he is hoisted aboard."

"I tell you, no!" growled the king, although he was surprised at her vehement interest in the elf's fate. "Let us talk about this when we have him wrapped in our chains."

The galley rocketed forward as the rowers put their backs into accelerated strokes. The ogre king licked his lips, anticipating his enemy's humiliation, imagining the slender sailboat cracking under the impact of the mighty galley. *Goldwing* drew closer, as the vulnerable sailboat sat motionless, save for its gentle bobbing in the swells. Now Grimwar could see several people scrambling about on the deck. Obviously, they knew they were helpless, and it pleased him immensely to imagine their fear.

The collision was only minutes away. Grimwar laughed aloud at the revenge he had savored for eight long years.

The wind had fallen away completely. The sails hung limp. The ogre galley loomed larger with each passing heartbeat. Kerrick felt a sensation of utter helplessness, knowing he couldn't budge his boat, couldn't evade the warship.

"The paddles?" Strongwind asked desperately. "You have two of them—can't we try to row?"

"Bah!" Kerrick declared in disgust. "The oars can maneuver us around in a harbor, but they're no match for that!" He pointed at the ship surging toward them under the power of two hundred oars.

"By the gods, what would I give for some wind!" he cried in exasperation.

Moreen suddenly looked up. "What did Dinekki give you?" she asked. "That wreath she gave you when you set out for your home . . . she said it had some kind of power."

"Yes," Kerrick said, trying to remember the old woman's words. What had she told him?

The chiefwoman had already darted through the hatch, down into the small cabin. Moments later she came out, carrying the delicate circlet woven of slender, almost threadlike fish bones.

"She said it would help if you were in trouble and needed protection."

Yes, she had said that it would protect his boat, somehow. The details escaped Kerrick. Then he remembered.

"Throw it on the water, she said, and it will hide the boat!"

Moreen's one good eye flashed with hope as she looked at him. She cast the object over the side and into the rising swells of the Dracoheim Sea. She murmured something, a prayer to Chislev Wilder, he imagined.

Immediately fog churned upward, a white veil of mist erupting like a funnel cloud. The vapors were silent but roiled and swelled like living things, sweeping outward with churning frenzy to wrap the sailboat and the surrounding sea in a murky embrace, expanding quickly, shrouding them from view in all directions. It swirled through the air, explosively expanding until it surrounded them, rising upward to form a shield that obscured all glimpse of the sky, the sun. Even the top of the mast vanished in the haze.

Motioning to Randall and Moreen, who had joined him in the cockpit, Kerrick pulled the two oars from their racks. He explained urgently, pointing toward the bow.

"Stay as silent as possible, but row! Push us in that direction! We'll try to slip out of the galley's path and hope they can't see us in the fog!"

Moreen nodded. "It's worth a try," she noted hopefully.

Strongwind, meanwhile, had drawn his great sword and stood resolutely atop the cabin, straining to see through the unnatural fog. The berserker and chiefwoman took their paddles and began to stroke, striving not to make the splashes too noisy, as the elf used the tiller to guide them. Gradually, *Cutter* began to glide through the rolling waves.

Kerrick had another idea. He went to the mainsail and quickly pulled down the great shroud of white canvas. Carefully he draped the sail over the boom, tugging it down over the gunwales. He pulled more of the material toward the stern, encompassing the cabin, then draping it, tentlike, over the cockpit and the tiller, allowing Moreen and Randall to row from beneath the sheet. Except for the tall spire of the mast, the ship might as well have been painted white, a ghostly shape shifting with the mist.

Kerrick strained his ears, listening for signs of the galley. He felt exposed and vulnerable, angry about cowering in the mist, yet desperate to remain unseen. The two oars splashed softly, and the sailboat continued to move—very slowly, it seemed—through the mist.

"There! Look and listen." He heard Randall's words, as soft as the waves lapping against the hull, and the elf followed the Highlander's pointing finger. A shadow moved through the white fog, a barely visible darkening as the great shape moved past. They could hear the oars of the galley stroking the water and splashing, and Kerrick could only pray to Zivilyn Greentree that *Cutter* remained invisible, that the ogre ship would sail heedlessly past.

"By Gonnas—where is that devil-boat hiding?" demanded the ogre king, roaring into the billowing fog that had swelled to surround them. The pall masked everything in all directions, and when Grimwar looked to the rear, he couldn't even see the stern of his own lengthy vessel.

"We would have a better chance of finding them, my king, if we remained silent and listened," whispered Stariz, her tone dangerously close to insolence. She remained rigid, arms outstretched, face turned skyward, as she tried to concentrate on sustaining the wind-killing power of her god.

Grimwar cursed—loudly—because he knew again that his wife was right. He lapsed into sullen silence, straining to discern something through the murk. The water, darkened almost to black by the unnatural vapors, slid past the hull as the galley continued to plow forward.

"Hurry!" demanded Stariz. "The force of the spell will not last much longer."

"How can I hurry when I don't know where the elf is?" snarled the king, still trying to hear or see something.

For a long time the king strained to see something in that impenetrable mist, then he could stand it no more. Surely they had rowed too far!

"Come about!" he called to Argus Darkand, who passed the order on to the helmsman. "Conduct a search, back and forth, until we find that boat! We'll sink the damned thing and use the elf as shark-bait!"

The ogre galley curved through a wide turn, oarsmen grunting and churning as they reversed course, but still there was nothing to see but the enveloping cloak of fog.

"You must find him—my strength fails, and he will escape!" declared the queen, staggering in weariness as she strove to maintain the powerful spell.

"I forbid you to weaken!" roared the king, turning to face his wife, spittle flying from his jaws. "We are so *close!*"

With a moan, the queen staggered backward. Her eyes rolled upward, and suddenly she tumbled to the deck, unconscious.

The king felt a wisp of breeze blow the fog past his cheek.

———◆———

"Wind!" Kerrick whispered, not daring to believe. In another moment it was plain that the fog was blowing away, moist droplets landing on their skin with a welcome chill.

"It's getting stronger!" Moreen said, elation raising her voice. She reached out to take Kerrick's hand, her dark eye flashing in triumph. "Let's make a run for it!"

Infused by her spirit, he nodded and raced to the boom. Quickly they raised the sail again, choosing haste over silence now. By the time the sail was up, the mist was thin enough that they could discern the position of the sun, low near the northern horizon. *Goldwing* was still out of sight.

Quickly the canvas filled with air, and *Cutter* started to glide through the water under moderate speed. Kerrick hastily raised the foresail. The mist thinned enough that they could see the galley, about two miles away, now wheeling toward them with strokes of those long oars.

The wind continued to pick up, swelling the sail, pushing the little boat through the water with increasing momentum. The ogre galley gave brief chase, but soon *Cutter* was pulling away. For long minutes they watched, heartened, as the enemy warship trailed smaller and smaller behind them. A few hours later they had gained enough distance that the galley vanished from sight astern.

"Now we turn to the southwest," Kerrick declared confidently. "That's where the galley was coming from. If this wind holds, we'll be able to reach Dracoheim before *Goldwing* can even get in sight of the place!"

For another day they sailed westward under fair skies and pleasant winds. They saw no signs of land, however, leading Kerrick to deduce that the Sea of Dracoheim was larger than the White Bear Sea. When at last a black shape rose from the horizon before them, he felt relief.

"That's it—that's got to be Dracoheim," he said. Moreen and Randall nodded in agreement. A rocky, volcanic island, with a mostly precipitous shoreline, took shape before their eyes.

The Highlander's attention was directed to the water off to starboard. "What's that?" he asked, after a few moment's scrutiny.

Kerrick looked and had the impression of a silvery flying fish leaping from the water. He waited, expecting the shiny thing to fall back into the waves. Instead, it kept coming up toward them. It was now angling directly toward the hull, approaching with astonishing speed— there was not even time to turn the sailboat from its path.

"Hold on!" cried the elf, in the instant before impact. Something powerful jarred his boat, shoving them sideways and rocking the hull. Sickened, Kerrick heard timbers snapping, then felt the deck twist under him as the keel of his beloved boat wrenched apart. Water surged over the gunwales, bursting out of the cabin door.

Instinct took over, raw fear propelling Kerrick. He dove through the door of the cabin, fighting the water surging upward through a great gash in the hull. The turbulence was savage, and the elf banged his head on the table, flailed, felt the square solidity of his treasure chest as the cold sea tried to suck the warmth from his flesh.

The water pressed against him, icy chill penetrating to his bones, darkness blinding him as he groped at the latch, allowing the lid to float free. His map drifted past, his spare clothes floated free, and he tore through them, feeling until his fingers closed around his small lockbox. Only then did he kick free, swimming back through the door, toward the surface that was a blur of brightness far above him.

Still clutching the box containing his father's magic ring, he propelled himself upward, breaking the surface just as his lungs were about to burst. He drew a breath and collapsed back into the rolling waves. Exhausted and shivering, he floated on his back, turning his head to look for his companions.

Cutter was gone, vanished below them into the unseen depths, leaving only a few bits of flotsam to mark her watery grave. Kerrick kicked weakly, gasping for breath, vaguely relieved to see that Moreen, Strongwind, and Randall had splashed free of the rigging. Like him, they were floating, stunned and disbelieving, in the icy sea.

20

The Iron Whalefish

Here—grab the ring," cried Kerrick, splashing through the water, seizing one of the flotation rings that had bobbed to the surface. Moreen kicked over to him, gasping, teeth chattering, as she seized the flotation ring. Randall was nearby, clinging to a buoyant crate, looking around curiously as the deep sea swells lifted and dipped.

"Where's Strongwind?" shouted the elf.

"Over there," Moreen said, gesturing with a flailing hand. "I saw him a minute ago."

Randall let go of his crate, swam toward the place where his king had disappeared. In the next instant Strongwind Whalebone surfaced with a great splash, treading water and gasping for breath. Kerrick saw that he had the hilt of his great weapon clutched in his hand.

"Almost lost my sword," the king explained with a groan, gratefully slinging an arm over the crate Randall pushed to his side.

"What happened?" asked the chiefwoman. Her face was shockingly pale, her lips blue and trembling.

"We hit something. *Cutter's* gone," Kerrick replied,

numb and disbelieving. Only then did the reality sink in: His beloved boat, all his gold, everything that mattered, was lost at the bottom of the sea. He sagged in the icy water, too weary to do anything but acknowledge defeat. The fatigue was insidious, a voice whispering in his ear. Just relax, sink back, descend into the inviting sea. It would be so easy to join his boat in the depths of these icy waters.

Vaguely he remembered the lockbox, still clutched in his hand. It startled him out of his lethargy. He remembered the powerful instinct that had driven him to dive after it, to rescue the ring, of all his possessions, from the fate of his doomed boat. He must have saved it for some reason.

"Something hit *us*, I'd say," Randall corrected, kicking his feet, pushing closer to the others, with Strongwind swimming behind. "I'd like to know what it was."

"Does it matter?" Kerrick treaded water listlessly as the sea swell lifted and lowered him. "It has ruined our plans, sure as any ogre galley." He looked at Moreen, wanting to say something to apologize. He wanted to express his sorrow, his guilt, but already the cold was suffusing his mind, thickening his thoughts, slowing his tongue.

He barely noticed Randall splash past, the berserker kicking with surprisingly strong strokes. Following him with his eyes, the elf noticed a round, smooth shape breaking the surface of the water. His first thought was that *Cutter* had rolled over, that he was looking at a section of hull, but vaguely he knew that wasn't right. The thing was too smooth, shiny, and shaped somewhat differently.

"It's metal!" cried Randall, who had reached the object and smacked it with his fist, producing a dull clang. He reached, trying to pull himself up, but couldn't find a hold.

"That's what sank our boat," Strongwind declared, swimming awkwardly toward the round silver thing, for he still grasped his great sword.

Moreen barely had any strength left, so Kerrick grabbed the life ring that she clutched, and towed her with him, sidestroking toward the strange object. Randall and Strongwind found a set of rungs and used them to pull themselves free of the water. Randall stood up, while the king knelt and probed at the metallic surface with his sword. The elf pushed Moreen before him, and the two Highlanders pulled her to safety. He climbed after.

They were all soaked and shivering, drawing precious little heat from the summer sun, but at least they were out of the freezing water. The elf rolled up on his knees.

He heard a loud clang and looked up to see that some kind of trapdoor had abruptly flipped open from the center of the metal tube. A head, the face obscured by a bristly white beard, popped into view.

"Hey!" cried the stranger in an angry squawk. "Get off of my *Whalefish*!"

———◆•◆———

Kerrick stood in a dark compartment, shivering and dripping. Moreen was seated next to him, wrapped in a blanket that Randall had borrowed over the furious, sputtering protests of the same disgruntled gnome who had accused them of trespassing on his *Whalefish*. The irascible fellow had condemned them vociferously until Strongwind placed the tip of his long sword at his throat. The four castaways had pushed their way through the trapdoor and down into what seemed to be a very clammy and constricted metal tube. Kerrick had to bend his neck to stand, while the strapping king elected to squat uncomfortably, after banging his forehead on several obstacles.

An oil lantern cast a dim glow over the scene, illuminating an array of pipes and valves, as well as the furious expression of the gnome. He stood barely waist high to the elf and humans but was apparently fearless as he resumed barking at them.

"What kind of manners do you have? Barbarians, pirates—that's what you are! Forcing your way into my *Whalefish*! Why, I have a good mind—"

"You'll shut up, if you have any kind of a mind at all!" snapped Kerrick. "What do you mean by sinking my boat? You're lucky I don't tie an anchor to your feet and send you straight to the bottom of the sea!"

"I—I didn't sink anything!" retorted the gnome. "If you can't build a hull that will float, then it's pretty foolish of you to go sailing about on these deep waters! I should think you'd count yourself lucky—"

Kerrick seized the gnome by his long beard and leaned close, staring into watery blue eyes.

"*Cutter* was built by my father, and carried me along the coast of Ansalon and across the Courrain Ocean. She was going to take me home again, too—and she would have, if your god-cursed *Whalefish* hadn't rammed her and cut her in two!"

The gnome spluttered something else but couldn't articulate his words because Kerrick was pulling his beard upward, lifting the little fellow a few inches off the deck.

"Who are you anyway? What is this strange thing?" Moreen's voice, calm and forceful, cut through the commotion. Shaking his head, Kerrick relaxed his grip. The gnome pulled away, darting behind a small table. He regarded the trio with wide, accusing eyes.

"This is my *Whalefish*," he finally said, with an unmistakable pride. "A submersible boat of my own invention, powered by steam, and unique in the annals of Krynn's seafarers—as far as I know—though it is my sincere hope that, someday, undersea travel inspired by my design will be commonplace across the oceans and seas of our world. I am her master, Captain Pneumatic-operationspressurefitterandchydraulicmakerwelderextraordinairephilosoph—"

"We will call you Captain Pneumo," Kerrick interrupted quickly, having had enough experience with gnome appellations to realize that the recitation of the name would likely have continued through the better part of the next three days. "Are you claiming that you didn't sink my sailboat intentionally?"

"Well, yes, I am . . . that is, if you're certain I *did* sink it!"

"Quite certain," Randall said. "I spotted that sliver blade on the bow of your, er, submersible. It swam through the water, then cut right through our boat. Sent her straight down, more's the pity." He looked at Kerrick with genuine sympathy. "She was a beautiful vessel, she was," he declared.

"I assure you, that was not my intent!" Pneumo declared, coming out from behind the galley table. "You see, there are still a few, not exactly flaws but, well, unexpected wrinkles in *Whalefish*'s design. Such as, it's rather difficult for me to see where I'm going. But I can always get there at very high speed!" he added.

Kerrick glanced around the narrow, tube-shaped hull. There were compartments fore and aft, both secured behind metal hatches. The air was surprisingly warm and very humid, smelling faintly of coal smoke and steam. A dull roar of sound emerged from—he guessed it was the stern, though he couldn't really be certain—somewhere.

"Do you operate this . . . thing:"—Kerrick couldn't think of it as a boat—"by yourself?"

"No! I have a crew. Steady loyal sailors, both of them. Divid! Terac!" called the gnome, his voice a piercing screech.

A hatch opened, revealing a narrow compartment in the direction Kerrick guessed was the stern. A billow of black smoke emerged, followed by two rotund figures who tumbled through the hatch, then scrambled to stand at attention.

"Close the hatch!" demanded the gnome, and one of the sailors immediately lunged back through the passageway while the other slammed the door shut, turning to rub a grimy fist against his soot-covered eyes.

"This is Divid," explained the captain, drawing a deep breath as the other crewman came back through the hatch, releasing another cloud of smoke before he shut the door behind him. "And Terac."

The two small figures stood in the shadows. At first Kerrick thought they were more gnomes, but as his eyes adjusted he noted the weak chins, barely covered with peachfuzz beards, and wide, staring eyes. Terac's jaw hung slackly, allowing a trickle of drool to dribble from his mouth, while Divid had a finger buried past the first knuckle within a great beak of a nose.

"Gully dwarves? Your crew is *gully dwarves*?"

"They work very hard, mostly, and they come cheap," Pneumo declared proudly.

Before Kerrick could say anything else, *Whalefish* suddenly angled sharply downward. A great stream of icy water spilled through the still-open hatch atop the hull, and the elf had the sickening sensation, once again, of a deck dropping away beneath him, starting a plunge that seemed likely to carry them all to the bottom of the sea.

"The elf is coming! For all we know, he's here already! We have to be prepared, guard against . . ." Grimwar stalked around the great hall of Dracoheim Castle, bellowing wildly in alarm. Only when he heard the echo of his voice coming back to him did he realize he didn't know what to say, what the real danger was.

"Guard against what?" testily demanded Stariz, who was still out of breath after the hasty climb up from the harbor. *Goldwing* had arrived in port barely a half hour ago. She stomped over to the hearth, held her hands out to soak up the warmth from the glowing embers. "We managed to beat him here. What do you think he can do against all your soldiers?"

"Yes, my son. What exactly are you worried about?" Hanna's voice was maddeningly calm, but the fact that she echoed his wife's irritating question was like a second knife in Grimwar Bane's guts. He leaned back and roared his frustration at the vaulted ceiling, while the two ogresses waited with infuriating patience for him to regain his composure.

"Reports! I need reports, from all around the island! These are still the days of the midnight sun. He cannot bring that boat into shore under the cover of darkness. When there is fog I want guards standing shoulder to shoulder, every place he could land! I need trusted ogres watching every inch of our shoreline, alert for any sign of that cursed boat."

"We have watchmen out now," Hanna said, "regular patrols around the whole island. We can increase the number, but my son, he is one elf, with only a few companions. It would have been good if you captured him at sea, but I don't see how he represents a serious threat."

Grimwar growled. His mother was right, of course. What could one elf and a few of his friends do? Still, he had a gut feeling that something was amiss.

There was a staccato rap on the heavy door.

"Who is it?" demanded the king, spinning on his heel to glare at the entryway.

The door was already open, and the Alchemist was halfway across the great hall. In another second he had reached the trio and was bowing to the king.

Grimwar blinked, nonplussed by the fellow's surprising quickness. Even as he was standing still he seemed to be quivering, ready to bolt in any direction.

"I came to report on the status of the orb," the Alchemist stated quickly, barely drawing breath. "The components will be assembled and purified by the end of the day—and by tomorrow morning I will have them inside the orb, and I will be ready to melt the bead of gold around the rim, to seal it. After that, it will be ready for use."

The king nodded, as though distracted, whereas the newcomer had actually helped to focus his thoughts. He pointed at the Alchemist and spoke to the two ogresses.

"He is coming here to stop the Alchemist," Grimwar Bane declared firmly. He waited tensely, half-expecting his wife or his mother to mock his statement. To his surprise, they looked at each other, eyes widening in understanding.

"Oh, you are right," said Stariz in a genuinely awed voice. "Your insight is keen, my lord. Indeed, that is the only explanation that makes sense." She looked at the slight, trembling figure and nodded in appraisal. "He seeks to stop you—kill or cripple or capture you, somehow."

"But I don't understand," declared the now twice as jittery Alchemist. "Why would this person you speak of try to do that? Why should I fear him? What is this all about?"

"You should fear him," Grimwar Bane said in cold triumph, utterly certain now. "Because he, too, is an elf!"

<hr />

"The hatch!" cried Kerrick, lunging past the flailing gnome. He clawed his way up the small ladder, fighting the force of rushing water until he found the handle on the inside of the trapdoor. He wrenched it down, and the water pressure helped slam it shut, though the elf was knocked down the ladder and sent sprawling on the metal deck.

Captain Pneumo rushed past him, scrambling up the ladder to turn a metal valve that apparently cinched the hatch in place. Water ceased to spill down the hatchway, but the deck was still angled steeply downward. Something barreled into Kerrick, sending him sprawling into a tangle of metal pipes, and he realized that one of the gully dwarves—Terac, it looked like—had bowled into him.

Light flared as Pneumo adjusted the flame on a wildly swinging lantern. Kerrick coughed, breathing steamy fumes, then blinked as he saw the gully dwarf dive headfirst into the water churning in the downward-pointed bow.

"More fire!" cried the gnome. "Feed the boilers! Scoop the gold! Plunge the ballast! Strike the vanes—no, strike the ballast and plunge the vanes!" The bearded captain seized a great hammer and raced away from Kerrick, pulling open the constricted hatchway leading into the stern. The other gully dwarf, Divid, remained amidships, spinning some of the bewildering array of valves. If the little fellow knew what he was doing, his frantic gestures gave no clue.

Kerrick raced after Pneumo, using his hands to pull himself up the steeply canted deck. He cast a glance behind, saw there was no sign of Terac in the water churning in the bow. Strongwind had found a rope from somewhere and was headed in that direction, Moreen at his side. Randall, his expression almost bemused, trailed the elf.

Cracking his head on a low bulkhead, Kerrick cursed, then reached for a handhold that turned out to be a scalding hot pipe. Only Randall's strong hands against his back prevented him from falling, but quickly the elf recovered his balance and continued to move upward, scrambling toward the rear of the seemingly plummeting *Whalefish*.

He found Pneumo in a large chamber that was illuminated by red light spilling from the open door of a boiler. The gnome was frantically pitching chunks of coal into the furnace, releasing thick smoke that brought tears to Kerrick's eyes. He blinked, saw familiar brightness shining among the sooty black, and realized that there were nuggets of pure gold mingled with the fuel.

"That valve!" shrieked the gnome captain, pointing to a great, spoked wheel as the elf drew near. "Turn it—we need more pressure!"

"Which way?" Kerrick asked, taking the metal rim in

his hands. The surface was warm, slick, and oily, but he felt it budge under the pressure of his grip.

"How should I know?" demanded the gnome, still pitching gold-laced coal into his boiler. "Just turn it!"

Kerrick gave the valve a hard twist, and immediately a gout of steam exploded from an unseen vent. The eruption blasted Pneumo away from the boiler, sent him tumbling across the narrow, cylindrical chamber.

"Not *that* way!" shrieked the gnome.

Reversing the direction of spin, Kerrick opened the valve, feeling a thrum of power as steam somehow hissed through the system of pipes. Randall, meanwhile, slammed the door of the boiler shut, leaving the room in an eerie darkness split by the crimson glow of several glass panels around the boiler. The Highlander pulled the sputtering gnome to his feet and brushed him off.

"You lost a little hair, fella, but you'll be okay," he said.

"The vanes! We have to turn the vanes!" cried Pneumo, breaking away, racing back the way he had come, down the steeply tilted deck.

"Vanes?" Kerrick repeated, trying unsuccessfully to imagine what the gnome was talking about.

"I'll tend the fire here," Randall offered. "See if you can help."

The elf lunged after Pneumo, sliding down the sloping passage, ducking under the bulkhead to find himself back in the *Whalefish*'s lamp-lit central compartment. Despite his initial impression of a tightly cramped space, after the hellish confines of the boiler room this now seemed to Kerrick like a spacious cabin.

Water still sloshed in the forward section of the submersible, and he spotted Moreen and Strongwind, holding their rope, staring futilely into the murky liquid. The chiefwoman caught his eye when he entered and shook her head.

"No sign of the other little one," she said grimly.

Pneumo, meanwhile, had seized a crank mounted high on the bulkhead and was kicking and straining to try to turn it. The mechanism, so far at least, seemed unyielding. Kerrick suspected this was one of the "vanes" that must be turned, and as he advanced to help he spotted a similar apparatus on the opposite side. He went to that one and gave the handle a pull.

He got it down a few inches, against tremendous pressure, but found it would move no farther. Pneumo was jumping up and down, tugging on the handle but having no visible success with the crank.

"What do the vanes do?" Kerrick asked, shouting, then wincing in surprise as his voice boomed and echoed though the narrow hull.

"Point us up—or down!" shrilled the gnome. "Now, they're steering us to the bottom!"

Frantically the elf tugged at the mechanism, but he couldn't get the crank to move much. When he loosened his hold to adjust his grip, the pressure on the vane spun the handle back to its starting position.

"More power!" screamed the gnome, bouncing up and down as he tried, still without success, to rotate his own handle. "Feed the boilers! Drive the propeller!"

Kerrick suddenly halted, went to the gnome, and wrenched him away. He shook Pneumo by the shoulders, kneeling to stare the captain in his wide, watery eyes.

"You say the vanes are steering us downward?" he demanded.

The gnome gave a frantic affirmative nod.

"Then why do you want *more* power?" cried the elf. "Won't that drive us down—faster?"

Pneumo opened his mouth, beard bristling, eyes bulging. Abruptly he clamped his lips together and nodded. "Right," he said. He shouted toward the stern. "Less power! Starve the boilers! Stop the propeller!"

Leaving the gnome, Kerrick scrambled back to the boiler room to find Randall awaiting him expectantly. The elf went to the large valve he had opened scarce minutes earlier and quickly wheeled it shut. The plunging momentum of the boat slowed perceptibly.

Back in the control room, Moreen and Strongwind were hauling a blue-faced Terac up from the flooded bow section. The gully dwarf spewed a great lungful of water, coughed, and retched but looked as if he would be all right.

Only then did Kerrick notice the water spilling along the deck, draining from the bow as the boat, recovering from its headlong dive, gradually leveled out. Slowly they floated upward. A pair of thick crystal panels revealed the increasing illumination of the water as they ascended through indigo, blue, and soft emerald depths. The light continued to grow until, long minutes later, the *Whalefish* popped to the surface, and the glass panel brightened with the almost forgotten light of the wonderful sun.

"We need more gold," Pneumo announced, after he had inspected his metal watercraft. "That's the only thing that will power the boilers enough to get us out to sea."

"Gold? You burn gold?" asked the elf, incredulous.

"Yup. Otherwise, the smoke infects the fish, and we can't eat any, and we all die," the gnome explained.

"Even gully dwarves, who can eat just about anything." He lowered his voice to a whisper, leaning away from Divid and Terac, who were gobbling some vile porridge at the galley table. "They're my third crew. The first two pairs, well, let's just say that it wasn't pleasant."

"Where did you get them?" Kerrick asked.

"Why, Dracoheim, naturally. There's lots of 'em living under the mountain there, and they make good, loyal crewmen." Pneumo lowered his voice to a hoarse whisper. "Dumb as two lumps of bricks, of course."

"You've been to Dracoheim?" Kerrick should his head in amazement. He had a hard time believing this was all happening, but his bruises and burns—and the memory of his beloved sailboat's loss—convinced him that the experience was real. "And gold? You burn gold in your engine? How do you get that?" he demanded.

Pneumo looked at him as if he was a stubborn student who simply refused to learn. "Why, where else would *you* go if you needed gold? Dracoheim, of course!"

The two halves of the golden orb lay open on the Alchemist's workbench. One of them would soon be filled with the lethal powder mixture. The other would be filled with the potion, then the halves would be sealed together.

The Alchemist had some work to do before he finalized the powder, and for that he needed to concentrate, to forget about the new danger menacing him. After all, he had guards—six bull ogres of the Dowager Queen's personal escort—and was high up in the tower of the lofty castle. He ought to be safe, beyond the reach of any intruder.

He set to work with a vengeance, his movements swift and precise. At least, such was his intention. Increasingly, however, his fingers trembled, or he found himself leaning on the bench to catch his breath, fighting dizziness.

He proceeded, as best as he could. First, he distilled acid over a low fire, allowing the caustic material to sizzle through a series of tubes until it collected in a glass decanter. He mixed gold dust with the sacred ashes in a great vat, while sorting other elements into a centrifuge powered by the pedaling of an ogre watchman.

In fact, all six of his guards crowded his lab, stood too close, stepped on his toes, and generally got in the way. His impatience grew until finally the Alchemist barked at them.

"Stand back, you louts! Do you want to call down the wrath of the Dowager Queen?"

The warning had the desired effect. The guards, all afraid of the elder ogress—with good cause, he knew—withdrew to the far side of the laboratory. There they watched him with narrowed eyes and muttered growls. He ignored them, focusing anew upon his work.

He found his attention wandering again, musing on the danger presented to him by this elf the king had called the Messenger. For more than a decade the Alchemist had feared such a vengeful visitor. He had long expected that, somehow, the elves, his people, would find him and punish him.

He felt like weeping. Couldn't they *see*? It was a matter of survival. He just did what he needed to do, in order to stay alive! The Alchemist strayed to the window, looked across the barren landscape as if he expected to see his elf nemesis creeping down a mountain toward him.

Finally, the preparations were done. The precious powder had been carefully and completely mixed, rinsed with pure acid. The Alchemist gingerly collected it in a several shallow dishes. At last, he sat down, crossed his arms before him, and cradled his head in the bony crevice of his elbows, trying to calm himself. His limbs finally ceased their trembling, and he rose and reached for one of the dishes.

An ogre guard standing near the door sneezed, and the Alchemist started, jumping back from the bench, the dish wobbling precariously on the lip of the work surface.

"Imbecile!" he cried, pointing a trembling finger at the ashen-faced guard. "You could have killed us all!"

"I beg your lordship's pardon!" pleaded the ogre, bowing abjectly.

"Out of here! I want you all out of here, now!" cried the Alchemist. "It's the only way I can work."

"We are supposed to guard you, lord," said one of the other brutes, the sergeant in charge of the guards.

"Then stand outside my door! I cannot function like this, with you all sniffling and snorting and growling in here! Do you not realize a single mistake and we could all be blown to pieces?"

Apparently that dire possibility was enough to convince the ogres. In any event, they pushed and elbowed at each other in their haste to depart the laboratory. The last one to leave shut the door very gently behind him.

The Alchemist was glad to be left alone. Looking around, he leaped to the window and closed the heavy wooden shutter that held the Sturmfrost at bay every winter. Latching the barrier, he allowed himself to feel reasonably well protected against intrusion by guards or a vengeance-seeking elf.

He turned back to his work, tried to summon the will to lift the dishes of powder, to pour the grainy substance into the orb. But he didn't have the desire to move. A terrible ennui seized him, dragged him down, cemented him in place. His consciousness wavered until he finally crumpled forward, as though tumbling into a pit of merciful oblivion

Something caused him to lift his head from his arms and to stare in the direction of the sea. It was as though a chill wind pressed through those walls, numbing his flesh.

Slowly, unsteadily, he pushed himself to his feet and lurched toward the door. His invention was ready, the great weapon needed only to be sealed, but that was unimportant, now.

The Alchemist knew, somehow he knew, he felt it in the pit of his soul, that the elf was coming for him.

———◆◆◆———

Kerrick was surprised by the ease of underwater travel, as—in spite of a few fits and starts and one more harrowing, unplanned plunge into the depths—Captain Pneumo guided his cylindrical craft into the very shadow of the great, dark massif that was Dracoheim Island. Finally, as *Whalefish* moved into the shallows, Kerrick felt the deck begin to pitch and roll under his feet. This was a reaction to the surf billowing around them, the gnome explained.

Face pressed to a hooded aperture, Kerrick was amazed at the view provided by a device of mirrors that, Pneumo explained, was thrust above the water, allowing the crew of the submersible to examine their surroundings. He called it a "Perry-scope," for reasons Kerrick had not yet learned. In any event, the elf was more concerned with what he saw than with how he saw it.

They seemed to be in a narrow cove, sheltered by brooding cliffs to port and starboard, with a shelf of steeply sloping beach before them. He couldn't tell if that shore was sand or fine gravel, but he was struck by the dark, almost pure black, color of the ground. Beyond the beach the island's land mass rose steeply, in some places precipitously, though the bluff was broken by a series of narrow ravines that rose inland for at least a short distance.

Whalefish was submerged in these shallows, close enough to the surface that each breaker lifted the vessel as it passed, then dropped it again to rest on the sandy bed of the cove. The elf pulled his face away and saw that Randall, Strongwind, and Moreen were watching him expectantly, waiting at the base of the ladder leading up to the hatch.

"We should be able to swim from here," Kerrick said. "We're not more than a hundred paces off shore."

"Help me little bit?" Divid asked, tugging on the elf's sleeve. "Me not much swimmer."

"Yes, we'll get you to shore," Kerrick agreed. "Then it will be up to you to show us where the Alchemist can be found."

"Me know the Alk-ist," nodded the little fellow. Then he scowled. "Know where him live. Him don't like us kind." Again the gully dwarf reached a blunt finger into his nose, rooting around vigorously for some offending obstruction.

"I can't understand why," the elf said, looking away with a grimace. He noticed Moreen laughing at him, her single eye flashing, and he couldn't help but grin back.

They had a plan, though Kerrick knew it would take some really good luck for them to pull it off successfully. The gully dwarf would lead them into the castle through a small tunnel used only by his people. They would go ashore in three relays, leaving Terac to watch the submersible. Pneumo assured them that the gully dwarf could guide the boat to the bottom of the shallow cove, and wait there as long as necessary for the others to return—or until he ran out of warquat, which would take about three days according to the gnomish inventor. Pneumo would make his way along mountain trails to a mining village, a place he had visited previously.

Strongwind and Moreen would strike out overland and distract any ogre patrols they encountered. Randall and Kerrick, guided by Divid, would sneak into the castle, up to the Alchemist's chamber, and . . . and do what was necessary.

He and Mad Randall were prepared for the Alchemist to put up a fight. If he did, they would kill him. There was no choice—the very survival of Brackenrock, perhaps of all human civilization in the Icereach, depended on stopping the manufacture of another golden orb.

"Did you see any sign of ogres or anything else through that Perry-scope?" asked the chiefwoman.

The elf shook his head. They heard a clank of metal and turned to see Captain Pneumo emerge from his small cabin. The gnome was wrapped in a great coil of rope and draped with pouches and packs. A metal helmet, several sizes too large for him, was perched on his head, drooping forward so that it covered one of his eyes.

"What's this?" asked Kerrick cautiously.

"I'm dressed for any eventuality," declared Pneumo. "I've got pearls for trading, here in my beltpack, and these other sacks I'll fill with gold. I've got to bring enough for a long voyage, you know."

"Makes sense," Randall agreed with an easy nod.

Kerrick had misgivings but decided not to argue. After all, the gnome's mission—gaining fuel for his arcane boilers—was important to the submersible, and the submersible represented their only chance to escape from Dracoheim.

"All right," the elf said. "Let's get going."

With a boost from Randall the gnome made it to the hatch, turned the release valve, and pushed it open. Squirming upward, he vanished from sight. Divid went next, followed by Randall, Strongwind, Moreen, and Kerrick, each scrambling up onto the slick, round hull. After the elf pushed the hatch shut, he heard Terac cranking the valve behind him.

Outside of the *Whalefish* , the sky seemed impossibly bright. The submersible rested in relatively shallow water, but they still had a way to go before reaching dry land.

"No time for delay—let's go!" said Moreen, the first of the companions to slide down the curved hull into the sea.

A moment later Pneumo, buoyed by his many pouches, which served as floats, was splashing around in the surf, while the four survivors from *Cutter* swam toward shore, nervously scanning the dark island for signs of ogres. The elf, the strongest swimmer, kept one arm around Divid, dragging the gully dwarf along with him. Divid kicked and squirmed but couldn't break Kerrick's grip.

Finally the elf's feet scuffed against the rocky beach. Divid peeled away, springing out of the water with surprisingly good balance as, crawling and sputtering, Kerrick pulled himself out of the surf. He saw that Moreen and Randall were emerging to his right, while Strongwind—his sword at the ready—strode out of the water to the left.

"Where's Captain Pneumo?" Kerrick asked, turned to scrutinize the breakers.

The next big wave trundled in, and the elf spotted the gnome, tumbling in the shallows. Kerrick grabbed the coughing captain by the scruff of his neck and pulled him to his feet, then helped him stumble forward until all six of the companions stood next to each other on the shore.

The black beach consisted of fine sand interspersed with small rocks. In places patches of lighter material swirled through delicate spirals, but the overall effect was of eerie darkness. It was near midnight, with the sun low in the south, hidden behind the heights surrounding this cove.

They made haste inland, jogging across a fringe of flat ground and into the mouth of one of the ravines leading upward. Crouching amid some large boulders that had tumbled to the base of the draw, they made their final plans.

"Which way from here?" Kerrick asked Captain Pneumo.

"To the top of this bluff, for starters," the gnome explained. "The village where I get my gold is just on the other side of the pass. I'll head there, fill my pouches, and be back here before the sun makes a full circle. Don't worry—I'll wait for you, even if it takes you more time.

"You'll be able to see the castle from up there," Pneumo continued. "There's lots of broken ground—you should be able to get close without being spotted. It will be up to Divid to show you the way into the castle."

"If we are spotted, Strongwind and I will lead the ogres on a merry chase, while you and Randall and Divid stay hidden," Moreen said firmly. She pointed a finger in Kerrick's face. "You have the most important job. Somehow you have to find this Alchemist and stop him. We'll do everything we can to see that you succeed."

The elf and Randall nodded solemnly.

"Anyway, we all have to make this climb, so let's get going," suggested Strongwind Whalebone. "We should hurry away from here, in case anyone noticed us coming ashore."

With Randall in the lead, they began to climb. The dirt in the ravine was soft, black in color but grainy like sand, prone to cascading down on them they tried to scramble up. It caught in their fingernails, scuffed and abraded their hands and knees. Once Divid tumbled backward, thumping into the elf's chest, and the two of them slid down for twenty or thirty feet before Kerrick could arrest their fall.

An hour later the berserker was the first to reach the crest. He turned to assist Moreen and Pneumo. Strongwind, the gully dwarf, and Kerrick came last, arriving at a rocky plateau. A lofty castle, spiderwebs of arched bridges connecting slender, tall towers, rose from a knoll a few miles away. Commanding a view in all directions, the place was dark and forbidding. The elf turned to Moreen, ready to express his apprehension, and saw that she was looking off in the other direction.

"I think I see trouble," she said in a low voice.

"You're right," Randall said cheerfully as he followed her gaze. Four large figures, each armed with a sword and a spear, were jogging toward them along the top of the bluff.

"Looks like a welcoming party," the elf said grimly.

"The orb is nearly complete," declared the Dowager Queen, looking down her nose at her son as though she expected him to quibble. "My guards tell me that the Alchemist needs only to seal the two halves with a bead of gold."

"Good," Grimwar snapped. "We can get out of this place and get on with the business of destroying Brackenrock. We leave today, and we take the orb with us!"

His mother and his wife glanced at each other in the fire-warmed study high within the fortress of Draco-heim. The king didn't notice. He was standing at the window, gazing at the pale shimmering sun. More than two months of constant daylight had already passed this summer. It would be at only three more weeks, he knew, before the golden sun vanished for the duration of the year. His attention was sharply drawn back to the room by Stariz.

"Your mother has decided to return to Winterheim with us," she announced.

The king wheeled in surprise, and after a moment he remembered his manners, forcing a smile.

"That is splendid news, indeed," he said, with a dignified nod of his head. "I am glad you have decided to be more . . . flexible."

Hanna snorted and glared at him, a look that he wished he could decipher. He flushed under the feeling that his mother could see right into his soul, could discern all of the emotions mingling there, emotions that right now centered around another ogress, far away from here.

"I am not pleased," said the Dowager Queen—apparently she *was* reading his mind!— "that you have chosen to ignore my wishes in the matter of the harlot Thraid Dimmarkull. You know that she humiliated me and made your father behave like a fool!"

Grimwar drew himself up to his full, eight-foot-plus height. "I am the king now, and she has done nothing to me to call reproach down upon herself. I repeat: I shall not have her punished simply to soothe your need for vengeance."

"I know this," Hanna said sternly, "and yet I have decided to return in spite of your stubbornness. Your wife has convinced me that it is the gracious thing to do. I trust you will see that my dignity is not affronted."

"Ahem. You will be welcomed in Winterheim as the Dowager Queen, of course. You shall have your choice of apartments in the Royal Quarter and will be treated with honor wherever you go in the city. These are my commands, and you know that I have long sought your return." He crossed the room and took his mother's hands. He looked her in the eyes and was able to speak sincerely. "I'm glad you are coming home, Mother. Truly."

The elder ogress's expression softened, and he felt a glimmer of affection, affection such as he had not known for decades. He searched for something else to say, but before any words came to him an alarm horn brayed through the halls.

Moments later there came a knock at the door, and Stariz yanked it open to reveal a breathless ogre dressed in the gold and scarlet of the royal guard.

"What is it?" barked the queen.

"Intruders, Your Majesties! Six of them landed on the northern shore of the island!"

"A sailboat! Was it a sailboat that brought them?" demanded the king.

"No, sire. Rather, the watchman said it was as though they rose out of the water, walked on waves at first, then came swimming ashore."

"Bah," declared Grimwar, waving his hand. "The watchman is an idiot! Such tales! They *must* have come by boat!"

"Surely," Stariz agreed with the king, rather surprising him. "But where are they right now?"

"We . . . er, one of the wretches slipped away," the guard stammered. "He was nothing—a gully dwarf it looked like, though his beard was a bit long. He headed west. The others are headed this way, toward the castle."

"What is the nature of these intruders?" demanded the king. "Did you see an elf among them?"

"One is a human woman, Sire. That is plain. The others we took mostly to be men—though we weren't close enough to see for certain. There was another one, too, who seemed to be a gully dwarf."

"Five, and a gully dwarf? The elf is among them—he must be!" gasped Stariz, clapping a hand to her mouth and sagging into a large chair. She looked wide-eyed at Grimwar. "The Messenger is here. He has come at last, and some strange plan is afoot."

"Find them!" screamed the king. "Find them and kill them all, at once, without mercy!"

22

Way of the Gully Dwarves

Kerrick crouched, watching Moreen dash over the rounded ridge. As soon as she disappeared from view he raced after her, staying low as he dived across the summit, rolling a few times down the grassy slope on the other side. The last of the companions to make the harrowing passage, he sprang to his feet quickly, looking anxiously around.

"I don't think they saw us," Randall observed. The Highlander was sprawled on the ground, spying through the narrow gap between a couple of square boulders.

"Nope, they're not coming this way—they're still moving along both sides of the creek down there," he reported. "Their attention is focused on the valley floor. In a few minutes they're bound to wonder what happened to us."

No less than three ogre patrols were converging on the plateau above where the companions had come ashore. The first group to spot them had sent some kind of signal and summoned other comrades from their watch posts. The companions had just evaded at least a score of pursuers.

"Those rocks gave us good cover," Moreen said. "We must have made it up the hill without being seen. When they meet up at the bottom of the other side, it'll take them a while to figure out which way we've gone.

"What about Pneumo—did he get away?" asked the chiefwoman.

"I think so," Randall said, still peering over the crest. "I lost track of him across that broken ground, but he seemed pretty certain about where he was going. I hope he's already trading his pearls for the gold he needs. I'd bet he'll be the first one of us back to the cove."

"We've got to keep moving," Strongwind Whalebone chipped in, "if we don't want them to come up here, catch us out in the open, or at least pick up our trail."

"Me hungry!" Divid declared, sitting down and crossing his arms. "No eats, no go to castle. We make swim, spit water out, and you say no eats. Now we do long climb, and still you say no eats. So me ask, when eats?"

"You've been very brave and smart, also, to lead us around this island," the chiefwoman said gently. "As soon as we find a place to hide, you can have some eats. We'll all stop for a rest." She indicated the pack carried by Randall, containing several days' worth of dried fish cakes, as well as two flasks of water. "Our friend is carrying plenty of eats."

"Eats now, or no go to castle," Divid repeated, glaring upward. "Stay right here. Yup!"

"No go to castle, and you end up stuck on an ogre spear," Moreen said calmly. "Would you prefer that?"

The gully dwarf scowled, then frowned as he considered his options.

"Okey dokey, go to castle," Divid decided, popping up to his feet. "This way." He stopped and pointed at Moreen. "But you promise—then we eat!"

"I promise," she agreed.

The little fellow led the elf and the three humans down the slope. They dashed across the grassy tundra, momentarily in full view of the castle before they dropped out of sight against the walls of a narrow ravine.

"Where does that valley go?" Kerrick asked, as they carefully made their way down a steep, rocky stretch of the ravine.

"See path?" Divid asked. "Goes from castle to fish-camp on shore of island. Ogres use it alla time."

As if to confirm the gully dwarf's remark, they heard a shout from below. Kerrick saw figures on the winding path down there, a full company of ogres streaming along the track on the valley floor. One was pointing up the hill-side, and the elf dropped out of sight onto the ravine floor.

"They spotted me—only me, I think," the elf said, as all the companions gathered behind a large rock. "A big one at the front of the line got a good look at me."

"He saw me, too, I'm afraid," Strongwind said. The Highlander king peered around the corner of the rock. "They're coming this way at a pretty good clip now."

"Tough spot," Moreen muttered. "We can't go up, or the ogres on the other side of the ridge will see us."

"Okay, we go this way now," said Divid, suddenly. He pointed into a shadowy alcove beneath the base of the boulder, right where they were hiding. Looking closely, Kerrick could see a small hole leading into darkness.

Moreen looked at it with wry distaste. "I guess it's better than being captured, but I don't want to be caught in some animal den, either. Where does that cave go?"

"Goes to castle, yup! Me take you to castle," their gully dwarf guide declared. "Good ol' Divid."

They all looked skeptical. The castle was at least a mile, probably more, from here.

"Sure! Good path, used by gullys alla time! No ogres in there neither, you betcha! Tight squeeze for them. Now come along, or me go alone." He looked longingly at the backpack carried by Randall. "Me could carry some eats, okay?"

"Sure," said the berserker with an easy grin. He shrugged out of the shoulder straps, lowering the pack to the ground as he adressed Kerrick and Moreen. "You two better get moving, don't you think?"

"We're all going!" Moreen declared.

"There are two of us who won't fit," Randall said firmly, shrugging his broad shoulders, casting a meaning-ful look at the king. Kerrick knew he was right. The two muscular Highlanders would have to stay behind. He and Moreen were slender enough that they could make it—not easily, certainly not comfortably, but they could make it.

"Randall is right," Strongwind announced. "He and I will make use of ourselves out here in the open."

"What do you mean?" asked Moreen, shaking her head. "We should stick together!"

"No," Strongwind argued. "You and Kerrick go with Divid. Randall and I will try to draw the pursuit away from here."

Randall was already dividing the food cache, putting some of the supplies in a smaller rucksack that he handed to Kerrick. The elf slung it over his shoulder.

"Come on," Divid urged, peering around the edge of the boulder, then drawing back from his vantage. "They comin' up here, right quick! Time for me to go—you comes if you wants to!" With that, he dropped to his hands and knees, and vanished into the dirt-lined hole. Moments later his dirty head popped out. "Bring eats, eh?"

Moreen stomped her foot but said nothing.

"The king is right," Kerrick said, taking her hand.

"Go!" Strongwind said urgently, stepping forward to put his hands on Moreen's shoulders. "We'll meet you back at the cove, when this is over. Promise me you'll be there?"

"Yes—but you be there too, dammit!" Moreen declared, touching the king's cheek affectionately. He squeezed her fingers, then turned away with Randall. Kerrick waited as Moreen knelt down to crawl behind Divid, then the elf, too, dropped to the ground and crept into the rank and muddy confines of the gully dwarf hole.

"There they go—back up the ridge!" cried Grimwar Bane. "After them, my Grenadiers! I pledge a full cask of warqat to the ogre who brings me the elf's head!"

"Are you sure we should chase them, Sire?" asked Argus Darkand, at his liege's side, reluctantly eyeing the steep slope leading upward. "Perhaps we should head them off up at the castle, take the path back that way. Thene can make sure that they don't circle around us."

"We've got them on the run," declared the king, scorning his helmsman's advice. "By all means we'll chase them—run them into the ground. You ogres, keep going up the hill." He pointed, uttering a cry of delight as he saw a flash of movement high on the slope above them, a human figure dashing across a shallow draw, closely followed by another. "Look, there they are! In that ravine up there!"

Already the two dozen ogres of his detachment, every one of them a seasoned Grenadier, had turned from the path they were following along the valley floor. The ogres crossed the tundra to the base of the steep ridge, moving in a loose skirmish line. Even in this broken ground, there was no way the fugitives could slip through the ranks.

The king scanned the valley floor behind them. He could see another group of ogres, thirty or more about a half a mile behind his band, led by his wife. Stariz strode along energetically, bearing a tall wooden staff, the warriors jogging to keep up with her. With her billowing dress and broad, stomping stride, even Grimwar had to admit she looked powerful and intimidating. He was satisfied her party would be able to cover the low ground.

Beyond his wife rose the forbidding bulk of Castle Dracoheim, perched on its rocky knoll, commanding a view of this and all surrounding terrain. Grimwar was comforted to know that his mother was still in the fortress, the Dowager Queen keeping a careful eye on the approaches. Grimwar smiled cruelly, knowing that the Alchemist was safe—and busy crafting the final seal around the rim of the golden orb. The explosive weapon had been nearly complete when they started in pursuit of the intruders.

Content with the disposition of his warriors, Grimwar hurried to catch up with his strapping young Grenadiers, who were scrambling upward almost as quickly as they had moved across the level ground. Even with a measured pace, the king was startled to find himself breathing heavily after a few dozen paces up the steeply ascending ground.

Still, he made progress, creeping upward, within hailing distance of his faster warriors. Looking up the slope, Grimwar spotted a bearded man carrying a great sword. The bearded fellow paused near the summit and glanced down on his pursuers, then whirled away. Other ogres shouted in alarm, increasing the pace of their climb.

The king didn't see any signs of the other intruders.

His scouts had reported a party of five coming this way.

"Be sure to look in all these gullies!" Grimwar shouted. "Don't let the cowards hide, or sneak past!"

By the time the monarch crested the ridge, he was sweating profusely and gasping for breath. "Stop . . . here!" he ordered, plopping down onto a flat-topped rock. He mopped his brow. "Any sign of them?" he called to one of his warriors, who had advanced to observe from a high rock twenty or thirty paces away from the ogre king.

"I saw at least two heading along this ridge," reported the Grenadier, a veteran called Three-Tusks because of the unique tooth growing out of the middle of his lower jaw. It was a trait that caused him to spit when talking, so Grimwar was pleased to speak to the fellow from some distance away.

"Go after them, my friend," the king said. "Argus and I will keep a lookout here, and come along in a moment. Argus," he called to his trusted lieutenant, who had made the climb at his side. "Can you see where the queen's party is?"

"Her Highness Queen Stariz leads her company down the path we vacated," Argus reported, indicating a score of ogres even now making their way down the valley floor. "It looks as though she intends to go all the way to the sea."

"Good," grunted the king. "That will cut them off along the shore. We chase up here, she's down there. Let him cast a fog or pray for wind—this time the Messenger won't get away!"

From somewhere he found the strength to push himself to his feet. Grunting, shaking his head, and once more wiping the sweat from his eyes, he started forward at a fast walk, following the ogre Three-Tusks and the detachment of Grenadiers.

Kerrick's knees felt as though they had been scraped raw. His hands were caked with dirt. An unidentifiable odor of remarkable rankness coated the inside of his nostrils, so thick that even if he ever got out of here he was certain he'd smell it for the rest of his life.

He had no idea how long they had been crawling through these close, muddy confines—hours, at the very least, maybe even days. He was vaguely aware of Moreen in front of him. Occasionally his hand would touch her boot, when she slowed down or he crawled faster. He could only wonder at her courage, advancing resolutely even where she probably could see nothing in front of her at all.

Divid muttered periodically, usually about being hungry, and his voice was the only confirmation Kerrick had that the gully dwarf was still leading the way. Several times they squirmed through narrow bottlenecks, getting scuffed and scraped on all sides, and twice they reached slightly larger chambers, confluences of several tunnels. In each of these they stopped to stretch and, briefly rest. When Kerrick looked around he noticed several passages leading in all different directions.

When it was time to resume, Divid displayed no hesitation in selecting one of the apparently identical tunnels. Kerrick could only hope that the dwarf knew where he was going, for they certainly had no choice but to follow him.

Abruptly Moreen stopped and as the elf came up behind her he heard voices from ahead.

"Hey, Croaker? That ole you?"

"Divid? Where you go? How you come here? Got eats?"

"Got boat job," said the gully dwarf guide proudly,

before sighing. "Sinking kinda boat. Lousy eats, though. Whatcha got?"

Moreen moved forward, and Kerrick came behind, seeing that they had entered the largest subterranean chamber yet. The chiefwoman rolled to the side, then sat with her back against the muddy wall, while the elf squirmed forward, then knelt at her side. They were in a circular room, perhaps twenty feet across. At least a dozen low tunnels led away from here in as many directions.

"Who dat?" asked the strange gully dwarf. This was apparently the redoubtable Croaker.

"These guys go castle," Divid said. "I show 'em the way."

"Oh yeah? They no ogres?" Croaker asked, peering suspiciously at the elf and the woman.

"Nope, no ogres," their guide assured his companion. "Nice smellin' one is a lady! Married to skinny one, me thinks."

Kerrick winced. "Friends," he corrected. Moreen chuckled softly.

"All gullies friends," declared Croaker, whacking Divid on the back with enthusiasm. "This one even when we hates him for taking my eats. And my girl-gully."

"My eats!" Divid declared, bristling. He stood close to the other, chest puffing out aggressively. "You take my eats! And Darknose *my* girl-gully!"

"You take eats and my girl-gully," Croaker said. "Oughta bop you a good one-two!"

"Yeah? Me bop you, two times!" Divid raised his grimy fists, ready to swing.

"We have eats," Moreen said quickly, reaching out to Kerrick. He handed her the small sack of provisions that Randall had given them when the two groups parted. "Is anyone hungry?"

"We hungry! Always hungry!"

Kerrick was astonished to see that there were suddenly at least a dozen gully dwarves in this chamber. They came scrambling out of holes, eyes wide and shining in the darkness. "Whatcha got?" asked one grubby female, swaggering forward and poking her face into the satchel.

"Here. We have some fish-cakes. I think there's one for everyone," the chiefwoman replied, gracefully pulling the bag away, then soothing the scowling girl-gully by offering her the first cake. The others crowded around, and soon the whole group was munching on the nutritious, if rather dry and tasteless, food, the traditional fare of travelers in the Icereach.

"What is this place?" Kerrick asked Divid, glancing around. "Somebody's, er, home?"

"This fine inn!" declared their guide. "Called 'Wayfare House.' Gullies come here for good eats, good talk. Meet girls, too," he said with a wink.

"Meet my girl," Croaker said sullenly, apparently unwilling to let that transgression go unmentioned. "Two times!"

"This is an inn, eh?" the elf said. He looked around the place, now crowded with gully dwarves. There was no furniture, no fireplace, just a few rotting logs and big stones and a slab of rotten meat lying along one wall of the room.

Kerrick assumed from its odor that this latter was garbage, but one of the gullies, having consuming his fish cake, pulled a piece of stringy flesh from the slab and gobbled it down with a great smile. The elf suppressed a gag as he saw maggots crawling on the morsel, just before the cheerful gully dwarf smacked his lips over the white, pasty grubs.

"How much farther," Kerrick asked Divid with a gulp. "How long before we get to the castle?"

"What castle?" asked their guide, chewing innocently.

"Dracoheim Castle," the elf replied, trying to hold his temper. "You know, where you promised to take us."

"Sure, sure, I promise."

"When? How far is it?" repeated Kerrick.

"We here," said Divid, leaning his head back.

"Where?" asked Kerrick, looking up, noticing for the first time that the roof of the "Wayfare Inn" was high overhead. Moreen was already standing up, pointing to a shaft leading upward, a rickety ladder extending down from the opening in the ceiling all the way to the floor.

"Castle Dracoheim! We right under big castle. What you think, anyways?" said Divid, before turning back to dig in, with visible relish, to a bite of maggot-infested dessert.

———◆◦◆———

"Do you think we should cross over the ridge?" wondered Randall, as he and Strongwind paused for sips of water and a bite to eat. They rested on a patch of sun-warmed grass, catching their breath, making sure the ogres didn't fall too far behind. "That might make them worry a little . . . pick up the pace of their pursuit, you know?"

"Maybe, but I think we should stay where they can get a good look at us now and then," the king suggested. "I wouldn't want them to give up and head back to the castle." He gazed off toward the citadel, now a good distance away. He hoped Moreen was safe, but knew there was nothing he could do for her now except keep these foolish ogres away from her.

"Time to go," the king said, rising to his feet, adjusting his sword so that it hung easily from his belt.

"Suits me," Randall agreed, also rising to his feet, easily hefting his axe. The ogres were coming on below. One of them shouted something as the two men showed themselves, and the cat-and-mouse chase resumed.

"How many of them did you see?" growled the ogre king, panting for breath, as he squinted toward the place where the humans had dropped out of sight again.

"Just two, Sire," reported Argus. "I don't know if they are the same two, however. More and more my eyes fail me—"

"No, that's what I saw, too," Grimwar declared. Squinting, he looked back along the ridgecrest, toward the looming height of Dracoheim Castle. "Come to think of it, I've never seen more than two, not since this chase started."

The castle was now a good ten miles away, in the opposite direction of their pursuit. The king tried to think, always a strenuous effort. He furrowed his brow and looked first toward the fleeing men, then back at the castle. If the intruders were after the Alchemist, and the Alchemist was back at the castle, surely he was safe.

But if they were chasing two humans, where were the other three people who had crashed the shores of Dracoheim? Where was the Messenger?

Suddenly, Grimwar had the feeling he had made a terrible mistake.

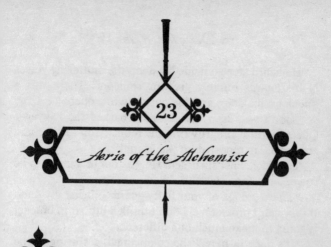

The bead of gold sizzled under the spurt of blue torch-flame, the metal glistening as it heated, slowly becoming liquid, dripping from the end of the malleable strip to flow into the groove around the seam of the golden orb. The Alchemist worked slowly and carefully, not because he was worried about wasting the precious material, but because he dared not overheat the sphere of soft, yellow metal.

One final turn, a sprinkle of water bursting into steam, cooling down the surface, and he was done. The orb gleamed like a giant, emotionless eye, resting on a wooden pedestal on his bench. It was heavy, weighing more than he could ever hope to lift, but that was no longer his problem.

He chuckled at a grim thought. The king would have to select a very diligent ogre to carry this precious object down the stairs from this lofty laboratory. One slip and the orb would start to roll, and on the first bounce, or the second, the glass bottle of potion enclosed in the sphere would crack, the liquid would mix with the powder, and the destruction would transform Dracoheim Island.

He heard steps outside his door, the muttering voices of his guards humbly greeting someone. There was a knock on his door, and the portal swung open.

"Don't you keep this locked?" barked the Dowager Queen, striding angrily into his room. "You know there are intruders reported on the island!"

The Alchemist shrugged. He was not in a mood to be cowed or deferential.

"There are six of your hefty guards outside my door. If they can't protect me, I don't think a little iron bracket is going to make much of a difference."

"It's dark in here," she complained, gesturing to the shuttered window.

"Safer that way," he replied.

Only then did her eyes fasten on the gleaming metal sphere. She came forward, licking her lips, placed her massive hands on either side of the orb. "Gonnas be praised," the elder queen whispered, awestruck. "So much power in such a small package. It is completed?"

"Ready to be carried down to the ship," the Alchemist said quietly, wishing that she would just pick it up and go.

Queen Hanna shook her head. "It is better to keep it here for now," she said. "Until we have the matter of these intruders taken care of and the elven Messenger is caught and skewered on a spit. My son has taken his warriors in pursuit on the highland, and Queen Stariz leads a full company through the valley. I have no doubts but that the blood of these insolent wretches will soon be soaking into the ground."

The Alchemist nodded, strangely ill at ease with this conversation.

"Bah," Hanna said, seeing his expression. "You are a pathetic weakling. I will be glad to leave you behind!"

"Leave? You are leaving here?" he asked, surprised.

She snorted in amusement. "Yes. I return to Winter-heim with my son. You will be fending for yourself from now on."

"But . . ." Cold fear gnawed at the Alchemist. "Can I not accompany you? I have heard so much about Winter-heim. I would like to see it!" His need was suddenly so acute that his hands were shaking. "There are things I could do . . . serve the crown. I know that the *Hornet* is lost. I could supervise the building of another galley!"

"My son's carpenters did well enough with the plans you provided. They still have the plans, if not the ship!" The Dowager Queen smiled a tight, wicked smile. She looked as though she were enjoying herself immensely. She had never liked this strange man, and he was one of the things she would be happy to leave behind in Dracoheim.

"But I have other skills. Tell me—" He was begging now, and Hanna cut him off with a stinging slap, knock-ing him back against the bench to look at her through teary eyes.

"Perhaps someday we will have need of you again and return," she sneered. "If that doesn't happen I, for one, will be glad to be rid of you. You make me sick, with your craving, your pathetic weakness!"

"When are you leaving?" the Alchemist wondered numbly. Where would he get his potion from now on, he wanted to ask, although he knew that she wouldn't care.

"As soon as the Messenger and his companions are slain," she replied. She glanced at the cask of elixir—the potion of haste—which was still half full. "You'd better try and make that last as long as you can," she observed cheerfully, a glint in her eye. With that, the Dowager Queen stalked out and slammed the door behind her.

He looked at the cask of potion, which suddenly seemed much emptier than it had before. How much? How many more sips? It would last through the summer, perhaps. He remembered there was a little left in the small bottle, the potion of gaseous form she had made for him earlier in the spring. Two swallows, perhaps, a few more precious days of enhanced existence.

Suddenly the winter looked very dark and very cold.

"Let's hurry," Kerrick said, touching Divid on the shoulder, nodding to the gully dwarves still gathered around them. "I thank all of you at the 'Wayfare House' for your hospitality. Now it is time for us to continue on our way.

"You climb, me stay here with pals," the gully dwarf said. He offered a two-eyed wink, nodding to the grimy female who had gotten food from Moreen. Now that gracious damsel was snuffling about in the dirt, nostrils pressed to the ground, as if she sought to confirm some intriguing scent there. "That Darknose," Divid whispered. "She hot for me!"

"She's, er, lovely, but we still need your help," the elf declared sternly. "We don't know the layout of this castle. Please show us how to find the Alchemist—then you can hurry back. I'm sure the, er, lady will wait for you!"

The gully dwarf looked at his comrades, many of whom were cheerfully gnawing on the piece of carrion, wrestling back and forth, occasionally flinging maggots at each other. Cloaker was sound asleep against the wall, and apparently that was enough to convince Divid that he could risk leaving his lady-love alone for a trifle longer.

"You give us pretty good eats," the gully dwarf admitted. "Guess me show you which way to tower."

"Thank you," said Moreen.

The elf, looked skeptically at the ladder, which leaned precariously and seemed barely capable of supporting their weight.

"I'll go first," Kerrick told Moreen, feeling he should take the greatest risk. "Divid can follow, and you bring up the rear."

He took hold of the ancient ladder, feeling mildew and mold on the lower rungs. Suppressing a shudder of disgust, he started to climb. Hand over hand, step by step, he made his way upward.

The ladder was surprisingly sturdy, and soon Kerrick spotted a hole overhead, a circle of grayish darkness. Pulling himself up the last stretch, he emerged through a gap in the floor of a stone-walled room.

"This be cistern, water for castle," Divid announced, following him out of the ladder shaft.

Moreen came last. They stood on a ring of cold flagstones, a circular underground chamber around a pool of deep, clear water. Another ladder, this one formed of iron rungs planted in the stone walls, rose from here, toward light glimmering above.

"Up," pointed their guide. "We gullies not usually go here. Ogres see us, they stick us with spear. No good."

"You are very brave," Moreen said, patting him on the shoulder. The praise made Divid beam, and as he started after Kerrick the elf reflected that, indeed, the grubby little fellow was performing an act of no small heroism.

This time when they reached the top, they climbed through a hole in the floor into an alcove off of a darkened corridor. Stone archways supported the ceiling, and a stairway of wide steps led upward. Divid took the lead, and they gingerly followed him, ascending at last into a large, dry room. A flickering of oily flame cast light from some unseen space just beyond the arched entrance.

"This one of favorite places . . . castle dungeon," the gully dwarf explained in a loud whisper. "Sneak in here sometimes, but gots to run if ogres come."

"Just show us the way to the tower," the elf replied, gripping Divid's arm in an gesture that was meant to be encouraging.

"Ouch!" protested the little fellow. "No grab!"

"Sorry," Kerrick said replied quickly. He heard a rumbling sound from around the corner. Cautiously he peered around the edge and saw a large ogre lying on a bench, snoring loudly. The elf's attention immediately went to the wall behind the bench, where several spears and a couple of swords stood haphazardly in a wooden rack. Beyond the bench the corridor was blocked by a barred iron door with a large lock.

This was a perfect opportunity. Kerrick had lost his sword when his boat went down, and he was weaponless.

Gesturing for his companions to wait, the elf crept forward as soundlessly as possible. The sleeping ogre snorted and half-rolled over, and Kerrick held his breath, afraid the lout would fall off the bench and wake up. Apparently the turnkey was used to his narrow perch, however, for he curled around and resumed his sonorous breathing.

The elf reached over his flabby belly, selecting the smallest sword in the rack. He lifted it out without managing to rattle any of the other weapons. The sword was a little long for him, heavier than his elven blade, but still a prize. He thrust it through his belt.

Divid led them away from the sleeping guard and the locked door, to another flight of steps. As they climbed Kerrick felt a heart-pounding excitement. They moved into a brighter hall, a place illuminated by the genuine light of day!

They emerged into a covered entryway next to the castle gatehouse, an arched passage leading directly to the wide courtyard around the keep. The trio pulled back into the shadow of the arch as a troop of twenty or more ogres marched past. Kerrick's hand clenched around his new sword, but he knew that if they came this way he and his companions were outnumbered. He didn't breathe for a full minute until the patrol had moved well out of sight.

"Up there," said the gully dwarf, pointing to indicate one of the towers. "That where Alk-ist lives. Alla way to top."

"We can climb from the gatehouse, then cross on that bridge," Moreen suggested breathlessly, pointing to a stairway that the elf hadn't noticed before. It seemed to lead up within the large, square building where they found themselves. That route offered some conceal-ment. It was certainly better than a dash across the open courtyard.

"All right," said. "Let's do it."

He turned to thank Divid for his help, but the gully dwarf was already gone.

———◆◆◆———

"They're giving up," said a dismayed Strongwind, watching the ogre pursuers milling around more than a mile away. "It looks like they're turning back to the castle."

The ogre party started down the long slope toward the path on the valley floor. Strongwind saw the brutish warriors waving, apparently signaling to the larger party that had progressed toward the coast. Now those ogres, too, reversed course and started toward the looming castle.

"I wonder if that one, the big fellow wearing the black cape, isn't the king, himself," Randall mused, chewing on a blade of grass. "Didn't Lady Moreen say something about a black bearskin that he captured from her tribe?"

"Yes. It was a tribal symbol, a bear slain by her ancestor as I recall. I've never heard of any other black bear. I bet you're right."

"There's got to be a way to get their attention, to keep them chasing us," Randall suggested. The berserker scratched his chin, a wry smile upon his face.

"I fear not. What do you propose?" asked Strongwind, anxiously.

"Well," said the berserker, with a mild chuckle. "Up until now we've been fleeing. We could always attack."

"This way!" hissed Kerrick, leading Moreen along a small, narrow passageway. They had ascended a spiral stairway within the gatehouse tower and emerged from that route on top of the curtain wall. Now they followed this enclosed tunnel toward a battle platform, the outside rampart visible before them and bathed in bright sunlight.

At the end of the tunnel they paused, concealed behind the frame of the arch, watching as several guards strode along the parapet. One moved away from them, but two approached, so they shrank back into the shadows.

"That's the bridge over to the keep," Moreen whispered, touching his arm, pointing to a break in the parapet.

"Be ready," Kerrick replied, leaning forward to see the guards. The two that had been approaching stopped and turned, engaging in some muttered conversation as, step by step, they marched away on the continuation of their rounds.

"Now!" whispered the elf. Together he and Moreen scuttled out of the gatehouse, staying low so that they couldn't be seen beyond the wall. In seconds they were around the corner, crouched against the rampart of the bridge. The span itself was unguarded, empty. Even better, a hundred feet away it led to a doorway into the tower.

As quickly as possible they crossed the bridge, hunched over, racing toward the door. As they were drawing close, however, they heard tromping bootsteps and froze. A guard came into view, marching right past the door. They saw him plainly, marching from right to left, so close that if he glanced onto the bridge they were doomed.

Instead, the ogre walked past, and once again they scuttled forward. At the terminus of the bridge, however, they met an open space that they had to cross, a circular platform around the outside of the tower. Crouching, they heard ogres in conversation just a few feet away. The gap of open space was at least ten feet. They hesitated, uncertain what to do.

The piercing blast of a horn suddenly rang through the castle, originating from somewhere near the gatehouse. As the echoes faded, they heard heavy footsteps, stomping guards, the chaotic sounds of movement gradually receding.

"What's the fuss?" called an ogre nearby. "See anything down there?"

Kerrick guessed that the sentry was looking down over the wall, not toward the bridge. Grabbing Moreen he darted past the ogre, no more than five paces away, who was leaning over the wall, looking into the courtyard. Kerrick pushed open the door, and the two slipped inside the tower. Quickly the elf eased the portal shut behind them.

"I think they know we're in the castle," Kerrick whispered. Moreen nodded grimly.

"We've come this far. We can't very well go back," she said, with an easy grin that he suddenly found immensely heartening.

Another dozen steps brought them to an open arch leading into a larger room with no windows, the area lit by several flickering torches. A wide stairway led down and up from the chamber, while several arched passages on the far side apparently led deeper into the keep.

Footsteps clattered on the stairways, drawing closer, and once more the two intruders shrank into the shadows.

Some ogres were right outside. It sounded as if several had come up the stairs from below. They paused, and Kerrick's hand found the hilt of his sword. If any came through the arch, the two of them would certainly be discovered

Instead, he heard guttural voices arguing and questioning, then growing silent as more ogres came down the stairs. Finally he could make out some words.

"What you find up there?" demanded a bullish voice.

"Nothing, no problems," came the reply in a similar tone. "Guards up there saw nothing, heard no noise neither. Alchemist still in his room. False alarm, if you ask me."

There was a snort of disgust, then the original speaker continued. "You stay here, you and Bonebreaker. Keep watch. I'll take the other fellas down to the main hall."

"Okay. Move fast. The queen's not happy."

Immediately there came a clatter of heavy boots going down the stairs. They heard a sniff of broad, clogged sinuses, then a disgusted spit.

"What's up?" asked an ogre.

"Some humans running around outside," replied another. Kerrick and Moreen exchanged looks. "Somebody come in by the cistern. They found muddy tracks."

"I hope them humans come this way," said the first. "My blade is thirsty!"

Crude chuckles followed. Kerrick glanced at Moreen, whose one good eye was bright, staring at him. "The Alchemist is up those stairs!" she whispered.

He nodded. Suddenly he was overwhelmed by the reality of the challenge they faced. What could the two of them do, against so many hulking guards? What had he expected? That the Alchemist would be alone in his room and invite them in? The elf slumped against the wall, overwhelmed. To come so far and be defeated. It was too much!

Moreen touched his arm, then gestured. The gesture was clear. The Arktos chief wanted him to put on his ring.

He knew that was exactly what he had to do. Nodding, he reached into his pocket and slipped the golden circlet over his finger. Immediately his fear and weariness fell away, replaced by a vibrant energy fueled by rage, hatred of the two ogres who stood between him and his objective.

With a quick smile at the chiefwoman he drew his sword and raced through the archway to confront a pair of very startled ogres. One died, stabbed through the heart, with the surprised look still etched on his face. The other marshaled a great shout and lowered the haft of his stout spear, holding the weapon crossways to block the attack.

The elf's heavy blade whistled down, cutting the spearshaft cleanly in two. The ogre gaped at his broken weapon and was still gaping as the sword slashed back through his throat, leaving his head barely dangling from his gashed neck. With a gurgle, the ogre toppled backward.

Unfortunately, he had been standing at the top of the stairs. The limp body smashed down the steps with a clang of armor and weaponry. The ogre's metal helm, slick with blood, also tumbled down the stairway. The clatter was more alarming to Kerrick than a hundred bells or a thousand clarion horns.

"Come on!" cried Moreen, racing past Kerrick, tugging at his arm. Without a backward look, his sword still red with gore, he turned and raced after her up the stairs leading to the top of the keep, and the laboratory of the Alchemist.

———◆———

"You're right—that's the king himself!" Strongwind said, when they got close enough to recognize the enormous ogre wearing the black bearskin cape. The golden breastplate was the same one the ogre leader had worn at the battle of Brackenrock—the Highlander could even see the hole where Kerrick's sword had pierced it.

"Let's go! We'll take him in a rush!" Strongwind urged boldly. They could strike quickly, maybe even hurt the king himself, then break up the hill. He felt giddily hopeful that he and his companion could distract the ogres with the crazy attack proposed by Mad Randall.

"Let's go, then," said Randall cheerfully. "There's only twenty of the bastards. Shouldn't be much of a problem." Strongwind noticed the twitch of his old friend's lip, saw the light of war come into his eyes. The madness of battle-frenzy was coming over him now.

The two men burst from concealment, sword and axe upraised, racing down the hill. "For Kradok!" shouted the Highlander king, invoking the name of his people's god. "And for all the Icereach!" he added, allowing himself one last, fond thought of Moreen. Randall's voice rose in that shrill, ululating scream that had terrified so many opponents of the past, as if a great predatory bird swooped down on the ogres.

They ran full tilt toward Grimwar Bane and his band of stunned, disbelieving ogres.

"They're in the north tower!" came the cry, as the Dowager Queen scurried through Dracoheim's great hall. She was ahead of her bodyguards, who were still buckling on their swords. She herself carried a massive cudgel, a heavy weapon of cold, black iron, the studded head imbued with the crushing power of the Willful One himself.

She came to the base of the winding stairway to find a group of guards standing around staring at a bloody helm and nearby a still form sprawled across the steps.

"It's Bonebreaker," one ogre guardsman said. "Head mostly cut off."

"By an elf?" grunted another, astonished.

"Not just an elf—an enemy my son has battled for eight years!" snapped Hannareit. "Today, he dies!"

With a roar, she started up the stairs, heartened by the sounds of a dozen of her warriors rushing close behind.

———❖———

Moreen's lungs strained for some fresh air. Her limbs were leaden, her eye stinging with the sweat trickling off of her forehead. Her already blurry vision was reduced to a small patch of light before her, and in that light she seemed to see only an endless string of steps leading upward.

Kerrick was at her side. When she stumbled he reached out, finding the strength to bear them both. She remembered his ring and dreaded the price he would pay for this magical sustenance, but she also understood that, for now, it was their only chance to reach the Alchemist.

They had to stop and catch their breath. It was then that they heard shouts from below and the unmistakable sounds of pursuit—heavy boots clomping on the stairs, weapons clattering, butts of spears cracking against the flagstones.

Kerrick was looking at her oddly, his expression remote. She drew a breath, steadied her nerves. "Let's keep going," she said. "I can keep up."

"Wait," he said abruptly. "We have to slow them down somehow."

"How?" she asked. He went to a large stone table, one of several placed at the various landings. It must have weighed a few hundred pounds, but he pushed against it and toppled it over, then shoved it across the floor until he had wedged it firmly atop the flight of stairs. Giving it a final push, he fixed it in place as a barrier. He turned and gave her a grin.

Once more they flew up the steps, around corners, one after the other, until they came to a landing. There were two arches leading to a sunlit outer parapet and one door in the opposite wall. Most importantly, there were six ogres standing in front of the door, staring at them in shock and disbelief, scrambling to lower spears and draw swords against an attack they had clearly thought inconceivable.

Kerrick didn't hesitate. He rushed forward across the narrow landing, his sword raised. Two ogres were slain in quick stabs. The other four roared and closed in, spears thrusting, blades chopping. One by one they howled with pain, falling to the whistling blade, the steely determination of the elven Messenger. In a few seconds four of the ogres were dead, and the other two were crawling away, bleeding and moaning.

Kerrick thrust the sword through his belt and raised his fist, furiously prepared to smash the door down. Only then did Moreen rush forward, restraining him. She reached out, lifted the latch, and pushed the unlocked door open.

The elf rushed into the room, Moreen at his heels. The chamber was thick with shadow, smelling of arcane fumes. She saw a man seated at a cluttered bench looking up at them. There was a large globe of pure, immaculate gold just behind him, the only brightness in the room. The chiefwoman couldn't read the expression on the thin, withered face, but slowly the man, on wobbling legs, stood to face them.

"Are you the Alchemist?" she demanded.

"I am called that, yes," he replied. His voice was weak

and reedy, yet somehow familiar. His features were also distinctive, vaguely reminiscent of . . . what?

Silvanesti!

She turned to Kerrick and saw an expression of shock mingled with horror on his face. All at once she understood.

"Moreen, Lady of Brackenrock," Kerrick almost spit the bitter words, in that same accent, the silky elven tongue. "This is my father, Dimorian Fallabrine, once a hero of Silvanesti, a leader to make every elf proud. Now, you see, he is the Alchemist, pawn of an ogre king."

M y lord king, beware!" cried Three-Tusk, pushing Grimwar Bane to the side.

Those were the last words the loyal Grenadier ever spoke. The ogre king stumbled, dropped to one knee, and the next thing he knew the berserk Highlander was pulling his axe away, leaving Three-Tusk lying on the ground fatally bleeding from a slash through his neck.

The human, his voice shrieking weirdly—the familiar shriek the king had heard at the gatehouse of Brackenrock—was clearly not finished. Another ogre stepped into the bearded man's path, and he, too, was cut down. A third Grenadier swung his sword, slicing a deep gouge in the attacker's arm. The maniac didn't even seem to react. Instead, he yelled even louder and spun himself through a circle, slashing his axe like a spinning top, leaving bloody wounds in several burly ogres.

Another human, a blond swordsman of impressive physique, also charged in a short distance behind the berserker. Neither of these intrepid attackers was the elven Messenger, the ogre monarch noted grimly, as he tried to rally his men.

"Fight, my Grenadiers!" he commanded. His veteran warriors formed a wall around the king, pressing shoulder to shoulder to prevent either attacker striking directly at Grimwar Bane, shielding the royal personage with their own flesh.

Both humans stabbed and chopped at the ring of the ogres. One ogre threw a spear, piercing the thigh of the berserker. Even then the man didn't fall. He turned and lunged at the spearman, almost striking him with his whirling axe. But the wound was grievous, slowing the Highlander's movements enough that another one of the king's guards had a chance to close in with a sudden lunge. This time the berserker's axe found ogre flesh, but at the same time the Grenadier's sword thrust plunged into the human's chest. Still howling his battle cry, the stricken warrior stumbled to the side, barely avoiding the next blow.

At the same time the blond-haired Highlander was trying to hack through the ogre ring from the other side. He was a skilled swordsman. His blade struck one Grenadier's wrist, almost cutting off the hand, then deflected a slashing blow from another of Grimwar's bodyguards. The force of that parry knocked the man off balance, however, and quickly a third ogre leaped close, swinging his spear like a club. The shaft, as thick around as a man's wrist, caught the Highlander on the side of his head and he dropped like a felled tree, sprawling motionless on the ground.

Seeing his comrade fall, the berserker's voice rose to a frenzy. Bleeding from many wounds, hampered by the spear still lodged in his leg, he nevertheless rushed the ogres and, with a single slice, killed the one who had felled his comrade, splitting his forehead with a savage downward chop of his axe.

That attack came at terrible cost, as the Highlander exposed his back for a moment. One ogre stabbed, another threw his spear, and the human fell on his face, pinned to the ground, the spear point emerging from his chest. Still he tried to fight on, pushing with his hands, struggling to roll over, as the rest of Grimwar's escort brought their weapons down in a gory orgy of murderous vengeance.

Only then did the king step over to the big blond human, who was bleeding from a wide cut over his ear. Grimwar rolled him over, looked at him critically.

"This one is still breathing," said the monarch. "Tie him up. I will interrogate him if he lives."

———◆◆◆———

"You created such a weapon? A device that could destroy an entire citadel, a whole community of people?" Kerrick demanded. His face was taut. He spoke tersely, stalking around his father's chamber, his eyes never leaving that withered, cadaverous, and eerily kindred visage.

"I am sad to see that it is happening to you. I should never have left it for you. Nor would I, if I had understood . . ." Dimorian's voice was wistful, rambling, distant as though he heard not a word his son had uttered.

"What are you mumbling about?" snapped Kerrick. "Listen to me. Don't you understand that you are a pawn of evil?"

Dimorian, who was the Alchemist, sighed, gazing at the metal sphere with its cold, almost obscene beauty. "Evil, yes. You speak, of course, of the golden orb. Yes, I fear that was my handiwork. I had no way, of course, to know it would be used against my own son or his friends."

"But if you had, that wouldn't have stopped you, would it?" It was Moreen who spoke now.

"No, because . . . because I had to have . . . I needed . . ."

Moreen gave Kerrick a look at once so fierce and compassionate that he was taken aback.

"Take off your ring," she said quietly, and in that instant she understood.

He was like his father: seduced by the urge. He moved his right hand over his left, as if he was about to ease the circlet off of his finger. Touching his skin, he toyed with the metal circle, considered removing it.

He couldn't.

"You had better see to the door," said Dimorian, gesturing vaguely. The words barely penetrated Kerrick's consciousness, but Moreen responded. She stepped to the entry and pushed the door shut, turning the latch to lock it. Spotting a heavy beam, the chiefwoman picked it up and dropped it across the portal, securing it in place.

They heard ogres rush onto the landing, roaring in rage. They were outside now, pounding against the door. Kerrick turned back to his father.

"You were their puppet. You did so much for them! Grimwar Bane's ship, the *Hornet*—that was your design too, wasn't it? That's how the ogres were able to make another galley!"

Dimorian nodded. "There were certain flaws, mainly because of the absence of any hardwood. Her hull was weak. I have an idea how to make the next one stronger."

Kerrick stared at him accusingly. Dimorian found Moreen with his watery eyes.

"I suppose that ship will never be built, now, will it?"

"We came to stop you," she replied. "Not from building ships, but from making another golden orb."

The elder elf offered a smile of immeasureable sadness. "You are too late to stop its creation, as you can see. I fear that this is a weapon even more terrible than the one Grimwar Bane used against your fortress. It is larger, heavier, more powerful in every respect."

A great boom echoed from the door as the ogres brought massive force to bear. The portal bulged inward, cracking, splinters flying loose. Kerrick turned to look, confused, his mind and heart were spinning wildly.

"My son . . . please believe me, I never expected to see you again, to see any elf. I am grateful that you are here, and we must talk about everything that has happened to me . . . and you . . . over the years. But now you must flee!" declared Dimorian Fallabrine, with a trace of the authority that once captained a mighty warship.

"We aren't going anywhere!" Moreen retorted. "Not while that orb exists and can be used against my homeland."

"I assure you," said Dimorian in a new, more serious tone, "I can address both of your concerns immediately. The orb will never be used against you, nor will my work continue to aid the king of Suderhold."

The Alchemist suddenly stood straight, his eyes clear, as if years or even decades had fallen away from him. He met Kerrick's gaze with an expression combining pride and a plea for forgiveness.

"What—what are you saying?" asked the chiefwoman. Then she understood. Moreen turned to Kerrick. "Can we trust him . . . your father?" she asked the younger elf.

"Yes," said the son softly, studying his father's resolute expression. "I believe we can."

The quivering door showed cracks and splinters. The din was powerful, as if a hundred ogres were breaking it down. "Is that the only way out of here?" asked Kerrick.

"There is another way. Here, you must drink this to take advantage of it," said the Alchemist, lifting up a small bottle and removing the stopper. He handed it to Moreen. "It is a powerful elixir, too powerful for me, but for you, it can have a profound use. It will allow you to escape, to live."

"What is it?" the chiefwoman asked suspiciously.

"A treasure, in its own right," replied the Alchemist, allowing himself a wry smile. "Ironically, it is a gift from the Dowager Queen herself."

Moreen stepped forward, warily took the proffered bottle. The Alchemist went to the window and threw open the heavy shutter. Sunlight spilled into the room, pure and bright and wholesome.

The chiefwoman lifted the neck of the vial to her lips and drank from it.

Instantly her image began to wave, the black of her hair, the tawny buckskin of her shirt fading into a misty gray even as she set the bottle down on the bench. The rays of sunlight passed through her as she grew incorporeal, until finally she grew barely visible, floating in the air, a cohesive but gaseous cloud the color of pale steam.

A heavy blow struck the door, an axe blade plunging through, twisting and ripping as its wielder pulled it back for another strike. Kerrick stepped forward, reached for the bottle but spoke pleadingly to his father.

"Come with us," the Messenger said. "We can destroy the orb, and without you they'll never be able to make another one. You can return with us to Brackenrock. Someday I could take you back across the ocean, to Silvanesti . . ."

His father shook his head, a slight gesture, dashing Kerrick's hopes. "I have no home there anymore," he said regretfully. "I turned my back on my people, my birthright, long ago when I made the choice to serve the ogre king in return for release from his dungeon. It was a choice your mother resisted. She died in that dungeon, her pride still intact. For that, I reproach myself above all. But when she was gone, I'm afraid I weakened. The lure of magic, the taste of power . . . I am ashamed to admit that I lacked the strength to resist. I must do something to atone. . . ."

"Yes," Kerrick said quietly, feeling that same warm pulse of magic in his own blood, the sensation of power emanating from the golden ring on his finger.

Dimorian gestured to the ring on his son's hand. "I see my ring on your hand. You must take it off now. I pray that you will recognize its danger and throw it away!"

There was such a stark terror in his father's voice that this time Kerrick did as he was told and slid the ring off of his finger. Immediately he staggered with the onset of weakness and despair, the familiar sensation of bleak hopelessness, as he held the little band of metal in his hand. Every nerve in his body, every ounce of his desire, urged him, begged him to put the ring back on. He swayed.

Then he surprised himself by reaching forward and dropping the ring it into Dimorian's trembling, outstretched hand. Quickly Kerrick took the last swallow of the drink, the liquid searing his throat and the warmth spreading through his body as he grew light and immaterial.

Moreen was already drifting away, slipping out through the window, and he turned to follow her, flying free, sweeping outward to the sunlit sky. The two of them swirled into the air beyond Castle Dracoheim as the Alchemist's door burst, and the hinges broke free.

———◆———

The Dowager Queen could not believe her eyes—six of her finest ogre guards mangled and bleeding, most of them dead. Blood everywhere, while three of her burliest guards continued to hack and chop at the resistant door.

"An *elf* did this?" grunted one of her attendants, biting back any further questions as she flashed him a murderous look.

"Break it down!" she cried. "Out of my way!" She raised her iron cudgel and swung a mighty blow.

With her help the splintering barrier finally gave way, cracking down the middle and collapsing in two halves. The first three ogres charged through with vengeful roars, and Queen Hannareit pushed behind them—then they all froze, paralyzed by fear.

"What are you doing?" she gasped, trying to comprehend the scene.

The Alchemist was alone in the room, the window wide open. If the Messenger had been here, he was gone.

Somehow the craven and feeble elf who had been her pet, her slave for all these years, had found the strength to lift the golden orb. He had hoisted it in his two hands, balancing it on the windowsill above the hundred-foot drop to the courtyard below. The elder queen and her ogre guards stood aghast, then began to back away.

"I had a chance to talk to my son," he said, "I found strength I didn't even know I possessed."

"Put that down—carefully," Hanna said, her voice like an iceberg grating against the hull of a ship. "Put it down, and I will forgive you . . . for this . . . for everything. You shall have . . . everything you want . . . need."

"I think that for the first time in a very long time, I have everything I need," said the Alchemist.

He seemed strangely content—happy, Hanna would have said, if she had time to say anything. Dimorian Fallabrine leaned out the window and let go of the golden orb.

———◆◆◆———

Stariz was red-faced, puffing for breath, as she jogged up to Grimwar Bane. "I saw the fight," she said. "I hurried as fast as I could. Was it just two men who attacked?"

"Yes," replied the king with irritation, looking down at his prisoner. The blond Highlander had regained consciousness and now sat on the ground at Grimwar's feet, hair matted with drying blood, hands bound behind his back. Several watchful Grenadiers stood nearby with weapons poised, ready to abort any aggressive move.

"Why did you and your comrade attack us?" demanded the ogre king. "What could you have hoped to gain?"

"A measure of vengeance for a very good friend," the man retorted, his jaw set and his eyes blazing with pride. "That's her father's cape that you wear over your shoulders. I wished to get it back for her."

"What nonsense is this?" Grimwar unconsciously reached a hand to his shoulder, touched the bear pelt, that black color unique among all the bears of the Icereach. "Who are you?" he demanded.

"Just a man from the Highlands," said the prisoner with a dismissive shrug.

"Don't be a fool!" Stariz snapped to Grimwar, her disrespect toward their king provoking growls and startled glances from the ogres gathered around the royal couple. Grimwar himself flushed with fury, but his wife continued without breath. "You dolt, they were trying to keep you from getting back to the castle! Away from your duty, your station! Look up there! Look! The elf is probably striking now, even as we stand here uselessly!"

Surprised, the king looked up the valley, to the lofty citadel five or six miles away. It stood black, tall, and impervious on its rocky height, yet it looked strangely vulnerable against the pale blue sky. He had a sick feeling in his gut, a fear that his wife, as usual, was right.

The queen was not finished with her rebuke. "I tell you, we should be there, right now—"

Everything vanished. Grimwar's vision went blank as it was seared by a flash of brilliant light. He felt heat against his face, as if a furnace door had burst open just a few feet away. He gaped, trying to see, but even though he blinked and rubbed his eyes he could not restore his vision.

Then came the second blast, a wave of force that knocked the wind from his lungs, sent all the ogres smashing to the ground, rolling like tenpins. He tried to breathe but felt only that awful, crushing pressure. After interminable seconds of this punishment the third wave, the sound, reached them, a horrifying blast pounding their ears with the same brutal force that had impacted their bodies.

Grimwar was vaguely aware of screaming, groaning ogres to all sides. He himself was roaring and screaming. Finally, after long minutes or hours, the burning, the noise, the fiery whiteness began to fade. Though he saw only a bright wash of whiteness in the middle of his field of vision, he began to make out images around the edges. There was smoke, a billowing cloud of dust besmirching the once clean sky . . . but that was not the worst of it, not at all.

As he looked up, toward the knoll at the head of the valley, his ultimate fear, his impossible nightmare, was confirmed.

Castle Dracoheim was gone.

Kerrick felt himself blown toward the sea, the force of the blast propelling his gaseous form through the air like a piece of feather-light rubbish. He rode the blast, feeling no pain, just a numb sense of horror. Moreen was lost in the gale, but he believed that she was nearby, borne along like him by the force of the magic weapon his father had created.

As the tumult waned, he finally discerned the cloudy image of the chiefwoman drifting nearby. He floated over to her and reached out, tendrils of vaporous limbs embracing, linking themselves together. Gradually they drifted downward, angling themselves toward the shadowed waters of the cove where the *Whalefish* had landed them.

Moreen alighted on the shore of black sand, and she became a woman again, looking dazed and battered, but a human female of flesh and blood, muscle and beauty. In another instant Kerrick was there beside her, whole again, feeling the magic drain from him to leave only a weakness and emptiness, a gnawing hunger he would never satisfy.

But both of them were again whole, corporeal beings. They embraced, relishing the miracle of their lives.

Never had Kerrick found such comfort in the touch of another person. Moreen cried, as he pressed her head against his shoulder, stroked her hair, desperately tried to soothe her.

Just off shore, the top of the submersible's hull rose from the placid waters with a gentle splash. *Whalefish* bobbed in the shallows, rolling gently from side to side.

"Do you see Strongwind or Randall?" asked the elf, looking worriedly around.

Moreen's expression was stricken. "When—when we were floating . . . up there," she said, her voice choking with grief. "I think I saw Randall, his body . . . horribly slashed. It was down on the ground, near a whole band of ogres. I didn't see Strongwind, but . . ."

"But they would have stayed together," the elf said, feeling a weary sadness permeate him. He wanted to collapse, to lie down and sleep for many days. "Both of them lost. It doesn't seem possible."

The hatch atop the steel hull popped open, and Captain Pneumo waved. "I've got gold in the boilers and steam in the pipes," he called. "There's some kind of madness going on around here. C'mon, let's go!"

"None of this seems possible," Moreen said quietly. "Even you—you found your father, and lost him again."

"Yes," Kerrick said, turning, wading into the water. He stopped to look back at the island, barren and bleak as ever, now with a huge smoke column billowing upward, marking the pyre of an elf, a weapon, and a reign of terror.

He choked on the words, as he drew a breath. "Now, at least, I know he died a hero."

Gathered together for the first time in fifteen years. . .

The magic of DRAGONLANCE® brought to life by the world's most renowned fantasy artists!

The world of DRAGONLANCE has captivated readers around the globe for almost twenty years. Now you can once again experience the visual wonders of this epic saga in this new collection of some of the most stunning art in the fantasy genre.

The Art of the Dragonlance Saga, Volume II
September 2002

Featuring pieces by top fantasy artists such as:

Brom • Jeff Easley • Daniel Horne
Todd Lockwood • Matt Stawicki • Mark Zug

. . . and many more!

Tales that span the length and breadth of Krynn's history

The Golden Orb
Icewall Trilogy, Volume Two • Douglas Niles

The Arktos prosper in their fortress community, while the ogre king and queen seethe and plot revenge. Humans and highlanders must band together to defend against an onslaught that threatens mass destruction.

February 2002

Sister of the Sword
The Barbarians, Volume Three • Paul B. Thompson & Tonya C. Cook

The village of the dragon is under siege. Riding hard to the rescue is the great nomad chief Karada. Can her warrior tribe overcome a raider horde, mighty ogres, and the curse of the green dragon?

May 2002

The Divine Hammer
The Kingpriest Trilogy, Volume Two • Chris Pierson

Twenty years have passed since Beldinas the Kingpriest took the throne, and his is a realm of unsurpassed glory. But evil threatens, so Beldinas must turn to a loyal lieutenant to extinguish the darkness of foul sorcery.

October 2002

The Dragon Isles
Crossroads Series • Stephen D. Sullivan

Legendary home of metallic dragons, the Dragon Isles attract seafaring adventurers determined to exploit the wealth of the archipelago, despite the evil sea dragon that blocks their success.

December 2002

All-new editions from Margaret Weis & Tracy Hickman

The Second Generation

Meet them again for the first time – the children of the Heroes of the Lance, those who inherited the sword, the staff, and the legacy of the heroes who came before them. This all-new paperback edition features stunning cover art from DRAGONLANCE® artist Matt Stawicki.

February 2002

Dragons of Summer Flame

When the father of the gods returns to Krynn, the world is shaken to its core. The battle that rages in this hottest of summers will change the people and deities of Ansalon forever. Striking cover art from Matt Stawicki graces this all-new paperback edition!

February 2002

Legends Trilogy Gift Set

A handsome hardcover case surrounds this trilogy of classic titles from the foundation of the DRAGONLANCE saga. Each title in this collectible boxed set features paintings by Matt Stawicki and is a must-have for any DRAGONLANCE fan.

September 2002